LOST BOYS

SLATEVIEW HIGH #1

EVA ASHWOOD

ONE

TWELVE O'CLOCK, pre-dinner preparations underway. Guest rooms cleaned, first course prepped.

Three o'clock, grounds inspected, driveway tidied, decorations begin going up.

Five o'clock, Mom and Dad prepare for the evening, dressed and groomed for greeting guests.

Six o'clock, guests arrive. Cordelia begins getting ready. Cocktails served downstairs in main hall.

Seven o'clock, Cordelia downstairs. Pre-dinner socializing.

The itinerary repeated in my head: twelve, three, five, six, seven. Mom always liked our dinners running smoothly—and for my mother, that meant every minute, every *second*, was planned down to the letter, every 'i' dotted, every 't' crossed and absolutely nothing out of place.

Least of all, me.

I sat in my room at my vanity, the sounds of orchestral strings and tinkling brass drifting up from downstairs where my mother and father's guests were surely sipping from flutes of expensive wine, helping themselves to hors d'oeuvres, and talking amongst themselves about their next big investment or whose heiress daughter was going to marry their sons.

It was a scene I was intimately familiar with. After all, this had been my life for the last seventeen years.

I'd been born into this world, and I knew my place in it. As the only child of Elizabeth and Gideon van Rensselaer, I was to remain poised and proper at all times, with never a hair out of place, a lash uncurled, nor a stray comment from my mouth that could bring some unspoken shame to my parents. I was the perfect vessel to carry on the family legacy; the only thing that could've made me more perfect in my parents' eyes was if I had been born a boy.

"There we go Ms. Cora. Ah, aren't you stunning?"

Ava stepped out from behind me where I sat at my vanity. She'd been with my parents for as long as I could remember. A kind woman in her forties, her fawn-brown hair was always pulled back in a thick bun, and her warm, round face always with a smile that could melt the coldest of demeanors.

In some ways, she was like a second mother to me. She had taught me how to tie my shoes and how to braid my own hair—before my actual mother had declared braids too "common". When I'd started my period, she was the one I'd gone to, and the one who'd gone out of her way to make sure I had everything I needed to weather that particular storm. I talked to her about boys, because it was just... easier. Knowing my mother, it wasn't hard to see why.

I smiled at her in the reflection and looked at her handiwork. My hair fell in thick blonde ringlets around my face, which was lightly made up with just the right amount of product to highlight my natural features. Heavy makeup, according to my mother, was gauche. Choosing to live on the wild side, Ava had even given me a bit of a glow this evening—a dusting of shimmery silvery powder at my cheeks and along my exposed collar bone, just for a slight pop. It contrasted well with the deep green dress my mother had chosen for the evening, one that matched the shade of my eyes. Rensselaer jade, they were called among my mother and father's peers. Our social circles knew them well.

My red painted lips quirked, and I stood up, turning to Ava.

"It looks incredible. You always make me look lovely," I said. "That's good. I know Mom and Dad want tonight to go perfectly."

"Hm." Ava pursed her lips, something she did when she had something to say but was too polite to actually say it. "Well, if there's going to be anything perfect tonight, it's going to be you, my dear girl. And just think—all the handsome young men I'm sure your father's invited. They won't be able to take their eyes off you."

I flushed.

"Well, I know that Dad invited the Kings. Their son is... Well, I haven't met him personally, but I'm sure he's nice."

Ava chuckled and nudged me toward my door.

"I'll clean up; you go on. Your mother has you on a strict presentation schedule. Wouldn't want to do anything to disrupt that," she said, her mouth twitching into an almost-smile.

I laughed a little, leaving her to tidy the vanity and clear away the clothes I'd been wearing before I'd put on the green dress. I knew that by the time I came back up to my room later tonight, tired from socializing and ready to collapse into bed, the room would be spotless again, not a thing out of place.

Ava took care of me like that.

My family's manor was expansive. We—my family, the van Rensselaer line—were often referred to as American Royalty, and if that were true, our home was definitely our palace. My father's family were old steel and oil tycoons who had diversified over the years; Dad had his hands deep in real estate and investments these days. My mother, a Stratler before she married my father, came from a family of textile producers, though there wasn't much money left to the Stratler name these days. She barely ever talked about her side of the family—anytime I asked about them, she told me there wasn't anything worth talking about.

Leaving my bedroom at exactly 6:55 p.m., I walked through halls of mahogany and gilded oak, decorated with tapestries and paintings of our ancestors, knowing that one day it would be my job to do what my parents were doing now—make sure our legacy ran strong and true with every new generation, and that no one could have a reason to forget or talk ill of the van Rensselaer name.

I doubted that would happen during the festivities tonight. No one who'd been invited this evening had any reason to dislike my family—and they had plenty of reasons to want to get along well with Mom and Dad. My father's friendship and good word had started business empires.

As I descended the large set of double stairs to the sounds of voices, laughter, and music, I shoved down the little thrill of nerves that ran up my spine. I was no stranger to these kinds of events, but part of me still hated being put on display like this. My parents always made my entrance the final and grandest one. Given the volume of conversation drifting up toward me, it felt like the entirety of the Baltimore elite was in our house.

Well, to be honest, they likely were.

The adults were already well into the merriment, with a few of the sons and daughters mingling with their own flutes of wine and champagne. Rules could be bent when it came to a van Rensselaer party. Guests turned when they saw me appear at the top of the large, curving staircase. It had been built for just this sort of grand entrance, and I made sure not to glance down at my feet as I walked down, my dress brushing each step as I descended with perfect grace. More than one appreciative glance came my way, and with each one, no matter who it was from, I returned a smile. Just like

Mom had taught me. *Appreciation given deserves appreciation in return.*

I passed by the Carlsons, giving Mr. and Mrs. Carlson a sweet nod on my way past them. Then the Remingtons, the Ellises, the Beaumonts—families that had almost the same clout that Mom and Dad had. *Almost*, because Dad always had just a little more. It was a status that the van Rensselaer family had always ensured they were able to boast.

Eventually, I found Mom and Dad, a pair of divinity in the crowd.

Mom was a vision in red. A deep wine gown perfectly complemented her blonde hair, which was the same color as mine—white-gold, like spun flax. Dad stood next to her, his tailored black suit embellished with accents of the same wine red that Mom's dress carried.

They matched, a perfect set, and I was the combination of the two of them. Mom's blonde hair and grace, and Dad's green eyes and resilience.

When I reached them, I dipped my head slightly. I didn't have a close relationship with either of them, but whatever affection we might show on a normal day was turned down even further at an elegant party like this. Over-affection was the enemy of poise, and for one of Mom and Dad's parties, poise was always paramount.

"Mom, Dad," I greeted instead. "I hope I haven't missed out on too much?"

"Cordelia." Dad beamed at me, his hands on my shoulders as he kept me at arm's length, appraising me. "My, my, you were right, Elizabeth; the green certainly brings out the beautiful shade of her eyes." He fingered a coil of my hair, smoothing it out before giving a nod. "Perfect. Now, let's see if we can find Sebastian. I wanted you to meet his son, Barrett."

I nodded and took Dad's left arm as he moved through the crowd with Mom on the other side of him. It was always how we made our rounds; Dad in the center, the head of the house, the pillar that kept the van Rensselaer family together, and the two prized women of the house— his wife, always prim and dutiful, and his daughter. Like my arrival, our trek through the grand entrance was marked by greetings, smiles, compliments given, and compliments paid.

When we walked up to Sebastian King, something shifted.

Dad straightened out his suit, preened himself almost, as though he were the one who needed to go out of his way to impress. My brow rose, but only for a moment as Dad began the pleasantries, his deep voice smooth and commanding as ever. Sebastian, a charismatic man with salt-and-pepper hair, grinned at the three of us. I would never say it aloud, but he looked almost wolfish. I could say the same for his son, Barrett.

Barrett had hair longer than most boys in our circles, neat and slicked back from his face, save for a few strands that fell over his eyes—like his father's eyes, they were a deep, warm amber. I'd seen him in passing before, and where his father gave off a jovial, effortlessly confident air in the way he held himself, Barrett had a different aura about him.

More dangerous.

Lascivious.

Suddenly, I felt less eager to meet him properly, no matter how handsome he was—but I knew that simply leaving was out of the question.

"Ah, Sebastian, I almost forgot. You've met my daughter, Cordelia. But I don't believe that she and Barrett have met?" My father smiled even more broadly as he made the introduction.

"*Pleasure* to meet you," Barrett said before his father could speak. He took my hand, pressing a kiss to the top of it. His lips lingered there as he looked me in the eyes with that wolfish gaze of his.

If I thought him a wolf, what did he think of me?

A little rabbit to be slain?

I pulled my hand from him politely. Dad and Sebastian exchanged a look, Dad giving a nod and Sebastian smirking before the two older men and my mother slipped from us. And just like that, I was left alone with Barrett.

It's strange, the feeling of isolation when you're surrounded by people.

"Likewise." Forcing a smile, I ignored the way his touch had made my spine tingle, and not in any sort of pleasurable way. "It's a shame I've known your father so long, but we haven't been introduced."

Barrett laughed, a cocky, lecherous grin tilting his lips.

"Well, if we had, I'm sure we wouldn't be spending the evening hammering out pleasantries. At least, not in a room full of people." His head tilted as he sized me up. "It is a shame though. I've heard so much about the van Rensselaer's gem. I can see why people call you that with those eyes of yours. You must be popular with the other sons."

The only indication that the comment stung was the slight clench in my jaw—but I knew better than to let it show. Instead, I did what I knew. I smiled.

"Only with the ones I choose," I said. "Though—if you'll excuse me. I think my father's trying to get my attention. It was nice to meet you, Barrett."

Before Barrett I-Don't-Know-How-To-Act-In-Public King could say anything else in response, I gave a slight curtsey and slipped away.

I had a feeling that wouldn't be the last I saw of him, but for now, I could at least curb some of the discomfort of being in his presence. And the easiest way to do that was by removing myself from it.

Of course, Dad hadn't called to me. In fact, he'd be angry to know I excused myself from talking to Barrett so quickly, given the fact that he'd sought the boy and his father out specifically to make the introduction. But that was okay. Just this once, I was willing to risk Dad's ire. I didn't want to let him think for a second that I liked Barrett—I knew he was starting to give consideration to my future, to finding a good match for me, and I'd rather chew my own arm off than go on a date with Sebastian King's creepy eldest son.

I intended to slip outside, just for a moment. Just enough time to allow Barrett to find someone else to speak with, and for me to scan the crowd to actually find my father and mother. I also needed to come up with a reason for walking away from Barrett like I had. I knew there was more than just an innocent reason that my father had introduced the two of us. He would have questions, and I would need to be able to answer them smoothly.

Just a moment alone, just a moment to breathe.

With the number of people in the mansion, it would be easy to disappear—

But before I could do any of that, a commotion from the front foyer made me stop. Raised voices carried even over the music, until the musicians my father had hired stopped playing entirely. A ripple of shock went through the air, palpable.

One by one, several large, uniformed men—*armed* men— parted the crowd of partygoers. *What's the phrase people like to use? Like the Red Sea?* Only there was no Moses, and certainly nothing biblical in the sight before me. Disbelief clouded my brain, almost refusing to let me believe what I was seeing was real.

"Everybody stay back," the officer in the front said. His voice boomed, echoing deep with authority. Everyone in the grand entrance was silent, keeping their distance from the imposing figures filing into my home. Uniformed officers gave way to a man and woman in pressed suits, badges attached to their chests.

"Gideon van Rensselaer. Can you please step forward?" that same officer in the front said.

What the hell was going on?

I scanned the room quickly, waiting to see if my father would come forward as commanded. In my entire seventeen years, I had never seen that man obey commands in his own home.

He gave them. Always.

But tonight, the world turned upside down. Dad moved forward out of the crowd as the officer had demanded, our guests parting for him as surely as they had parted for the officers in question. The room was completely silent, as if the sudden appearance of what amounted to nearly an entire SWAT team in our home had snuffed out all the sound in the house.

As my father came to a halt, my attention was pulled between him and the man who had called to him.

The man was bigger than my father. Taller. Broader. Scarier.

"What's the meaning of this?" Dad asked. Confusion and anger filled his expression, but he still sounded calm—like he was still the head of his house and he knew it. Confidence and relief flooded me at the sound of my father's voice. That sound had reassured me ever since I was a little girl, because when Dad spoke, the bad things went away.

For the first time since the officers had invaded the party, I was able to take a full breath.

It's okay. Everything is going to be okay.

"The meaning of this is you're under arrest, Gideon van Rensselaer."

My father paled.

"Arrested? Arrested for what? On what grounds?"

"Felony fraud, Mr. van Rensselaer."

TWO

THE WORLD STOPPED in the moments after the officer made his declaration. Felony fraud? My father? No. They had to have the wrong man. Business could be messy, I knew that much, but my father would never—

Officers began to spread out in our home as guests made prompt exits. People who had been friends with my family for years slipped off as though they would rather be anywhere else but here. Even Sebastian... I saw him as one of the first to leave, with Barrett at his side. He didn't even look at me. For all his posturing earlier, it was a cold slap in the face.

I made my way over to my father. He was surrounded. My mother looked shaken, her brown eyes wide like a deer caught in headlights.

"Dad—"

"Miss, I need you to back away." The female officer in the

suit held me back, her hold on my shoulders firm, her eyes calm.

"That's my father!" I insisted. I'd been taught never to yell, and especially never to yell at my elders, but fear made it hard to control my tone and volume. "Why are you arresting him? What are you doing?"

Panic rose in my chest as my father's eyes cut to me. Those jade green irises, the exact same shade as mine, were sharp.

"Cordelia," he said stiffly, just shy of a snap. "Calm yourself."

Right. People are still around. This isn't the time for hysterics.

I looked up to the officer. "Please?" I said softly. "He's my father."

She gave me a look like she was trying to evaluate whether I might have some kind of concealed weapon or something—trying to decide if I was dangerous. Finally, with a sigh, she let me go. I rushed to my father, who kept his distance from the officer that'd first come in.

"This is a mistake," Dad said again, lowering his voice without losing any of the strength in his tone. "Fraud? I've never committed any crime, let alone a felony fraud—"

"With all due respect, Mr. van Rensselaer, we've been conducting an investigation for the last year and a half." The man's triumphant smile made my stomach twist. "I've read you your rights, I would suggest you say nothing more until you've spoken with your lawyer—"

"Hey!" Dad's booming voice interrupted the officer, and I jumped, my heart slamming hard against my ribs. He'd just told me not to shout, not to lose control and make a scene, but now my father was doing both, his face set in hard lines of anger... and fear. My gaze followed his, tracking over to a group of men who were making their way up the curved staircase leading to the rest of the house.

"You can't go up there!" he thundered. "What are you doing—?"

The officer in front of us put his hand on my father's chest.

"We have a warrant to search and seize any evidence relevant to this case," he explained, his tone flat. My hands clenched into fists as I pressed my lips into a line. He didn't care that this was our home his people were violating. "Including items purchased fraudulently—"

"Excuse me," Dad interrupted. "Fraudulently purchased? This is my family home—"

"And those are the terms of the warrant." A self-satisfied smirk curved the man's lips again. I hated it. I didn't know why, but his confidence made my blood run cold. "I would hate to have to add obstruction of justice to your list of offenses, sir."

My father quieted, but I could tell he didn't want to. He was too prideful to take being told what to do in his own home without a measure of indignation. The crowd of guests around us had thinned, but many people were still watching us, intently observing every moment of my father's degradation.

For the first time, my mother spoke up.

"Please, surely there must be some mistake," she said. Her usually musical voice had a slight rasp to it, as if she were pushing the sound out past closed vocal cords. "Perhaps we can settle this without all of this disruption—"

"Ma'am," the officer interrupted, shifting his focus to her. He looked irritated, but I had the strange feeling that was an act. That he was enjoying this the way Dad enjoyed a fine, aged whiskey, savoring every moment of it. "I think I've made myself about as clear as I possibly can. I'll have to ask you not to interfere, unless you'd like to be arrested along with your husband."

My mother's already pale skin whitened like a sheet. I forced my feet into motion and went to her, not knowing what else to do as our home was overtaken by federal agents, who marched through the halls with purposeful steps.

As the remaining party guests slipped away into the night, the agents dismantled our home.

They went into the rooms, taking things seemingly at random. After about an hour of that, our massive front foyer was filled with our belongings. Mom, Dad, and I were still gathered near the base of the stairs. Dad stood stiffly, a muscle in his jaw jumping as he clenched his teeth in anger. Mom had her arms around me, and to any officer who glanced our way, it might look like she was comforting me— but the reality was, she was clinging to me.

I was helping her remain upright.

And still, the men in the suits didn't stop. They gathered more and more items from upstairs, to the point that I had to wonder if they were really taking things as evidence, or if it was just to prove a point.

That they could do whatever they wanted, say it was for whatever they wanted, and we weren't able to do a thing about it.

My father, once the most powerful man I knew, couldn't do a single thing to stop them.

A WEEK LATER, the large mansion was empty.

Empty of people. Empty of belongings.

Empty of memories.

What hadn't been taken in the raid, Mom had to liquidate; it was the only way to get enough money to pay for Dad's lawyer. Nearly everything to my father's name was under lock and key. Mom had a small amount of money in savings, and that small amount, pooled together with what I had in my own...

Well. It was something. Meager, compared to what we were used to, but something. Just enough to pay for Dad's legal team and a small two-bedroom rental across town.

We'd lost our house. Our *home*.

I knew some people had considered the massive mansion to be too big and ostentatious—even Dad's wealthiest friends had exclaimed over the size and grandeur of our house—but to me, it'd always just been home.

The place where I'd spent my entire childhood. Where Ava had taught me to swim in the large pool house out back. Where I'd run down the stairs on Christmas morning, padding quietly on bare feet to make sure I didn't wake my parents up too early.

It still hadn't quite sunk in that this was real, although it'd been weeks since the day my father was arrested.

I was grateful it was summertime. I couldn't imagine going to school with this... scandal? Is that what it was called when your father was arrested for felony fraud?

Whatever it was called, I was glad I didn't have to face anyone at Highland Park Preparatory Academy with my father's trial hanging over my family like a guillotine blade ready to fall across our necks. But with the amount of money we needed, with everything that the federal agents took, there was no way Mom would have been able to keep the house.

Ava had stayed as long as possible. She'd helped us where she could, but without a steady paycheck, she had to move on to find another job. It broke my heart. It broke hers. We had said a tearful goodbye a few days ago, and out of all the things that had my heart hurting, her leaving was the worst.

Now, I stood in the doorway of our empty home, waiting for Mom to come downstairs. We'd moved what we could to the rental house; Ava had dropped off the few keepsakes and heirlooms we'd been allowed to keep there as her last favor to our family. The crystal glassware that had been used at my parents' wedding. The mahogany chair that'd belonged to my great-grandfather.

We couldn't take everything, however. Beside me were two suitcases with as many clothes as I had managed to fit in them. Enough for an extended holiday, but hardly everything. Not even half. Clothes, I knew, were the least of my worries, but after giving up so much of our lives, they felt like a comfort. They felt familiar.

It was silly. But at the moment, I didn't care.

"Mom?" I called up, hating how my voice echoed in the empty space. "We have to go."

A few moments later, she came down the stairs, her own suitcase held in one fragile hand. I watched her in silence, feeling helpless and awkward.

We hadn't spoken much since Dad's arrest. Without the comings and goings of a busy social life—because no one in their right minds would find themselves associating with us anymore, leaving us like a pair of castaways on a deserted island—without Dad, without Ava, the fact that Mom and I didn't really... speak to each other a lot became even more apparent.

I didn't know *how* to speak to her if I wasn't asking which cocktail dress she'd prefer me in, if I wasn't informing her that I had an event at school or had achieved some honor she'd be proud of. The emotional things, the things that came from the heart—my crushes on boys or fights with cruel girls at school or fears and doubts about the future— were things that I'd always spoken to Ava about. I would pour my heart out, and Ava would listen, hug me, and give me advice.

Reflexively, I turned, as if Ava would be standing at my side to reassure me that everything would be okay. No one was there. Nothing but cool air and the sinking feeling in my heart.

"Well... It's time to go," Mom said when she reached the bottom step. Her voice was heavy with weariness, reminding me that I wasn't the only one having a hard time with all of this. Mom was probably devastated, even if she didn't say it.

"Yeah," I said, injecting as much optimism into my voice as possible. "It's okay, Mom. I'm sure everything will work out soon. It's all just a misunderstanding, right?"

My mother gave a nod and a noncommittal hum. And that was the end of the conversation.

We loaded our suitcases into the back of the car, one of the few things we'd managed to keep. It was an old-school Bentley and had belonged to my mother's father. It was in her name; part of me wondered if the federal agents would have taken it if it'd been in my father's name, just out of spite.

Mom slid into the front seat as I climbed into the passenger side. We sat there for a few moments before I realized the problem.

She was staring at the steering wheel and dashboard, lost.

Oh, God. When was the last time that she had driven herself anywhere? Before I was born, I was certain. I reached over and took her hand, her knuckles white with the way she gripped the keys. I guided her movement as she slid the key into the ignition, turned it, and put the car in reverse.

"See." I smiled hopefully, even though it hurt my face. "Not so hard, right?"

My reassurance did nothing. Silently, my mother pulled us out of the driveway, and away from the only place I had ever called home.

THREE

OUR DRIVE WAS EERILY QUIET, void of music or speaking. I kept my head leaned against the window, looking outside as plush, manicured lawns and sprawling Baltimore mansions gave way to cluttered suburbs and over-crowded ghettos.

My stomach dropped as we left the familiar neighborhoods behind, heading deeper and deeper into the side of the tracks my father had always disparaged. Children ran up and down the sidewalks or rode bikes in the streets. More than once, people stopped to leer at my mother's car as we drove past.

They were looking at the car, not the two of us inside it, but it still felt like walking down the street stark naked and vulnerable. I shrank down in my seat, my heart thudding hard in my chest. I was used to being looked at, used to being the center of attention. But all my training for how to handle myself in high society had done nothing to prepare me for this. I felt wholly out of my depth.

Too soon, or perhaps not soon enough, Mom and I pulled into the driveway of a small house. It was squat and square, the cement of the front steps was crumbling, and the paint was faded and peeling. It barely looked like it could keep one person comfortably, let alone two.

My mother said nothing as she parked the car. We sat there for a moment, both of us staring at the house. From my understanding, my father's lawyer had helped her find this place. It'd been one of the only two-bedrooms we could afford, considering neither my mother nor I were working.

I swallowed. *Might as well get it over with.*

Mom was still sitting stock still beside me, and I had a feeling she wouldn't move until I did. So I was the first person out of the car.

The feeling of vulnerability didn't go away as I trailed around to the trunk, pulling out my suitcases. *It's okay*, I told myself. *It's just until Dad gets released.*

Because he *had* to be released. There was no way he could possibly be guilty of what he'd been accused of. Once he was exonerated, once this all blew over, we would get our things back—get our house back. We would be a family again. Whole.

I kept telling myself this, and as I lugged out both of my suitcases, I paused.

Someone was watching me.

Over the years, I'd gotten good at picking up on things like that. My mother had taught me to be aware of who was looking at me at all times—to navigate a cocktail party or ball with perfect aplomb.

My back straightened, and I glanced around, locking gazes with a boy standing across the street from me.

Shaggy brown hair fell into his face, but it didn't diminish the intensity of the hazel eyes that stared back at me. He leaned against a beat-up convertible, no shirt on and his jeans slung low on his hips. He was probably about my age, but he looked older somehow—like he'd seen more of the world in his seventeen or eighteen years than I had. His shoulders were broad, his muscles sculpted and defined.

The boy's head tilted as he openly stared at me, pinning me with his gaze as something like recognition flashed in his eyes. The thought of someone from here recognizing me sent a shiver of fear down my spine.

It's fine, Cora. He doesn't know you. Don't be ridiculous. He's probably just curious about the new neighbors. No one in this neighborhood probably had an inkling who my father was, let alone who I was.

Taking hold of whatever poise and haughtiness was left in me after the past several weeks, I turned my nose up. I wasn't usually snobby—not with people I knew—but this boy was a stranger, and I didn't have the patience to indulge his vulgar, rude staring.

Instead of looking away, he smirked, running his tongue over his bottom lip.

I flushed. *What the hell?*

Heat crept up my cheeks and then kept going, seeming to spread to every inch of my body, making me warm all over. The boy was undeniably good looking—one of the hottest guys I'd ever seen, actually—but something about him put me off-balance.

It wasn't like with Barrett, the way my skin had crawled when he'd touched me, making me want to flee his presence.

This was something else entirely.

Not repulsion.

Attraction.

Mom was still sitting in the car, and I couldn't seem to make my feet move. Couldn't tear my gaze away from the dangerous-looking, sexy boy across the street. He didn't seem in any hurry to look away either, and the longer we stared at each other, the harder it became to breathe.

Finally, the strange, buzzing connection between us was broken when two other boys approached the first. A bronze-skinned, tall one, and another with a shock of short blond hair. They were shirtless too, and the sight of them nearly short-circuited my brain.

It was too much to process at once. It wasn't like I'd never seen guys with their shirts off before, but there was something about the raw strength that seemed to radiate from their bodies, the dominating size of them, and the way they all stared at me in complete silence, that made my heart beat so hard I was sure they must be able to hear it from where they stood.

My mouth opened slightly as I tried to think of something to say—but no words came. If they had talked shit to us or catcalled me or something, I probably could've mustered up a scathing retort. But their quiet intensity threw me off.

The first boy, the brown-haired one, finally turned to murmur something to the boy with white-blond hair. It was too quiet for me to pick up his words, but I used the opportunity to wrench myself out of whatever strange bubble we'd all been encased in, stepping back toward the car and grabbing my bags again.

Mom was already inside—she'd gone in while I'd been distracted, leaving her suitcase behind in the trunk. She hadn't even bothered to close the door behind her.

Deciding to come back for her bag later, I followed after her. It took all my effort not to turn and look once more at the boys across the street, but I forced myself to keep my focus straight ahead even as their gazes burned into me.

I slammed the door shut behind me and paused inside.

Deep breath in, another out.

Our grand entrance had been larger than the space that took up the entire house, I realized as I looked around. The living room was smaller than some of our closets, the kitchen half the size of that. Not that I even knew how to cook.

Everything felt painfully claustrophobic as I made my

quick tour of the house. Small kitchen, small living room, one bathroom, two bedrooms.

I peeked into what I supposed counted as the master bedroom. My mother sat on an unmade bed, staring down at the floor.

"Mom?" I asked softly. I wondered if I should try to comfort her... she looked so lost.

She didn't look up at me as she answered dully. "Unpack. Ava brought groceries when she moved our things here. We'll make dinner soon."

We didn't, though.

Mom was fast asleep before dinner could even be considered. I finished unpacking the few things I'd been able to keep before I poked my head into her room again. She lay on top of the still unmade bed, curled in on herself. Her clothing was pristine, well kept, her hair still perfectly styled. She was still dressed like the blue-blood heiress who had been the envy of the Baltimore elite, but everything about her looked painfully out of place in this run-down little house.

Instead of waking her up, I decided to leave her be. Mom often claimed to have trouble sleeping, so if she was knocked out now, it was probably because she had a little help. I couldn't blame her. It would have been nice to lie down and simply think of nothing for the time being.

But when I thought of Dad sitting in some prison cell, it was hard to justify that kind of escapism.

Dad couldn't escape, so why should I?

Pushing down the guilt, I made my way to the kitchen.

Rifling through the pantry and the fridge, I saw that Ava had gone above and beyond stocking everything. There were boxes of dry goods, cans, frozen meats, veggies, and packaged meals. It struck me that she likely had paid for all of this with her own money. My heart seized once more thinking about her.

She was more a mother to me in some ways than my own mom. She'd gone out of her way to take care of me, to do what she could to ease this transition for us. And I had felt it in the way she'd hugged me goodbye that she still worried—that she would've done more to protect me if she could.

I spent ten minutes poking around the kitchen, utterly lost as to what I should cook for me and Mom, then eventually decided to say screw it. Today had been hard enough. Setting off the fire alarm and waking my mom up from an Ambient-induced nap would only make it worse. So I pulled out a box of cereal and some milk and headed to my room with a Tupperware-bowl full of Honey Bunches of Oats.

I settled on my bed, legs crossed, with my bowl of cereal in my lap. My bed was situated beside my window. Like Mom's, it had been salvaged from one of our old guest bedrooms at the mansion.

As I ate, I looked outside. My room was at the front of the house, and I had a straight-on view of the street and the house across from ours, where the three boys still stood on the patchy front lawn. They weren't paying attention to me or our house anymore. Now they stood close together, talking amongst themselves. The dark-haired, Latino boy with the beautiful eyes said something, and the shaggy-haired boy laughed, his face splitting into a wide grin.

For all the intensity he'd had when he'd stared at me, he looked surprisingly... soft when he laughed.

FOUR

GETTING USED to the new home was... a task.

A couple weeks had passed since we'd moved here, and it still felt like I was living in a stranger's home. I missed the familiarity, the comfort, of the winding halls of our family manor. The way the warm scent of the hand-crafted wood floors strengthened in the summer months, and how the light filtered in through the huge bay windows situated in almost every room, making the entire place feel ethereal.

Our tiny rental house smelled like dust and harsh cleaning products—as if the landlord had unsuccessfully attempted to bleach away the years of dirt that had accumulated. Whatever sun came in through the windows was off-colored and dull; the windows had a layer of fine grime over them, and I had no idea how to clean them properly.

I stared out the kitchen window as I ate breakfast slowly. It was Monday. First day of school.

Mom had taken her sweet time enrolling me in the public school that served this neighborhood. I think on some level, she couldn't fathom me going to a free school. Not like it mattered all that much—with Dad in jail, my going to public or private school was honestly the least of our concerns.

After finishing up breakfast—a bowl of overly sugary cereal, which was becoming my go-to as I avoided doing anything more challenging than heating up microwave dinners in the kitchen—I carefully cleaned the bowl and left it to dry on the small, chintzy dish rack.

Mom had so far refused to do any cooking or cleaning, as if that was her way of silently protesting the shitty hand life had dealt us. But with no more house staff to take care of things, it all fell to me.

I sighed, pushing down my irritation at my mom. She was trying. We both were.

And right now, housework was the furthest thing from my mind. For the first time, I was nervous about a first day of school.

I'd had friends at Highland Park Prep Academy. Caitlin Barrington, Felicia Prentice, and Allison Rhodes—we'd known each other since we were in diapers. We'd had plans to get married together, raise our kids together. The four of us had been the most popular girls at school, and that had cemented our bond even more.

Or at least, I'd thought it had.

I hadn't heard from any of them since my father's arrest.

Checks on social media told me they were still following me, still my "friends" as far as Facebook's algorithm was concerned. But none of them had called to see how I was doing. None of my texts or voicemails had been responded to. I'd given up after the first couple of days of radio silence, knowing what the quiet meant—that until my father was out of jail, my mother and I might as well not even exist to the Baltimore elite.

In some ways, I would've been more terrified to be going back to Highland Park today, knowing the kinds of whispers and stares that would be waiting for me in the pristine halls.

But going to a new school, a public school in a neighborhood I barely knew, was terrifying in its own way.

My heart thudded in my chest the entire drive there as I meandered down the cracked and dirty streets. Students trekked the sidewalks, laughing, joking around.

As I watched them, my thoughts went to the boys I'd seen across the street on my first day—and most days since. They didn't all live in the same house, I'd discovered, but they were almost always together. I'd started thinking of them as a unit, as if they were brothers or something. They clearly weren't, judging by the vast differences in their appearances, but there was something about the way they interacted that made it clear their bond was as close as blood.

Did they go to this school too? Would we be classmates?

Did it even matter if we were?

SLATEVIEW HIGH WAS APTLY NAMED. Its grey facade was broken only with mossy cracks and the smudge of graffiti paint. Someone had long ago given up on trying to clean it up; faded scribblings were covered over with newer, fresher paint.

Highland Park Prep didn't have a graffiti problem. The colorful scrawls were foreign to me, as were the shabby cars filling the uneven parking lot in the front of the school. Dented Mustangs and rickety station wagons were a common choice here, it seemed. I became uncomfortably aware that even the one car we'd managed to keep—our cheapest and oldest, nothing at all compared to the newer cars that had filled our garages—stood out, and not in a good way.

That was apparent immediately when I stepped out of it. I straightened my clothes and swung my backpack over my shoulder. The car I'd parked beside had a girl sitting on the back end, her feet propped on the bumper. A guy stood with her, settled between her legs with his hands resting on the swell of her ass. They both had their gazes trained on me, sneers on their lips.

"Hey, new girl." The boy narrowed his eyes. "You got something to say, staring so hard?"

Shaking my head, I looked away quickly. "No. Sorry."

I didn't want attention drawn to me. I just wanted to fade into the background and blend in. But I could already tell that wasn't going to happen. Even though no school uniform

was required at Slateview, my clothes alone singled me out as
an outsider. Everyone here had some kind of edge to them.
Hair dyed bright. Piercings. Clothes with rips, too much skin
showing to be considered within dress code. I was dressed...
normally. At least, what I'd *thought* was normal.

I could tell I stuck out as I walked from the parking lot to
the front entrance of the school. People wouldn't stop staring
at me. Even those that looked like teachers on their way to
their classes before the bell rang gave me lingering, quizzical
looks.

As I stepped inside the building, I was hit with the
cacophony of students talking, yelling, shoving their way
through the crowd, and the scent of what was very distinctly
cigarette smoke—and maybe another kind of smoke too.

The hall was so packed that I hoped I could slip through
the mass of bodies unnoticed, but my heart jumped into my
throat when someone yelled loudly, their voice cutting over
the cacophony around us.

"Hey! Fancy girl! The fuck you doing here?"

I didn't answer. I didn't even look back. My face flamed
as I pushed harder through the crowd, ignoring the new
voices that joined the first.

I didn't need to question who "fancy girl" was, and as the
day wore on, I realized that it was more than just my
appearance and my obvious disconnect from the other
students' social status that people had a problem with.

My class schedule resembled the one I'd had at Highland
Park Prep—if only barely. Slateview didn't offer honors

classes, let alone advanced placement classes, classes that I'd been in good standing in every year I'd attended Highland Park.

My first class of the day was geometry. There were at least thirty kids packed into the dingy room, and the teacher, Mrs. Wright, held me up at the front when I entered so she could introduce me. Her voice was bored and exhausted, like she was already tired of being here.

"Let's give a warm welcome to Cordelia van Rensselaer," she droned. "Cordelia—"

A girl in the front scoffed, interrupting her.

"Yeah. We all know who she is." She flipped her long, box-dye-red hair over her shoulder. Her makeup was heavy, and her blue eyes piercing. "Little Miss Rich Bitch. You here because your daddy lost all your money? Poor little fuckin' rich girl. Better tell your dad not to drop the soap."

I swallowed, staring at her. How did she know who my father was?

Mrs. Wright said nothing—not about the girl cursing, and not about her insulting my father. She just sighed and nudged my shoulder.

"There's a seat in the third row. Go on."

That was the last thing she said to me before she began the lesson. Nothing about the rich bitch comment. Nothing about the snickers, the stares, and the whispers that followed me as I made my way toward the empty seat either. One girl stuck her foot out, making me trip as I walked by her. My stomach pitched, and I grabbed hold of a desk to keep myself from falling flat on my face. The boy at the desk sneered at me, his lip piercing glinting under the dull florescent lights.

"Back off, bitch. I didn't say you could touch my shit. You think you just *own* everything here?"

I snatched my hands away and found my seat. My face burned, and if the lingering snickers from the rest of the class were any indication, everyone in the class could see the blush that painted my cheeks red. Embarrassment flooded me, and I forced my gaze up to the front, attempting to keep my attention on Mrs. Wright. It was hard; her lecture voice was incredibly boring.

Maybe that's why it was easy for the other students to allow their attention to drift back to me.

The staring. That was the worst part.

I could feel their gazes creeping over my skin like ants.

Slut, skank, whore—they whispered those words to me, their quiet voices cutting through Mrs. Wright's droning lecture. I was far from innocent and had heard them before, but the way they threw them at me with such vehemence made my stomach flip.

And this is only day one.

FIVE

SECOND AND THIRD period were about the same. My reprieve came in fourth—gym.

I was a little late, so by the time the other girls were filing out of the locker room, I was stepping inside. They gave me the same harsh looks, but I was at least able to change into my gym clothes in peace. And there were no opportunities for anyone to trip or shove me, considering most of my gym time was spent filling out forms.

Did I have any medical conditions the coach needed to be aware of? Did I have medications like an inhaler or an Epi-Pen that I would need to have access to when we did outside activities? Was I interested in sports? Would I like to have information on the track try-outs?

No, no, no, and no were my answers. And Coach Green was chatty enough that by the time we were done sorting out the first-day paperwork, gym was over and it was time for lunch.

Thank God.

Since we all left the gym at the same time, however, I didn't miss the other girls in the locker room this time. The redhead from my first class trailed in after me, talking loudly with a few of her friends. I ignored her and the other girls as they changed back into their street clothes, moving quickly to my locker to grab my things, intent on getting out of here without any trouble.

Maybe I should've known that was a hopeless wish.

I heard them too late. Without warning, I was flanked with my shirt off, jerked around to face the redhead and shoved back against my locker. The lock dug into my spine, the shock of pain making my eyes water. The girl was taller than me, though that was mostly due to the impressive heeled boots she wore.

"Well, well, well. If it isn't little Miss Rich Bitch," she taunted. "I thought they were lying when they said you'd been enrolled here, but holy shit, karma must be fuckin' real."

"Listen." I swallowed, steeling myself. "I don't know why you don't like me, but I promise whatever it is, I'm sure it's just a complete misunderstanding—"

The girl laughed. "Nah, it's not a misunderstanding, cupcake. We know who you are... and we know who your daddy is. You ever heard of Westhill Apartments?"

My brows furrowed. That was an apartment complex my

father had bought up a few years ago. He'd turned it into a luxury townhouse community.

"Yes. I—my father—"

"Your *father*," she sneered, imitating my voice. "Yeah. Your daddy bought that up for pennies and then turned it into some rich fuck establishment. You know how many families from that old complex got kids that go to this school? You know how many of us got thrown out on our asses when our landlords decided your daddy's pennies were worth more than ours?"

I blinked at her, not even sure what to say to that. Dad had said those buildings had been dilapidated. Abandoned. That he'd been doing the community a service when he bought them to bring in some higher-end buyers—

"Why don't we talk about Tenner's Bakes? Huh? Or the clothing swap on 24th? Or any of the businesses that were doing just *fine* before your daddy thought that he needed to gentrify what wasn't his?"

"There must be a mistake—"

The girl slammed her hand against the locker beside my head. I jolted from the rattling that reverberated through my body.

"Ain't no mistake, cupcake," she snapped. "My father lost his shop in your daddy's little buyout spree. You know how many years he worked at that store? And for what? Some ass that had too much time and money on his hands to know what to do with it, dangling all that cash in front of our landlord? You know we were three months out from being able to buy the place ourselves? Three. Fuckin'. Months. Dad works at Papa John's now." Then she snickered. "At least he ain't in jail."

Adrenaline surged through me, and I pushed back at her, shoving hard at her chest. "Don't talk about my father—"

The two girls that had flanked me took one shoulder each, driving me back into the lockers as the redhead gripped my chin. Her self-manicured nails dug into my skin.

"I'll talk about whoever the fuck I want, cupcake," she crooned, her lips curling. "And I'll do whatever I want to rich bitches that walk in here thinking their shit don't stink just because they come from money. You might have had a little mansion on the hill, but you're on the wrong side of the tracks now, princess, and we're not the only ones with a bone to pick with you."

She leaned in, getting close to my ear, the scent of her hairspray invading my nostrils.

"Just wait till the Lost Boys get their hands on you. Bish is gonna have a fuckin' field day with you. A daddy in jail won't be the worst thing to happen to you, cupcake, and your fancy car and your fancy clothes won't protect you from what's coming. Folks around here might not be able to get their hands on your pops, might not be able to take it out on him— but you'll do."

She and her friends tossed me away, throwing me to the floor before they turned and headed for the door, laughing loudly. No one else in the locker room had batted an eyelash the entire time. It was as if the scene hadn't even happened.

I sat on the floor, trying to breathe as steadily as I could manage. I pulled myself up once the locker room started to empty out, quietly and shakily changing out of my gym clothes and into my regular clothes.

The good thing was, it wasn't like I needed to be on time for lunch. Unlike the rest of my class periods, no one would care if I was late for that.

I took my time, waiting until the sick feeling from the adrenaline in my system wore off a little before stepping into the cafeteria. There were already a considerable number of tables taken, which was fine by me; I didn't want to sit around with these people any longer than I already had today. I just wanted to get my food and find somewhere quiet and deserted.

Lunch itself was as alien as the rest of the school. Nothing like the fresh salad bar or gourmet selections that'd been on offer every day at Highland Park Prep. There, I could've had shrimp scampi on Monday, a flat bread tomato mozzarella panini on Tuesday, and authentic French cuisine for the rest of the week.

The aroma that assaulted me as I stood in line wasn't that of succulent spices and fresh cooking meats, but of salt and grease and something slightly burnt. It turned my stomach even more than the encounter with the redhead in the locker room had. Disgust and anxiety compounded on top of each other as I came to the head of the line.

"Um, is there something else that I could order? Maybe a—"

"What you see is what you get, sunshine." The lunch lady, with her hair pulled back in a dingy white cap and her eyes trained listlessly on the screen in front of her, didn't even bother to look up at me when she spoke. Someone behind me laughed.

"Don't mind her, Miss Patricia. She thinks she's fuckin' special. Thinks maybe you got a special menu for royalty."

The twisting in my stomach got so bad I was afraid I might actually throw up. Grabbing the tray she handed me, I didn't even look at the food on it as I turned and hurried away, brushing past the boy who'd spoken without meeting his gaze.

At each table I passed, I was met with confrontational stares—*glares*, really.

I wondered if what the redhead had said was true. How many of these people were children of those who'd been put out of their businesses? Their homes? Or maybe that was all just a made-up excuse for why she'd attacked me. Maybe she was just using it to scare me, just like she'd tried to scare me with those boys she'd mentioned—the Lost Boys.

But they couldn't be that bad, could they? How could they hate me more than everyone else here did?

Since the lunchroom was off limits—my own decision, I decided to say, pretending that it had less to do with the people giving me disgusted looks and more to do with my personal desire to be left alone—I went outside. There weren't any formal sitting areas outside, but it didn't matter, since it wasn't like teachers were watching to stop anyone from slipping out either.

I found a spot near the outside wall of the cafeteria, away from the doors so I wouldn't be seen, but not too far away. Despite how horrible the day was turning out to be, despite my impulse to be alone, I didn't want to stray too far from the crowded lunchroom. Who knew when the redhead girl from earlier would decide she wanted to come at me for a second round.

Breathing a sigh of relief, I glanced down at my tray. My stomach pitched again. Out here, I didn't have to worry about stares or snickers or people throwing harsh words my way. Instead, I had another problem to contend with.

The food.

I wasn't sure what I was supposed to be eating. One pile of mush, another pile of slightly more palatable-looking mush, a carton of milk that I'd only just realized was already opened, or the fruit cup? The fruit cup was the one thing I thought I could stomach, until it occurred to me that I hadn't gotten a spoon.

My stomach rumbled; the breakfast I'd had this morning clearly wasn't going to last me all day, but I wasn't nearly desperate enough to eat this—especially not with my hands. And going back into the lunchroom to look for a spoon was out of the question.

I sighed and glanced around, spotting a trash can near the corner of the building. A few flies buzzed around it, as if they were just waiting for the chance to attack my ill-fated lunch. I'd have to remember to pack something to eat tomorrow.

As I dumped my food, tray and all, I heard a laugh. The sound sent a shiver up my spine—it was deep and velvety, but there was a hard edge to it too.

"What's the matter? Food not good enough for you, princess?"

I looked up, instantly on edge. I hadn't noticed there was someone around the corner. *Three* someones, to be specific—and I recognized all of them. They were the boys from my block, the ones who'd stared at me on my first day in the new house.

They leaned against the wall, looking every bit as dangerous and darkly beautiful as they had the first day I'd seen them. The shaggy haired one stood in the middle, his arms folded over his chest. The blond and the dark-haired one flanked him. I was instantly reminded of the girls in the locker room, the way they'd stood in the same formation before they'd attacked me.

I'd barely stood a chance against three vicious girls, and these three boys were all tall and muscled, each well over six feet. I was a petite 5'4", and even standing several feet away from them, I had to crane my neck a little to meet their gazes.

The boy with messy brown hair had asked me a question, but it felt like a bad idea to answer. I was positive there was no *right* answer anyway.

I took two steps backward, then turned on my heel and

started toward the side door I'd come out of. Maybe I'd take my chances in the cafeteria after all.

But the boys were fast.

Two of them reached me before I could even make it around the corner. Large hands closed around my arms, rough and warm, their grip tight.

God, no.

My heart raced, and I struggled against their hold. No one could say the rich bitch wasn't a fighter, even if she was punching above her weight. I dug my feet in, but all it did was slow our movements slightly as the blond boy and the one with caramel skin and dark hair brought me back to stand before the boy with enigmatic hazel eyes. He had yet to even move, standing just where I'd left him like a king surveying his domain.

I hated that he was gorgeous. Hated that they all were.

Maybe it would've been easier to despise them if they hadn't had a wild, almost feral beauty that attracted me as much as it terrified me.

I tried, though. I stared the boy in front of me down, refusing to look away or cower. He jerked his chin slightly, and his buddies let me go. I didn't try to run though; I knew better than that. I'd learned my lesson the first time, and I knew without a doubt that if I ran, they'd chase me—and they *would* catch me.

So this staring contest, this battle of wills, whatever you wanted to call it, would have to do.

We all stood in silence for several long beats. I could feel the other two boys at my sides and smell a faint hint of cloves and sage. It tickled my nostrils, and I breathed more shallowly, not wanting to take in any part of them.

"You didn't like lunch," the shaggy-haired boy said finally. "Not gourmet enough? Maybe it shoulda been served to you on a silver platter?"

I flushed angrily.

For the entire first half of the day, I'd put up with whispers and glares. I'd tried to keep my head down and ignore it all. But despite the fact that everyone here seemed to think they had me all figure out, these people didn't know me.

"It's not like that," I gritted out. "I didn't have a spoon... or a fork."

"You couldn't just go back inside and get one?"

"I didn't want to cut the line."

"Huh. Princess has manners."

His smirk lit a fire inside me. Heavy emotion flooded me, and I couldn't tell if it was fear, anger, or something more dangerous and forbidden. I clenched my jaw against the flush of heat spreading through me.

"It's not like that," I repeated.

The boy in front of me laughed. He looked to my left, where the dark-haired boy stood.

"What do you think, Misael?"

"I think princess thinks she's too good for what everyone else eats."

"Too bad. Rest of us have to deal with the cafeteria slop. Why don't you?" The one on the right, the blond, spoke up.

He was the biggest one, and I faltered when he nudged me. I glared at him, eyes narrowed. He smirked down at me. The muscles in his arm flexed as he folded them; a huge sleeve tattoo in the likeness of a snake caught my eye before I looked back to the boy leaning against the wall.

"What do you want?" I asked, trying to inject more confidence into my voice than I felt. "If you're here to whine to me about something my father did, or try to scare me with stories about the Lost Boys or whatever—"

"Oh, word travels fast. So you've heard of us already."

"Jesus Christ. That fuckin' nickname." The dark-haired boy to my left chuckled.

My stomach dropped.

I was sure my face had gone pale, but the boy in front of me didn't skip a beat as he dipped his head in a mock-formal greeting. "My name's Bishop. Bish to my friends, which you are not. Then Misael"—he nodded to the dark-haired Latino boy—"and Kace," he said of the blonde. "We call him Reaper. I don't think I need to explain why."

No, he didn't. With how built the boy was, and how violence seemed to radiate from his very pores, I didn't need to ask either.

"And why should I care?" I said, lifting my chin and giving a nonchalant shrug, even as my heart slammed against my ribs.

"Because," Bishop said. "We run this school. We *own* this school. So in effect, Princess, we own you too."

There was a dangerous truth in his voice when he said it.

Silky smooth, no room for question or argument. Whatever snide comeback I might've made stayed planted on the tip of my tongue, unwilling to voice itself under the finality of Bishop's statement.

I was lucky—I didn't have to force myself to speak because a few seconds later, the bell rang, signaling the end of lunch. Bishop didn't take his eyes off me, and for several long seconds, I remained stock still, frozen in place.

Finally, I backed away from the three boys and walked toward the school entrance as fast as I could, my skin tingling as I braced myself for their touch.

This time, they didn't stop me, but I wasn't stupid.

I knew this wouldn't be my last encounter with the Lost Boys.

SIX

THE REST of the day passed by in a daze. I didn't have any more encounters like the ones with the Lost Boys or the redhead girl—whose named I'd learned was Serena—but it didn't mean I wasn't ogled, sneered at, or shoved whenever the opportunity hit.

Not even my locker was immune from the awful treatment. I went to gather my books after my final class let out, and my stomach dropped as I noticed a group of people gathered around it, laughing loudly. When they parted to let me through, I saw that someone had written the words "Rich Skank" in red letters across the chipped paint of the locker door.

I didn't even bother to get a teacher, or to complain about it to anyone. Something told me tattling on my new classmates would end up being worse for me than just dealing with the tagging for the rest of the year.

It was a relief to finally slip into my car and pull out of the parking lot, blessedly alone for the first time all day. I wasn't sure I'd ever experienced a longer eight hours in my life.

I needed to do some kind of damage control.

First—figure out what the hell everyone was talking about when they said my father had destroyed their neighborhoods by flipping their homes and their businesses. I hadn't known anything about that, and I wasn't even sure it was true.

Second—do something to blend in a little more. If I could make people realize that Dad wasn't the person they thought he was, and maybe... look a little more like everyone else at my school, people might leave me alone. Or at the very least, maybe the redhead and the Lost Boys would stay off my back.

I didn't even want to think about the implications of them owning the school and therefore owning me. I didn't want to be owned by anyone, least of all by three boys who terrified and attracted me in equal measure—three boys who lived on my street and could literally watch my every move if they chose to.

No, thanks. Better to do what I could to become invisible at Slateview, to pass through my senior year like a ghost, than to attract the wrong kind of attention.

With fresh determination, I walked into the rental house, setting my bag on the kitchen table. The place was still and quiet.

"Mom?"

A muffled sound came from her room. I frowned and

made my way back, opening the door a few inches and peering inside.

She was curled up on the bed, snuggled deep down under the blankets. The small television in her room was on, some reality TV show playing, but I didn't think Mom was really paying attention. My stomach clenched, a new kind of tension filling me. All day at school, I'd been too busy dealing with the bullying and cruelty to think about what waited for me back at home.

I honestly wasn't sure which was worse.

Slipping inside the bedroom, I walked over and sat beside her. She didn't move or even turn her head to look at me.

"Hey... have you gotten out of bed today?" I asked awkwardly. I wasn't sure what I was supposed to do about this catatonia that my mother seemed to be in more often than not lately. She'd always been quiet, perfectly reserved and demure—but I'd never seen her retreat inside herself like this. Like she had lost a part of herself.

Well. I guess that's probably what it feels like when your husband is taken from you and your entire life crumbles around you.

I saw her shrug beneath the blankets. She didn't answer.

Okay. Guess we aren't going to talk about that then. Besides, I was pretty sure I knew the answer. She might've gotten up to eat while I was at school, but I was guessing that was the only time she'd left this room.

"Did you have a good day?" I pressed, hating everything about this. I hated the fact that I didn't know how to help her, and I hated the fact that she was so locked up inside herself, in her own grief, that she couldn't help me.

"It was okay," she murmured dully.

"Do you need to talk?"

"No."

I sighed. Fair enough. We'd never really talked much before all of this happened anyway. I decided to move on with what I had come in here for in the first place.

"I wanted to ask you something," I said, a little louder than my previous questions, so I would actually get her attention. "About Dad."

That finally jolted her out of her daze a bit. She actually looked at me.

"A lot of kids at school were saying things today," I continued. "Bad things, about Dad's work."

Mom averted her eyes, pulling the covers closer around her. "You know I didn't bother your father about his work, Cora."

"Yes, but maybe you knew some of the things that he was doing? People were saying awful things... that he was the reason a lot of them lost their homes, or their families lost their businesses—"

"I don't know anything about your father's work," she repeated sharply. "Stop asking me. This is giving me a headache, Cordelia. Don't you care? I don't want to talk about this. I don't know anything."

I deflated. Ugh, I should've known better than to try to talk to her when she was like this. I just wanted to know the truth. I'd stood by my father after his arrest, and I was still waiting patiently for him to be proved innocent—for this all to be dismissed as a horrible mistake. But I didn't like being kept in the dark.

Tugging my bottom lip between my teeth, I stared down at the lump under the covers that was my mother as silence stretched between us.

Thoughts and questions, doubts and fears, pressed at the edges of my mind. There were so many things I wanted to say, and I wished like hell I could say them to her. I wanted to tell her about my day at school and have her actually listen, maybe even give me advice.

But when had I ever talked to my mother about my bad days, or my good days, or my days at all?

Knowing that any more attempt at conversation would be talking to a wall, I left the TV playing and slipped out of the room, leaving my mom to her self-pitying stupor. I was on my own in this new world, and I needed to move on to phase two of my post-first-day damage control.

My clothes.

There was no way I'd be able to buy new clothes, even non-designer clothes, just to try to fit in with everyone else at Slateview. But I'd found a pair of scissors in the kitchen. If I could ruin the designer clothes in my closet enough, distress them and rip them up a little, then maybe I could at least make myself a little more incognito than I currently was.

I laid my jeans out on the bed alongside several expensive tops, then picked up the scissors. I hesitated just a moment, opening and closing the blades. Every piece of clothing before me was a reminder of a life I no longer had, a world I no longer lived in. One defined by excess, privilege, and wealth. In that life, I could've destroyed every item in my closet, and Dad would've replaced it all without batting an eye.

Now? This was all I had. The last of my father's money had bought these clothes, and I was about to deface them.

For survival. It was worth it. There was no point in nice clothes if I was going to have to suffer for it.

I attacked the jeans first, ripping and tearing into the fabric. I added holes to a few pairs and cut others into shorts.

Each cut felt like carving out a piece of myself, separating the new me from the old me, and I tried not to think about how pathetic that might have seemed to someone else as I moved on to the tops. I continued like that, altering the way my clothing looked until I was satisfied that the previous designer shine was no longer there.

I may have been a van Rensselaer, but I didn't have to look the part. I didn't have to give the other students any more reasons to look at me like a target. To hate me for what I'd once had. To associate me with my father in any way.

Because the truth was, I wasn't any better off than anyone else at that school now. I wasn't just trying to make myself look like them. I *was* one of them.

God, I hope this works. I can't make it through an entire year of days like today.

AFTER PLAYING FASHION DESIGNER, I put my clothes away. Since I was trying new things, I decided to attempt to make a decent dinner for Mom and me. Maybe a warm meal would make her feel a little better, although I doubted it.

I decided to go for one of the boxed meals. It had everything in there to make a dinner—some sort of quick bake. The directions were easy. *Open the can of meat and sauce, put it in a pan, sprinkle the topping over it, bake it.* It was a no-brainer, and I followed the instructions to the T as I sat down to do my homework.

But time must've gotten away from me. I finished my geometry assignment and was just beginning to draft a US history essay when I caught the scent of something burning.

"What the—"

Shit.

I stood quickly, darting frantically into the kitchen. It was smoky and hazy—why the hell wasn't the fire alarm working? I searched around for a pair of potholders, but couldn't find them, possibly because we didn't own any. I dashed to my room, got my bath towel, and used that to pull dinner out of the oven.

It was a crispy, unappetizing mess. My eyes watered and burned from the smoke that rose up from the pan. Shame bubbled in my gut. If I couldn't make something as simple as a boxed meal with directions, how was I supposed to make anything that was actually appetizing? Anything we could actually eat that wasn't out of a bag, a frozen box, or take-out?

Dejected, I threw the mess into the trash and decided to settle for cereal for the night. I'd try again tomorrow; maybe I'd have more luck then.

I'd spent enough time on my homework that the sun was already going down. Grabbing the garbage bag and tying it off, I headed out to the curb, not wanting to wait until it was fully dark. This neighborhood still creeped me out at night.

I tossed the garbage away, having no intention of staying outside longer than necessary—especially not with one of the Lost Boys living across the street. I didn't even let my eyes linger on the house across from ours; it felt as though if I even dared to think about him, Bishop would emerge through the front door of the dilapidated house like he'd been called from the shadows.

What did catch my eyes, however, was something much different.

The car that rolled slowly down the street stood out among the rusted, dented, scrap-metal junkers that were common in this area. A shiny black Bentley with darkly tinted windows. It clearly didn't belong to anyone on this block, let alone this neighborhood. It looked like—

My heart jumped. Maybe it was someone from my old life, coming to take Mom and me away from this place. Maybe it was Dad, somehow released from jail already, coming to surprise us.

A dozen hopeful thoughts raced through my mind, and I

wanted to believe that every one of them was true. That my horrific first day was the only day I'd have to suffer through at Slateview High. Quick as the hope came, however, it was dashed against the sidewalk pavement just as fast. The car drove right past me, the fading sunlight glinting off one of its mirrors like it was mocking me for daring to dream that I might be pulled out of this hell I hadn't asked to be put in.

I watched it, my shoulders slumping, as it drove a few doors down. It stopped in front of a two-story house and idled softly. Something in me felt like I shouldn't be watching this, but I was rooted to the spot as I watched a figure emerge from the front door of the house.

One of the Lost Boys.

The big one—Kace, with the light blond hair and muscles that looked like they belonged on a professional fighter more than they did a high school boy—strode down the walkway to the car. He was shirtless; even in the waning light, I could see the dark, colorful marks of his tattoo. Bold. Beautiful.

Dangerous.

The passenger side window rolled down, and Kace leaned over and spoke into the car. I couldn't make out what he was saying, but there was a smirk on his face. He said something else, nodded, and then reached into the car, pocketing something that was given to him.

Then, he looked my way.

It was a split second of eye contact. A split second that had my face heating as his gaze burned into mine. The way he looked at me—the way *all* the Lost Boys looked at me—

was like nothing I'd ever experienced before. It felt like he was looking through my outer layers, past every mask and defense I had, into the very heart of me.

I shivered, tearing my gaze away from his and abandoning all pretense of poise as I sprinted into the house.

A soft noise filtered through the door as I slammed it shut, and I swore it was the sound of Kace laughing.

THE NEXT MORNING, I spoke to my father for the first time since he'd been taken away. He and Mom both insisted that we not make visits. Neither of them wanted me at a prison—didn't think it was proper. I suspected, to a degree, that Mom simply didn't want to face the idea of people seeing her going into a prison, being in a place with actual, dangerous criminals. A place that her husband certainly didn't belong; it was undignified.

That, I could understand. But not hearing from him was hell.

He called early in the morning before I left for school. We put the phone on speaker and sat in Mom's bedroom, our heads slightly bent together. It was the closest I'd felt to my mother, both physically and emotionally, in a long time.

"Elizabeth, Cordelia. It's good to hear your voices." Dad's words were thick as they came through the speaker. He sounded tired. Mom remained quiet, blinking rapidly, so I immediately spoke to fill the silence.

"Hey, Dad. How are you? Is everything alright there? I've been so worried—"

"Cordelia, please. It's early, and I haven't got a lot of time to speak. They dole out phone time like it's more precious than gold."

I visibly shrank back. Not that he could see my reaction, I realized with a strange, weighted sadness.

"Sorry."

"Anyway. I called to check up on the two of you. According to Isaac, you've been settled in a rental home?"

Isaac was my father's attorney, and I'd bet the little money we still had that he and my father had spoken every day since Dad's arrest.

"Yeah... it's different," I said softly when Mom still didn't speak up. "It's nothing like home—"

"I'm aware. But it's what we're working with until I get out of this place and clear everything up. It shouldn't take long." God, I wished I had his confidence. "The whole thing is just a misunderstanding. Isaac is looking into it. He thinks it's a political maneuver to smear my name and undermine both me and my business associates."

Who would do something like that?

"Does it—I mean, is that why the people at school are saying some... awful things about why you were arrested?" I asked, hoping that unlike my mother, Dad would actually give me a proper answer.

"Things?" he asked. His tone shifted. Was that... worry? "What things?"

"Stuff about you buying out properties, making people lose their homes... their businesses—"

"Complete lunacy," he said immediately. "People always need someone to blame for their bad decision making—"

He cut off. Garbled speaking in the background came through, but I couldn't actually make out much of it.

"I have to go. I'll call you again when I can. Keep your heads up, both of you. I'll be out of this place soon."

"Dad—"

The call disconnected. Mom never even said a word.

SEVEN

THE CALL with my father had lasted less than five minutes, but I found myself turning every word over and over in my mind as I drove to school.

What was I supposed to make of any of it? Aside from Dad's confidence, his blunt reassurance, I had no real answers. His excuse about people just making things up because their choices had been bad didn't make sense to me. Why would they target a man they didn't even know if the loss of their homes was their own fault? And how could they have targeted my dad anyway? Who did he think had set him up?

Maybe Dad had gotten involved in some shady deals accidentally. He was ambitious, working twelve or sixteen-hour days for much of my childhood, but I'd always thought he was fair. Whatever aspersions people wanted to cast on men like my father, I believed he was a good man.

Still, questions and doubts plagued my thoughts as I pulled into Slateview's parking lot.

Like yesterday, all eyes were on me as I stepped out of my car. And like yesterday, I felt anxious and awkward, uncomfortable in my own skin. This time, however, it was partly because of the way I was dressed. I'd chosen one of the ripped pairs of jeans I'd distressed and a cropped top. It felt odd, being so exposed, but I hoped the effect was more chameleon than peacock.

That hope was dashed before I even reached the front doors of the school.

Maybe—*maybe*—if I'd shown up on my first day dressed like this, driving a different car or no car at all, I might've been able to blend in unnoticed. But I should've known it was too late to try to change anyone's mind about me. Everyone at this school had already decided who I was and what I was.

The taunts from yesterday didn't dissipate. In fact, they got worse. Snide remarks about me attempting to "slum it" mingled with thinly veiled threats about cutting up my body the same way I'd cut up my clothes, taunts and catcalls following me throughout the day. The only good thing was that the redheaded girl, Serena, wasn't in classes today. She'd apparently chosen to skip and spend the day with her boyfriend, who went to a different school. I didn't pay much more attention than that; I didn't need to know the sordid details of her extracurricular activities.

I also didn't see much of the Lost Boys—at least, not

directly. I saw them in the halls between classes. Now that I was hyper-aware of each of the three boys, I realized I shared a couple classes with one or two of the trio. But they never approached me, never bothered me.

I made sure not to bother them either, and I ate my lunch in a corner of the cafeteria so I couldn't get trapped outside with them again. But almost against my will, I found my gaze gravitating toward them whenever I was in a classroom or hallway with them—observing them, drawn by the dangerous energy and charisma they all exuded.

And what I saw made me feel certain they hadn't been lying. They really did own this school.

It was more the little things than the big things that convinced me. It wasn't like they paraded down the halls on red velvet carpets or anything. But *everyone*—students and teachers alike—moved out of the way when they walked past. When the three of them walked into a room, everyone shifted toward them unconsciously, as if every single person in this school existed in their orbit.

Whether that was true or just in my mind, I decided the best thing I could do was keep my head down and hope the novelty of the "poor little rich bitch" wore off quickly.

I was actually feeling pretty good when I pushed through the school doors at three o'clock. With Serena gone, her posse had mostly left me alone, and I was getting better at ignoring the taunts and cruel names.

Maybe I can do this. Just until Dad gets—

I stopped dead.

Ice flooded my veins, making me feel numb all over, as I stared at the spot where'd I'd parked my mother's car in the morning.

The car was still there. But it was totaled.

My stomach clenched, the granola bar I'd brought for lunch sitting like a lump of cement in my gut. The car was old, something my mom wouldn't have been caught dead driving in our old life—but it had been well taken care of. There hadn't been a scratch on the sleek black paint when I drove into the parking lot this morning. Now, it was riddled with dents, the glass of almost every window was broken, and the windshield was cracked in a spiderweb pattern. The tires had been slashed, and the entire car had been rolled onto its side.

This hadn't been just one person with a misplaced grudge; this had been a group effort to beat the life out of my car. And as a finishing touch, someone had spray-painted "rich cunt" across the undercarriage.

There were more tags on the car, more heartless works of art, but I didn't bother to read them.

Something in me broke. I felt the pang in my chest, like a knife through my heart.

It shouldn't matter. It was just a car. But it had been the last real, untouched thing from my old life—my *normal* life—and now it was barely fit to serve as scrap in a junkyard. A lump in my throat choked me, tears threatening to well over.

I didn't let them.

Clenching my hands so hard my nails cut into my palms,

I gritted my teeth and blinked hard a few times. People were watching me, laughing and shouting, filming my reaction and my car on their phones.

I'd only been going to this school for two days, but I already knew one thing with absolute certainty: I couldn't afford to look weak in front of the students at Slateview. It would make everything I was already going through so much worse, would make them see that they could get to me, that their cruelty affected me. And I couldn't let that happen. Next time, it might not be my car that got trashed. It could be me.

Let them have the car. Just let them have the damn thing. We can get a new one... someday.

At least, that's what I told myself. It was what I clung to as I turned and walked stiffly along the sidewalk leading from the school into the neighborhood, clutching my books in my arms.

The school buses had already left, and even if they hadn't, I didn't have a bus pass since I was supposed to be a driver. I wondered, somewhat bitterly, if I should just get used to walking. I couldn't imagine having to spend any amount of time on a bus with people that were willing to vandalize my car in broad daylight, let alone knowing that it would give more people a direct confirmation of where I lived.

Holy shit. I'm starting to sound so paranoid. It's ridiculous.

Regardless, I kept my head down as I walked, intent on

avoiding contact with anyone from the school. I pushed through some loitering crowds of kids here and there at the edge of school grounds, but blissfully, thankfully, they didn't bother me, too wrapped up in their own overtly jovial entertainment to care that I was even there.

Mom and I lived several miles away from Slateview. It was a quick drive in the morning, but it would take me at least an hour to walk home now.

A few kids yelled out the windows of their cars as they drove away from school, but once I'd walked for about thirty minutes, the streets grew mostly empty and quiet. It was a hot fall day, and humidity made tendrils of my blonde hair stick to the back of my neck. A drop of sweat tickled my back as it dripped down my spine.

I'd made it to the street our rental house was on when the back of my neck prickled for a new reason. My footsteps slowed, and my heart beat faster as I turned my head just slightly, unable to ignore the sudden uncomfortable feeling that I was being followed.

I was.

From the corner of my eye, I saw a car creep up alongside me. A beat-up convertible, just a little nicer than the cars that I was used to seeing, but not by much. My stomach dropped when I saw who was inside.

The Lost Boys.

I kept my face trained straight ahead, hugging my books close to my chest. If they thought I hadn't noticed them, maybe they'd leave me alone, thinking I just wasn't interested or particularly aware of them enough to care—

"Hey. You ignoring us, Princess?"

I took in a deep breath and turned to face them. Bishop was behind the wheel, Misael in the passenger seat, and Kace in the back. Misael typed away on his phone, looking up to me with a raised brow and a smirk when our eyes met. I pulled my gaze from him and shifted it to Bishop before continuing my walk.

"I'm just going home," I said flatly. "So if you'll excuse me—"

"What's with that get up?" Misael spoke up, jerking his chin toward my shredded clothes. "You look like you're trying to be somethin' you ain't, Princess."

"Stop calling me princess."

"Ain't that what you are? A princess?"

"No. It's not."

The trio laughed, amused at my indignation.

"Ain't what we hear, but that's fine. Can't hide what you are, anyway. You don't blend in well."

"Is there a reason you're telling me all this? A reason you're even talking to me?" I threw an annoyed look back at the car, faltering at the intensity of Kace's stare. I swallowed.

"You think you should be strollin' around on your own?" he asked. "Uptown girl like you... You don't really know the lay of the land around here yet."

I scoffed.

"I can walk from the school to my house by myself just fine, thank you."

"You're welcome, but it ain't a matter of if you *can* walk, but more about if you *should*."

My fists clenched. "Well, if you're so worried, you could always offer me a ride."

"No can do," Bishop spoke up. "Car's full up."

I looked at them incredulously, staring at the back where there was a perfectly empty seat beside Kace.

You know what, on second thought, I don't need that ride. I wouldn't take it even if they offered.

I turned away, nose up. "You're such assholes."

"Oh-ho." Misael laughed, grinning broadly and ducking down a little so he could meet my gaze through the driver's side window. "She swears! Your mama didn't teach you how to do that, I bet. See, Bish? She *is* starting to fit in."

I stiffened. *The nerve of this—*

Clenching my jaw, I drew in a deep breath through my nose. Misael wasn't exactly wrong. I almost never heard my mom swear, although I'd heard my dad let loose with plenty of colorful language—usually through his closed office door when some business deal hadn't been going how he'd wanted. And maybe I'd started to curse a little more often in the past couple weeks, but I'd die before I admitted that to the boys in that car.

So I said nothing, holding onto my resolve to ignore them all. I didn't have much farther to walk anyway, so I could put up with them for the last few blocks. I thought they might get bored and drive away, but they didn't—the car rolled along at a snail's pace beside me as they started joking among themselves about school and chicks. I rolled my eyes and left them to it. I was sure they were doing this just to annoy me, and even though it was working, I wouldn't give them the satisfaction of seeing me snap.

When we got to the house, I paused at the end of the walkway, looking furtively back at the trio. Misael winked at me.

"Have a nice evening, Princess."

All three of them laughed, and Bishop peeled away in the car, zooming off down the street—seemingly just for show, since they screeched to a stop again in front of the house I'd seen Kace coming out of the other day. I watched them pile out, unable to stop myself, until Kace turned and looked back at me. We stood there a moment, gazes locked, but I refused to be the first one to turn away.

I wasn't quite sure why I insisted on doing it. Maybe just to show them that I wasn't some little flower they could trample on.

Kace's lips tipped up in an almost feral grin, and he finally broke eye contact when he walked up into the house with Bishop and Misael.

He'd broken first... but something in my gut told me that wasn't exactly a win for me.

EIGHT

MOM SAID nothing about the loss of the car.

I think, somewhere inside, she cared. But these days she was so listless, so non-reactive, I could have told her that a meteor had decimated half of Baltimore, and she probably wouldn't have said a thing.

It was becoming unnerving; Mom wasn't the most talkative woman, but she'd never been so completely non-emotive as she was now. Worry and resentment grew side by side, battling for dominance in my mind. I was afraid that I'd lose my mother entirely to whatever depression or darkness she was sinking into, but I was also angry that she wasn't even fighting to make the best of our situation. Dad would know what to do to make her feel better; he'd always handled her perfectly, always knowing the perfect thing to say. I'd have to ask him to give me some pointers the next time he thought to call us.

Another night of homework and a microwave dinner came and went, and the next morning, I walked to school. I would have to see about getting a bus pass before the end of the day, but until then, I didn't really have any other options. I left a little earlier than usual, remembering how long it'd taken me to get home the day before. Part of me wondered if I'd have company again, but I saw no sign of the Lost Boys on the way to school.

I honestly didn't know if that was a good thing or a bad thing.

Having left the house too early, I arrived early. It wasn't like the students of Slateview High were clamoring to get to school more than a half-second before the first period bell rang, so the halls were fairly empty. It was nice, actually. Maybe I'd skip the bus pass and just walk to school every day if it was always like this.

The halls at Slateview always seemed overcrowded—not necessarily because there were too many students filling the space, but because everyone was always jostling, yelling, pushing or shoving. I hadn't realized how tense it made me, how much it felt like walking through a battlefield, until I could traverse the hallways in peace.

But just because there weren't many people here early, it didn't mean it was truly alone. And it was stupid as hell of me to forget that.

I was on my way to my locker to deposit the books I wouldn't need until later in the day when suddenly, rough hands grabbed my arms. I was pulled off to the side down a hallway near my locker.

Before I could even register what was happening, a boy I didn't recognize had me pressed up against the wall, his knee between my thighs and his hands on either side of my head as he leered down at me. My books fell out of my hands, and he pressed closer when I futilely tried to pick them up.

"Uh uh uh, none of that." He grinned widely, showing off a slightly chipped front tooth. His dark green eyes glinted with something malicious and gleeful—like a cat batting around a mouse before it goes in for the kill—and he smelled like cheap cigarettes. "You're that sweet little rich girl, huh? New kid. I'm Logan. You could say I'm the welcoming committee."

I swallowed. "Welcoming committee?"

"Yeah. You know. Welcoming the new meat to Slateview." His hand trailed up my stomach, under my shirt, and my skin crawled at the contact.

Oh shit. No.

This boy was like Barrett without the veneer of civility, without the mask of chivalry. As soon as that thought hit me, my blood went cold. I pushed at his chest.

"Stop! Get away from me."

He laughed. "Nah, I don't think so. I just told you I was the welcoming committee. And I haven't welcomed you properly, have I?"

Someone whistled, and with dawning horror, I realized

that other students were watching. Another person whooped, laughing.

"Yeah, Logan! Let's see a little more, yeah?"

"You heard 'em." The beefy boy leaned even closer to me, trapping me between the wall and his body. "They want a show. And I'm not sure if anybody informed you of this, but the rule at Slateview is, fresh meat does whatever it's told."

His hand pushed up further, and I felt a sinking, sick feeling brewing in my stomach. I knew better by now than to think anyone was going to see this and stop him. Everyone at this school had made it obvious they didn't care what happened to me unless it was causing me suffering. I stood there, unable to move, my heart pounding like a drum in my chest, my ears ringing, as his fingers shifted even higher.

I squirmed in his grasp, shame and desperation burning through me. It was bad enough to have a boy I didn't even know touching me like this, but he was doing it in front of other people, exposing me to them as he groped me shamelessly.

Oh God. Where will he stop? When will he stop? He wouldn't—in front of everyone—would he?

"Please. Stop! I said stop!"

I could barely hear my own voice over the ringing in my ears and the laughter around me. The noise seemed to swell, filling my senses as Logan's hands slid up my stomach, pushing my shirt up and over my breasts. Cold air hit the skin around my bra as rough fingers tugged at the straps, and I lost it. I could barely move with the weight of his pelvis pinning me in place, his body resting against mine, but I flailed and kicked, striking out with my fists as catcalls and whistles joined the roar of laughter—

"What. The. Fuck?"

Suddenly, Logan's weight was off me, and he was slammed against the wall beside me. It took me a moment to figure out what the hell was going on, a moment to put together that someone *had* in fact stopped this boy from... from...

I blinked as I realized that Kace had Logan pressed against the wall, his hand around Logan's throat. Misael and Bishop stood with him, eyeing the boy with the chipped tooth, their faces unreadable.

"What the fuck? I thought we were clear about what was gonna be done with little miss Princess." Bishop's voice had a hard edge to it. "And I don't recall giving you permission to touch, Logan."

Logan shrugged, moving only his shoulders since Kace still held him by the throat. But he didn't argue with Bishop—not that I thought he could. He was big and broad-shouldered, but Kace was even bigger than he was. I wouldn't want to try to fight the intense blond boy either.

"Must have slipped my mind, bruh. Won't happen again."

"Better not," Bishop said. "You know how shit's run around here."

Kace tossed Logan away, shoving him so hard he almost lost his footing. He stumbled and then righted himself, shooting a glance back at me. The hallway had gone oddly quiet, but that didn't stop Logan from giving me a smirk as he passed me by.

I swallowed, moving to bend down and pick up my things. But Misael had already grabbed them, and he held them out to me as the other two boys watched with their arms folded across their chests.

I didn't know what to say. Should I say thank you? Should I ask them why they'd helped me when I knew for a fact that they didn't like me? That they had... plans for me? Gratefulness warred with caution. I wasn't sure how I was supposed to act.

Misael grinned, and there was something both boyishly charming and threatening about it.

"Keep yourself outta trouble, Princess. We don't like having to do extra work for our investments."

Investment?

I wasn't quite sure what he meant by that, but I was too scared to ask. Whatever being an "investment" meant, was it worth it if it kept Logan's hands off me?

"I... right. Thank you."

I went to take my things from Misael, intent on hiding somewhere, maybe the bathroom, to calm down before having to head to class. Misael didn't hand over my things, however. He kept hold of them as Kace came up beside me, his hand on my upper arm. Bishop looked at me, his head tilted.

"I'm not sure why you think we're done here."

NINE

OH. Shit.

The Lost Boys had stopped Logan, but no one stopped the Lost Boys from dragging me outside. They were the law of the land, that much was obvious. And while they policed the halls of Slateview, no one policed them.

That wasn't reassuring.

Trepidation—no, real, unfettered fear—clawed through my veins as they brought me out back, pushing through the double doors behind the school. There was no one out here. No crowd of students leering and cheering. That was almost worse.

"Y'know, I thought rich people were supposed to be resourceful. Powerful." Kace pushed me against the wall, not releasing his grip on me. "You can't even go one morning without someone jumping you. Kinda pathetic."

"It's not my fault this school is full of psychopaths," I snapped.

Bishop laughed.

"That's rich, coming from you." Kace stepped back as the other two boys came to stand in front of me alongside him. "But maybe you're not quite so much Daddy's Little Princess?"

My face heated, fury joining the fear roaring through my veins.

"I don't understand your hatred of my father," I said, keeping my voice low and even. "He's not... what you or anyone else in this school say he is. I *know* my father. You've never even met him. You don't know anything about him—"

Bishop stepped forward suddenly, propping his hands on either side of my head, leaning in close to my face. Close enough that the heat of his body blazed against mine, close enough that the scent of woodsy body wash filled my nose as the intensity of those hazel eyes flecked in gold held my own.

"I know enough. I know your father is the reason a hell of a lot of people I care about are suffering right now," he murmured, his voice suddenly ice cold, dripping frigid down my spine. "I know enough to know that when a man like your dad goes and buys up health department buildings all through a state and turns them into luxury spas and health facilities for rich fucks, the people who actually need medicine, who need care, don't end up fucking getting it." He laughed, though it looked like he had more to say. And his words sounded personal somehow, making me think he wasn't talking about hypothetical people. "But of course, Daddy's little princess doesn't know shit about that, does she? Daddy should've kept all his ducks in a row. Then princess wouldn't have to pay the price for what her father trashed."

Vitriol dripped off every word Bishop said.

It was hatred. Pure hatred.

I had never heard another person speak like that. Not to me, not to anyone. And every bit of Bishop's anger and hatred was directed at my father.

How could the man who'd raised me deserve all that? I knew Dad was tough and demanding. I knew he pushed hard in his business deals. But had his ruthlessness really reached that level of cruelty? Of inhumanity? Bishop seemed to think so. Everyone at Slateview High seemed to think so.

"Bish?" Misael spoke up, his hand settling on Bishop's shoulder. Bishop stared down at me, that burning, hate-filled gaze holding mine until he sneered and pushed away from the wall.

My knees wobbled, and I had to fight hard not to let myself slide down the rough brick wall until my ass hit the ground. Bishop's hatred might be directed at my dad, but he seemed to have found the perfect conduit for his feelings —*me*.

"Let me lay it out for you," he said, running a hand through his shaggy hair. "I already told you we run the school, but maybe I should've been clearer about what the fuck that means. No one does anything we haven't sanctioned. You think it's lawless here? It ain't. We just decide what the law is. We decide what the hierarchy is. Who has the power. And Princess? You got none. Just about all the kids here have a reason to hate you. Whether their families were destroyed by yours, or they have someone close to them who was—just about everyone in this school would love to see you get fucked up, fucked over, or just fucked."

He let that sink in for me, not that it needed to embed itself further into me. It was obvious, wasn't it? The constant torment, my car, the incident this morning. I believed him when he said everyone hated me.

But I still didn't know what he was getting at.

"Yeah. I'm aware. You don't have to rub it in," I snapped.

Bishop shrugged, the movement lazy and predatory. "Ain't rubbing it in. Making it clear. There's only one way to keep what happened this morning with Logan from happening again... worse next time, probably."

I scoffed, trying to cover up the fear that swelled inside me like a balloon expanding. "Oh really? And what's that?"

"You need protection. We'll provide it," Misael said.

What?

This was the second time these boys had cornered me behind the school. Bishop had made no secret of the fact that he hated me, and neither of the other two seemed to have anything but dislike and disdain for me either.

So why the hell would they have any interest in looking out for me?

I blinked, shaking my head slightly as my mouth dropped

open. This couldn't be right. They had to be messing with me.

Misael laughed. "Ha. Told ya Princess wouldn't believe it."

"Why—why do you want to protect me?"

"It's less a matter of want, and more a matter of dibs," Kace said, his face scarily blank as he narrowed his eyes slightly. "We got as much reason to hate you as anybody else around here. But protecting you... that makes you ours. To dole whatever punishment you deserve without having to share."

I felt like I'd been drenched in ice.

"Excuse me?"

"It ain't that hard to comprehend, Princess." Kace huffed a breath, his muscles flexing as he crossed his arms. "We can't lay it out any clearer than that. But I can guarantee the three of us are better than a whole school-full of assholes like Logan running around looking to take out their anger on you."

I shook my head. *No. This isn't happening.* They couldn't possibly think it was sane for me to even consider their "offer". To throw myself at their mercy, hoping against all odds that they would be kinder to me than the other students here.

They wouldn't be.

How could they, when Bishop was still standing less than a foot away from me, angry energy pulsing from him with such force I could feel it like a physical blow.

They wouldn't protect me.

They'd destroy me.

Unthinking, I pushed at Bishop, shoving him as hard as I could before sprinting away. I needed to get him, get *all* of them, away from me. I needed to run, to escape this hellhole, to wake up from this never-ending nightmare—

But it was futile. I didn't know who grabbed me, but before I could make it to any kind of safety, I was pulled back. Strong arms held against one of them while Bishop stepped in front of me again, looking down at me.

"Well. At least you're a bit of a fighter," he said with a chuckle. I was shocked to hear a measure of respect in his voice. Then his hazel eyes hardened like glass. "But I'd encourage you to weigh your options, Princess. We don't give second chances."

TEN

THE HOUSE WAS quiet as I lay in bed that night, my thoughts tumbling around in my head too fast for me to sleep.

It was dark out. The stillness was something I still wasn't used to. It made it feel like our tiny rental house—or maybe the whole neighborhood—was haunted. The walls held that kind of creepy, oppressive feeling that made it hard to fall asleep. This wasn't the first night I had lain awake after a hot shower—or as hot as I could get it, considering lukewarm seemed to be the hottest setting for all the water in the house—staring up at my ceiling.

I had considered telling Mom about the Lost Boys' proposal earlier. There had to be something I could do about... that. Wasn't there? Some kind of rule against it, against that kind of blackmail and coercion.

But even if they existed, who could enforce those rules when the Lost Boys ruled the entire school?

Slateview High had a principal, dozens of teachers, and guidance counselors. There were people who were supposedly there to help the students get through their schooling, to deal with kids who broke rules or didn't play well with others. But I had never once seen the admins intervene, and the more I thought about it, the more certain I became that going to the principal would only make my position at the school worse.

And if it came down to whether I wanted to deal with three dangerous, unpredictable boys or a whole school full of people like Logan and Serena, the choice wasn't easy. I wasn't sure how long I could survive having the whole school after me. And if I refused their offer, then I'd essentially be up against the school *and* the Lost Boys, who would have even more of a reason to retaliate against me...

Ugh. This is stupid. Honestly considering taking them up on their offer is insane.

I would be theirs, belong to them, in exchange for protection. What kind of protection was that?

My mind drifted back to the incident in the morning with Logan. How he'd so easily tugged me down a hall. The way he'd laughed as he'd groped me in full view of everyone. How people had encouraged him. I wasn't stupid. I knew where that'd been heading. And if the Lost Boys hadn't shown up, I knew what would've happened. No one else would have stopped it; they probably would've thought it was what I deserved.

I sighed.

I wasn't even sure anymore what I deserved. Surely it couldn't be... whatever this fucked up situation was.

With a muffled groan, I rolled over, lifting my phone off its spot at the edge of the mattress to check the time. It was after one o'clock. I pressed the button to shut the screen off and forced my eyes closed. Maybe if I just kept them that way long enough, I might be able to drift off, to get some sleep. I'd need at least some kind of rest to be able to face the day tomorrow, with a school full of people who hated me and a trio of boys I still wasn't sure were the better option.

A sudden sound at my window made me sit up, my eyelids flying open—and then I gasped.

The smudged glass pane rose as it was pushed open from the outside. A shaggy head of chocolate brown hair popped through, and then an entire body.

Bishop.

I stared, mouth agape and unspeaking because... well, what the hell did you even say to some random boy breaking into your room in the middle of the night? I probably should've screamed, but a flash of fear for my mother kept my lips glued shut. I didn't know what Bishop wanted, and I had no idea what he was capable of—but I did know he hated my whole family, and I had to assume that would include my mom.

Whatever screwed up mess I was entangled in, I could at least try to keep her out of it.

Bishop didn't even say anything to me—just straightened himself up, glanced around my room, and started going through my things. He went to my dresser first, picking up and examining the small trinkets that I had managed to bring with me from home. He moved on quickly to my drawers, pulling one open and rifling through it lazily, like he had all the time in the world to kill.

Eventually, my brain and my indignation caught up to me, and before he could move on to my underwear drawer, I stood up, pushing him out of the way.

"What the hell are you doing?" I asked, snapping as loud as I dared to; it wasn't like Mom was sleeping on the other side of the house anymore.

He shrugged, nudging me easily out of the way.

"Seeing what my newest acquisition is all about," he said simply.

Irritation flared. "I'm surprised you even know what the word acquisition means."

He looked over his shoulder at me. Brow up. Smirk at the corner of his lips. I bet he could've gotten whatever girls he wanted if he wasn't such a blatant asshole.

"You obviously don't. Acquisitions aren't usually so... mouthy."

"You're not funny."

"I've been told I'm very funny, actually."

I scoffed. "Why are you here, Bishop? I'll scream, or—"

"Or what? Not like anyone around here would call the cops. I dunno if you noticed, but they don't exactly patrol here."

That silenced me. He nodded over to my bed.

"Sit."

I gritted my teeth but complied nonetheless, plopping down on my bed. He eyed me as I did, and I suddenly became very aware that the only thing I had on was my nightgown—a short, thin little slip. I grabbed a pillow and held it in front of me, wrapping my arms around it and shielding myself from him. His smirk deepened.

"Didn't peg you for a shy girl, given all that skin you've shown the last two days."

"Why are you here, Bishop?" I asked again, dodging his question and its implication.

"Morbid curiosity." He went back to rifling through my drawers.

"Sure you're not here for some... panty raid or whatever it is you inner city boys do?"

"Oh, trust me, Princess, rich boys are a lot nastier than the inner city ones. We're a lot more forward with what we want from someone, for starters."

As if that's a good thing, I thought skeptically. Still, I couldn't help but think of Barrett King, and as I did, Bishop's words rang true. Something about Barrett had made me uneasy, although on the surface, he'd acted like a complete gentleman.

"Seriously." I sat up straighter, tightening my grip on my pillow. "Why are you here?"

He was quiet, continuing to go through my things like he was searching for something. Honestly, I was pretty sure he just liked riling me up, stringing me along, not giving me answers when I demanded them. Just as my patience started to properly wear out, he turned.

"I'm here to make sure you understand your position. And what we're going to get out of you in our little arrangement. I don't like repeating myself."

I grit my teeth.

"Say what you need to say then."

He shrugged and leaned against the dresser, resting his elbows on top of it as he gazed at me with watchful eyes.

"How much do you know about this area?" he asked. "Did you even know about this place before you were forced to start slummin' with us peons?"

Peons. Another word I was surprised he knew. I kept that to myself.

"No," I answered honestly. "I'd never even been on this side of the city."

"Figures. Didn't think you would have." He leveled a hard look at me. "Lot of people around here have been fucked over by your father—"

"So everyone and their damn mother keeps telling me."

"You don't believe it."

"Why would I?" I scoffed, shaking my head. "I know my father is a man who gets what he wants. But that's just because he's good at business. He wouldn't... he wouldn't..."

"He wouldn't ruin people's lives if it meant he'd get what he wanted?" Bishop finished. "He wouldn't use people's ignorance about the law, or their desperation for what sounded like a good deal at the time, to make serious bank despite not even needing it? I hate to break it to you, Princess, but your father is all that shit and more, and the sooner you accept that, the sooner you can accept that what we're offering you is the best chance you have at surviving until someone decides if they want to let your daddy walk free or if he'll spend real, hard time in the clink."

I swallowed. Bishop spoke with such fierce certainty, it was hard *not* to believe him. But I had to remind myself that just because he thought he knew the truth, it didn't mean he was right.

"Why do you hate him so much?" I asked, deflecting. "You keep going on and on about other people getting screwed over. But no one cares about other people that much. Not even saints are that selfless, and I have a feeling you're no saint. You can't stand there pretending you're some humanitarian or something, standing up for the good of the people. You don't hate my dad because of what you think he did to the neighborhood or to other people. You hate him because you think he wronged *you* personally somehow."

This was personal. Way more personal than Bishop wanted me to believe. It was the only explanation that made any kind of sense.

His hazel eyes flashed as he scoffed.

"You really think you got it all figured out, huh, Princess? Maybe you think I'm jealous of your pops because he's got all that money and power, and I don't? You think that's all this is?"

He pushed off my dresser, striding over to me. I scooted

back on the bed as he neared, but I couldn't move fast enough to keep distance between us. He leaned down, bracing himself over me, his hands on either side of my hips as he looked me in the eye.

It was strange, how one person could fill an entire space in just a single move, but there he was, pulling my attention to him, making me hyper-aware of everything about him. His breath made the small, wispy tendrils of my hair dance as he spoke.

"My parents are dead because of your father," he said bluntly. "My mom got sick. She needed health care my dad couldn't afford. But... there was a facility, public health thing. It wasn't the best thing, but it helped. There was a treatment plan and all." He breathed in.

"It relied on donations and volunteer doctors. People that actually wanted to help others. The donors were usually rich fucks who needed to have some pet project to make them look good, but at least it helped people." His lips pressed together. His face was so close to mine that I could see the flecks of green and brown in his eyes. "Until your father came along. Promised all sorts of money, all sorts of support, bringing in new doctors, new tech. Except he never intended to keep the shit non-profit, and all that updated shit wasn't gonna be provided for free. Made some dumb shit program where people had to pay in—more money you were able to spend, better your care was. But if my parents couldn't pay for regular hospital care, how the fuck could they afford a program like that?"

"I—"

"That wasn't an invitation for you to speak, Princess," he interrupted. "Just making sure you understand me when I say your father is to blame. I don't just mean the system he's a part of—I mean him, period. He made the choices. He made the deals. He ensured only good press got out about his little operation. You get me?"

I nodded. How could I not?

"I get you."

"Good. Anyway. Few months after that, Dad went to get my mom something to eat from the corner store. Her appetite was shit, only a few things she could really eat that stayed settled in her stomach. He took a walk down to the corner store just for a sandwich and didn't end up coming back. Some drunk thought he'd bust in and steal some cheap beer... Dad ended up getting in between him and the store owner when he pulled an old pistol on the guy. Few months later, Mom followed Dad." He laughed bitterly. "They still hold events at that clinic. Wellness Events, they call them. You'll notice no one from this area ever goes there."

My mouth was dry. Even if I thought he was lying, I knew the clinic he was talking about just by what he called the events. I'd been to a few with Dad and Mom. I'd helped coordinate with Dad on a couple. Dad was always saying how much it had improved health care in Baltimore. There was no denying that.

But, for whom? Who had really benefitted?

"I..." I swallowed, my mouth suddenly dry. "I'm sorry."

"What are you sorry for? You're not your father."

I bit my lip. "Then why are you trying to punish me?"

Bishop's jaw twitched. He stared hard at me, as if he wasn't sure of the answer to that himself—or maybe he knew the answer, but he wasn't sure he liked it anymore.

My heart thudded unevenly in my chest as I gazed back at him.

The strange chemistry that always seemed to exist between us—the push and pull, the attraction and anger—flared hot and bright, filling me up with electric energy as if I'd been struck by lightning.

Suddenly, so fast I could barely track the movement, Bishop moved. He grabbed my legs and pulled, yanking me toward him, and then next thing I knew, I was on my back. His large, imposing body draped over mine, and the only thing between the two of us was my pillow.

But that small barrier was flimsy, soft... and temporary. Tugging it out of my grip, he tossed it away.

I didn't move. I couldn't.

He wasn't pinning me, not the way Logan had when he'd trapped me against the wall at school—I had room to move, enough space to slip out from beneath Bishop and escape if I wanted to.

So why did I remain completely still? Why didn't I take the way out that he'd offered me?

My breath came faster, making my chest rise and fall, almost brushing against his with every movement. Electricity buzzed through my veins, but I couldn't tell if it was fear or something darker...

Something closer to arousal.

Then Bishop's lips pressed hard against mine, and my eyes widened as I gasped, my entire body stiffening beneath him.

I had been kissed before, but only a few times. And never, *ever* like this.

Bishop kissed me like he was trying to hurt me—or maybe it was just the pain inside of him spilling out through his mouth, through the connection between our lips, infecting me too.

He kissed me like I had already given him and the other Lost Boys my answer. Like I already belonged to them.

His mouth moved against mine, his tongue tasted mine, and the weight of his body covered mine until there was nothing but *him*. Until the rest of the world ceased to exist, eclipsed by this dominating, cruel, broken boy.

"Why do I want to punish you? Because I can," he breathed against my lips. "Because I want to. Because I fucking hate your father for everything he's done to my family, and I can't kill the bastard myself."

My chest tightened with fear, and I opened my mouth to protest, or maybe to apologize again—but Bishop obviously didn't want to hear either of those things, because he kissed me once more, stealing the words from between my lips.

Heat pooled in my lower belly, and I felt something hard

and thick and hot as a brand pressing against my stomach as he rested his weight on me. His hands were moving over me, rough and demanding, touching every inch of skin he could reach.

There was something almost desperate about his movements, as if he was at war with himself, and every touch, every kiss, was a battle lost.

He wanted this. He wanted me.

But he was trying not to.

The feeling was entirely mutual, so I kissed him back the same way, my hands roaming over his muscled back and shoulders like they couldn't decide if they were trying to push him away or pull him closer.

I had kissed boys before, but never like this. Bishop's lips were firm and warm, his tongue demanding as it swept my mouth, tangling with my own. I was gasping for breath in the little half-seconds when our lips broke apart, but when he angled his head and took the kiss even deeper, I stopped breathing entirely.

Our lips moved in sync, and maybe it was the lack of oxygen, or maybe it was just the sheer, overwhelming force of the boy on top of me, but I felt like the world was spinning around me.

His hands moved over every inch of my body with impunity, sliding the soft fabric of my nightgown across my flushed skin as he groped me through the thin material. When his hand moved between us, slipping under the hem of my nightgown and pushing aside my panties, I finally broke our kiss. My lips wrenched away from his as I let out a strangled sound that was half gasp, half moan.

He must've liked that, because instead of pulling his hand back, he delved deeper into my panties, dragging one finger along my damp slit before working circles around my clit.

My back arched off the bed, both my hands grabbing onto his forearm as a loud moan was ripped from my throat. I pressed my lips together, embarrassment and worry filling me as I realized how loud I'd been. Mom was just down the hall. I couldn't let her wake up, couldn't let her see me like this.

Bishop didn't seem to give a fuck about any of that though. Ignoring my death grip on his arm, he kept moving his fingers, making my body buzz with the overload of sensations.

"Don't close your mouth. I like to hear you moan, Princess."

His command was spoken in a low, rough voice, but I didn't obey. I pressed my lips together harder, sealing them shut as my entire body began to shake. What he was doing felt good—*too* good. It was all too much. It felt amazing, but also like the punishment he had promised somehow, like he was trying to tear me apart from the inside out.

"Please," I whispered. "Please..."

The hazel eyes above me sharpened as Bishop pulled back a few inches to stare down at my face, his fingers still working my sensitive nub hard and fast. "Please what?"

God. He was going to make me say it. He was going to make me beg.

Maybe that was the punishment he'd wanted to inflict on me—making me admit that as much as I feared and despised him, I wanted him too.

"Please." My voice was a strained whisper, hardly more than a breath. "Don't stop."

And finally, he gave me what I needed.

His gaze stayed trained on me as his tempo increased, and the sensations ricocheting through my body peaked. My fingernails dug into his back and I lifted my head to bury my face against his chest, letting the warm, solid muscles there absorb the sound of my cry.

I could hear him breathing harder as I finally started to come down from my release, my muscles unclenching, melting back onto the mattress. His woodsy scent filled my nostrils like a drug, and when he pulled away, his pupils were so dilated his eyes looked almost black.

For a moment, we just stared at each other, neither of us blinking.

As the intense burn of pleasure receded from inside me, I became acutely aware of the way Bishop's weight rested against me, of the heat and strength of his body atop mine. We were touching everywhere, our bodies lined up from head to toe.

And then, suddenly, we weren't.

Bishop yanked himself away from me, blinking rapidly, almost as if he was shaking off some kind of spell as he scrambled off the bed. The bulge in his pants strained against his zipper, and I shifted my gaze away from it quickly, looking back up to his face as my cheeks heated. He was staring at me with an almost shocked expression, as if he couldn't believe what he'd just done any more than I could.

Then, without uttering another word, he strode quickly toward the window, slipped through it, and disappeared into the darkness outside.

Panting, I collapsed back onto my mattress, staring up at the ceiling. My nightgown was bunched up around my waist, my panties soaked and twisted from being shoved out of the way, and my clit was still throbbing from the aftershocks of my orgasm.

What the hell just happened?

ELEVEN

THE NEXT MORNING, my mind was a mess of confused thoughts—about Bishop, about what'd happened between us, and about something a little less ominous.

How to make oatmeal.

I occupied myself with pouring the milk, heating the pot, and letting it get warm before putting in the oats. I figured if I focused entirely on that and didn't let my mind wonder, maybe my thoughts would stop whirling. Maybe I'd realize that everything that'd happened last night had just been an insane dream brought on by my wild imagination, my intense attraction to the Lost Boys, and all the stress finally getting to me.

But I knew that wasn't true. Last night had been real.

I didn't just remember it—I could *feel* it in my body. Every single touch, every sensation Bishop had dragged out of me, every place his hands and mouth had touched my skin. I felt changed somehow, inside and out.

Marked.

Claimed.

My heart beat hard against my ribs as the entire night replayed in my head for the hundredth time, and I found myself gripping the counter, my breath coming faster. He had touched me like he owned me, like he knew my body even better than I did somehow.

He had hesitated, his fingers lightly brushing over the fabric of my panties, and his hazel eyes had burned as he'd stared at me, waiting. He'd given me a moment to say no, a moment to push him away—but I hadn't taken it.

A flush crept up my face, and I bit my lip so hard it hurt. The things he had done with his fingers, with his lips, with his sinful tongue...

"Son of a bitch!"

The acrid, bitter scent of burnt oatmeal stung my nose. I huffed, cursing again as I pulled the pot off the stove and set it aside.

Dammit. How the hell does anyone cook anything? I was having the hardest time getting anything right, and oatmeal was about as basic as cooking could get. Bitterly, I tossed out the scorched, blackened mess. This wouldn't be a problem if I'd been taught how to cook.

Then again, who would've taught me? Dad, who hadn't cooked a thing in his life, *ever*? Mom, who's culinary acclaim started and stopped with ordering the kitchen staff around?

I shook my head, pushing my hair back and rubbing at my temples. Maybe I was being a little testy—but in my defense, eating nothing but cereal and box meals was starting to get to me.

As I cleaned up, resigned to eating breakfast from a vending machine at school, I heard a car horn blare loudly outside. My brows furrowed, but I ignored it; random bangs, shouts, and other loud noises were common in this neighborhood at any hour of the day or night, something I was still getting used to after living in the bubble of quiet that had surrounded our gated mansion.

Another honk came just a few moments later, and a third one sounded as I was grabbing my backpack. Huffing an irritated breath, I pushed the door open and stepped outside, prepared to glare down whoever was making the racket as I walked past them on my way to school.

But as the door clicked shut behind me, I froze, blinking in surprise.

The Lost Boys' trashy convertible was parked in our driveway; all three boys sat inside, and all three were looking at me. Waiting. Bishop had his hand up like he was about to lay on the horn again, only to stop when he saw that I'd emerged from the house.

"Jesus! 'Bout damn time!" Misael called. "Hurry up. We're taking you to school."

It wasn't a question. Unlike the tiny window Bishop had given me last night, this time there was no room given for me to say no. I could have tried to resist—could've veered left and headed down the sidewalk until they physically forced me into the car or trailed behind me at a snail's pace like last time. But I had a feeling the boys wouldn't balk at taking either of those two options.

And if I was being honest with myself, I didn't really want to walk. I was exhausted and hungry, and the day was already uncomfortably humid.

Was I ready to face the implications of what accepting a ride meant though? To admit that I had accepted their bargain—that I was theirs?

"Come on. We ain't gonna bite." Misael grinned. "Bish even kept the front seat open for you."

My eyes flickered to Bishop, heat rising in my cheeks. He just gazed back at me with half-lidded eyes and an almost bored look on his face. There was nothing in his expression that gave any indication he was thinking about last night—or even that he remembered it.

A strange sort of pain clutched my chest at that thought. He couldn't have forgotten, there was no way that was possible. But maybe that sort of thing was so common for him that he'd already brushed it aside, added me to a long list of girls and marked another notch in his bed post?

The tightness in my chest got worse, making it hard to breathe, but I straightened my spine and forced my features into an expression matching his. I let a slight smirk play across my lips and arched a brow slightly. Bishop huffed and looked away, shaking his head.

Good. Better for him to think it hadn't meant anything to

me either. And really, what had I expected? That I was special? That what had happened between us had knocked his world off its axis just like it had mine?

It's not like that, Cora. Don't ever forget it.

"Uh, seriously, Princess. Any fuckin' day now."

Misael's laughing voice dragged me out of my thoughts, and I jumped as I shifted my gaze back to him.

I bit my lip. It was either walk or ride, and ironically, riding had fewer drawbacks than walking.

Besides... if I rode with them, it might mean that I wouldn't be bothered by other students today. That Serena and Logan and everyone else would leave me alone.

And I needed that win.

Sighing, I hiked my backpack higher and marched over to the car. Kace rolled his eyes and went back to his phone, Misael grinned at me, and Bishop—well, Bishop shook his head and sighed, peeling away from the curb almost as soon as my butt hit the seat.

"We'll be taking you to school every day from now on," he said. "So be ready on time. I don't like waiting."

I kept my bag in my lap as we rode to the school, uncertain of what to say, or even if I was supposed to say anything. Was I supposed to do something, other than just... sit here?

"Yo, Bish. Stop up there today for breakfast," Misael called from the back. I looked around, seeing the run-down Burger King that I passed every day on my way to school.

"You're gonna turn into a damn burger you keep eatin'

'em for breakfast, lunch, and dinner," Bishop muttered, shaking his head but changing lanes to head toward the fast-food restaurant.

"Yeah, well, it's better than getting Taco Hell. You know how insulting it is they try to pass that shit off as Mexican?"

"About as annoying as it is every time you point out it's not real Mexican, like we don't know that already?"

They went back and forth like that, and I sat back, listening quietly. It was weird to see them act like normal boys—or what I assumed was "normal" here, because they still didn't act like any of the boys I'd known in my old life. Every other time I'd interacted with them, they'd seemed so powerful and dominating, untouchable almost. It felt odd to hear them joke around and banter with each other so casually, and it almost felt like I was seeing something I shouldn't, peeking behind the curtain at something few people ever glimpsed.

Bishop pulled the car up, sliding behind another that was already in the drive-thru. *Burgers for breakfast, huh?* I couldn't even remember the last time I'd been at a Burger King. Maybe once when I was out shopping with Ava? But it'd been so many years ago that I couldn't remember what it tasted like at all.

It was strange to think of fast-food as a foreign thing. I had traveled to other countries and gotten used to their customs and cuisines, but this? This experience felt the most alien to me, and I was suddenly a little self-conscious about that fact.

I tried not to make it obvious that I was watching curiously as Misael leaned forward between the seats, rattling off a few items from the menu. He called them out by numbers instead of the item name itself and stipulated no onions on his. I said nothing; I didn't expect to be fed. But Bishop surprised me by glancing over at me after the crackly voice coming through the speaker asked if their order was finished.

"What do you want?"

I blinked. "What?"

Bishop sighed. "What do you want? To eat. For breakfast."

"Oh... I wasn't going to get anything?" I was confused. Why would they offer me breakfast? Was this even the food I wanted? It had to be better than whatever the ancient vending machine at school had stocked.

He shook his head and turned toward the speaker. "A number five on top of that. Actually—make it two."

"You got it. Total will be twenty fifty-seven. Pull up to the first window."

My brows furrowed as I looked to Bishop, but he didn't comment on the fact that he'd just bought me breakfast. A number five... what was that anyway? I wished I'd paid a little more attention to the menu so I knew what I was getting myself into.

We rolled up to the first window, and Bishop pulled out his wallet. Surprisingly crisp twenties were folded inside—more of them than I would've expected. When he caught me staring, his brow rose, and I looked away, my face flaming.

Shit. Was he some kind of gang banging drug dealer or something? Is that where he got his money?

I knew better than to ask, and a few minutes later, three fat paper bags with grease slowly seeping into the bag fibers were passed to us. Bishop tossed them to the back where Misael caught them with practiced ease, and then we pulled out of the lot. As we drove the rest of the way to school, Misael started divvying up the food.

"You ain't had a breakfast like this, I bet." He chuckled, passing up two wrapped burgers to me as he took a huge bite out of one that was twice the size of my own. Gingerly, I unwrapped my first burger, not sure if I wanted to dive right into it.

"Simmer down, Princess. It's not gonna bite you." Bishop rolled his eyes, sipping out of an extra large soda.

A frown tugged at my lips. I wasn't afraid of it biting me...

Then I shrugged, eyeing the burger before opening wide and taking a big bite. It was a greasy, cheesy, tomatoey mess.

But it was also delicious.

I actually moaned, unable to hold it back. It tasted amazing, better than half the fancy dinners our old chef had cooked. Was fast-food supposed to be this good? I'd always thought it was supposed to be convenient, cheap, and accessible. I'd had no idea it tasted like a greasy slice of heaven.

"Well, well, look at that. Uptown Girl likes her some

BK," Misael crowed from the back. "See? Bish told ya it wasn't gonna bite."

I flushed, saying nothing as I continued to eat. My gaze met Bishop's, and there was something like a smile teasing at the corner of his mouth.

His words from last night filtered through my head. *I like to hear you moan, Princess.*

This was a completely different context, but he still seemed pleased to have drawn that noise out of me. I half expected him to tease me, to say something crude about last night, to tell the other boys I was easy or something. But he said nothing, and neither did I. Instead, I found myself actually enjoying the last half of our short ride to school, my stomach full and my nerves oddly settled in the company of three boys I had no business spending time with.

Several minutes later, we pulled into the school lot, right up into the space that seemed to be the Lost Boys' personal parking spot—nice and close to the front. I wondered if there was a reason they'd picked this spot. The part of me that still saw them as some kind of lawless gang thought maybe it was for quick getaways if they needed to leave the school in a hurry. The logical part of my mind knew it was probably just because this was prime parking.

Probably.

I'd finished up both of my burgers already. I hadn't realized how hungry I was. I slid out of the car as Bishop, Misael, and Kace stepped out too. There was a moment of silence as I glanced at the three of them. Should I thank them for a ride and breakfast? It was the polite thing to do, but social conventions were so far from what I was used to in this situation that I really wasn't sure what the moment called for.

"We'll take you home later," Bishop said, steering the conversation before I could make up my mind. "Anyone gives you shit, you know where to find us."

Misael gave me a grin as the three of them set off. Neither Bishop nor Kace looked at me, but it didn't matter. Everyone in the vicinity was watching me, and everyone seemed to have gotten the memo already: the Lost Boys had an indisputable claim on me.

TWELVE

FOR THE REST of the day, I was left alone.

I got a few dirty looks, especially from girls, but that was the worst of it. Even Serena didn't bother me. She seemed to hate me more than ever, but she didn't so much as say a hello or goodbye to me.

It was such a relief, and such a huge change from how things had been that I almost couldn't believe it. The only thing Bishop, Misael, and Kace had needed to do was tell the school I was off limits, and suddenly I was. I was allowed to study in peace, walk the halls without incident, and come lunchtime, I was actually feeling hopeful that maybe I could get through the rest of my time at Slateview with relative ease.

And all I'd had to do to achieve this peace was give myself over to the three boys who terrified and intrigued me in equal measure.

Was it ideal? Hell no.

But it didn't have to be ideal. It just had to work.

I walked into the lunch room, very aware of the space I was allowed to have. Where people had actively put themselves in my way the first day, jostling and shoving me, no one bothered me today.

Damn. A girl could get used to this.

Without having to worry about watching my back, I slid into the back of the line and waited. I could have gone for another Burger King burger, actually, but fast-food wasn't exactly the standard of quality the cafeteria was boasting—which in all honesty, was a bit sad. I picked up my tray of unappetizing food and turned to scan the cafeteria. I spotted an empty table across the room and headed toward it, intending to capitalize on the peace I'd been afforded by eating alone and hopefully not being bothered.

But before I could reach the table, I was waved down by a girl with black hair and choppy bangs. She was sitting with a boy who had mocha skin and closely shaved black hair, and I vaguely recognized them both but didn't know their names. The boy was broad in the shoulders and looked easy-going compared to most of the people that went to Slateview.

Nervousness settled in my stomach, but I changed course nonetheless. I was learning that resistance was an action best suited for a last resort—and besides, I felt a little more confident knowing I had the Lost Boys on my side. So far, no one had dared to mess with me.

I slowed as I approached the table, chewing my lip apprehensively.

"Hello...?"

"Oh, don't look at us like that." The girl laughed. She had a throaty, raspy voice that made her sound older than she probably was, and her brown eyes danced with amusement. "We're friends with Bish, Reaper, and Misael. I'm Jessica; this is Liam. Bish told us to make sure you had a place to sit if they weren't at the table yet when lunch started." She smiled, her red lipstick shining with gloss under the harsh florescent lights.

There was something about her that I liked instantly, an openness that none of my friends back home had ever had, but I still hesitated. I wasn't sure if she and the boy beside her were genuine or not, and my first instinct these days was to distrust everyone.

Jessica shrugged.

"Hey, you can stand there until they show up, of course. I'm not gonna force you."

She went back to eating, forking a bite of meatloaf into her mouth. At least, I assumed it was meatloaf. It was hard to tell with school lunch.

Liam looked up to me, deep brown eyes understanding.

"Promise we're not gonna pull any shit," he said. "But people are gonna stare if you just keep standing here."

I flushed. I'd been doing well without too much attention focused on me, and although I felt safer with the Lost Boys' protection, it seemed wise not to present an easy target.

Against my better judgement, I slid onto the bench across from Jessica and Liam.

"See, not so hard, is it?" Jessica smirked. "You really aren't all that trusting, huh?"

"Bit of an understatement," I muttered. Why was she being so nice?

"Well, since the guys decided to take you under their wing, you could probably do with being a little more relaxed," she continued. "No one's going to hurt you. And if they do, well." She drew her thumb across her neck, her grin turning feral; I didn't need to ask what she meant.

"You giving her a hard time already, Jess?"

I jumped, almost knocking my tray off the table. When I glanced up, I saw Bishop, Misael, and Kace walking over with their own trays of food. Bishop sat to my left, Kace to my right, and Misael situated himself—obnoxiously, I might add —between Jessica and Liam. The broad-shouldered boy shot him an annoyed look, and Misael grinned. Liam just rolled his eyes and looked to me.

"See the shit I gotta deal with? Can't even have lunch with my girlfriend in peace," he said, but there was no anger in his voice. This must've been a typical thing among the group.

Feeling suddenly very surrounded, I tucked a strand of hair behind my ear and started to eat.

"So, you show New Girl the ropes yet?" Jessica asked. "I hope you three are being nice to her." She gave them all a look, like she was lecturing them more than anything.

Bishop huffed a breath beside me, but when I glanced at him, he was looking at Jessica, not me.

"Nice enough," he said evenly.

I kept my mouth shut, wondering if he was referring to the night before or this morning or something else entirely—and ever grateful that he didn't elaborate.

"Well, with the way everyone is around here, don't be dicks." She left it at that as she tucked in. Bishop shook his head.

"Whatever. Anyone give you trouble so far?" For the first time since plopping down beside me, he looked down at me. I shook my head.

"Nope. Everyone's... basically ignored me."

"Good."

That seemed to satisfy him. I didn't know if I should say anything else, but lunch went on without a hitch, and I wasn't going to complain about it.

THIRTEEN

"WE'RE HEADING DOWN to the warehouse district after school. You're coming with."

Bishop leaned up against the bank of lockers next to me as I pulled out the books I would need later for homework. I glanced up to him, confused.

"What?"

"Warehouse district after school. We're gonna chill. It's what we do, and you're coming with." He tilted his head, shoving his shaggy brown hair back from his face. "Come on Princess, keep up."

I leveled a look at him as I straightened, books in my arms.

"What is... going to chill? What does that entail?"

"You'll find out. Don't take too long."

"Yeah, yeah. I know. You don't like to wait."

"Nice to see you're learning."

The grin he shot me was almost flirtatious, and I hated that it made warmth pool in my belly, made my gaze catch on his lips. He lingered for a second longer, his hazel eyes growing serious as he dropped his focus to my lips too. Then he turned and strode away down the hall, leaving me to rush to my final class of the day.

I tried to take notes as Mrs. Hall lectured, but my mind was already skipping ahead to what would happen after school. Confusion and caution warred inside me as I waited for the day to close out.

Warehouse district? Who went to a warehouse district to chill?

Dumb question. Guys like the Lost Boys did, obviously, and I wasn't sure why I even bothered trying to figure them out anymore. I should've known by now it was a hopeless cause.

The thing was, it was the end of the week, and this was the first time they had mentioned anything like this.

Ironically enough, despite my terror at accepting their bargain, my days with the Lost Boys had been mostly tame. I rode with them to and from school, ate lunch with them and their friends, and fell into step with them when I saw them in the hall. So far, nothing strange had happened.

But maybe this was the moment when the other shoe was going to drop.

After all, no one went to an abandoned warehouse to do *good* things, did they?

Growing trepidation filled my gut as I made my way out

to the convertible after school, bag slung over my shoulder. The boys were already by the car, chatting as I came up to them. Misael looked over as I approached, and he grinned.

"Hey, there she is."

"Bishop said we were going to... a warehouse?"

Misael nodded. "Old canning factory that we hit up on the weekends sometimes. Cops don't roll around there, and they don't bother us. Good place to start the weekend off right."

"Is anyone else going...?"

Kace snorted. "Wouldn't be fun if just anyone was there. Call it an exclusive perk of being close to us."

My brow rose, but I said nothing to that. Kace barely ever talked to me, and every time he did, I felt an insane urge to agree with whatever he'd said. As if his words had so much power and force behind them that he could literally bend reality to his will. The Lost Boys all frightened and attracted me in different ways—Bishop was secretive and unpredictable, Misael was dangerously charming, and Kace was quiet and closed-off, a puzzle I shouldn't want to solve.

His use of the word "close" felt like an overstatement, but I supposed when it came down to it, our arrangement did make me close to them. Closer than I'd ever meant to get, that was for sure.

"Okay then." I shrugged. "Let's go."

I slid into the car, taking what was becoming my usual spot in the passenger seat beside Bishop, and we were off.

If things were like they used to be, I would've texted

Mom to let her know where I was going, that I wasn't coming straight home after school. But these days, she spent so much time holed up in her bedroom, buried under layers of blankets, or curled up on the couch asleep that I doubted she'd see the text before I was home anyway.

Honestly, I wasn't sure she'd care even if she did see it.

Figuring I should at least tell her something, I shot her a quick, vague text on the cheap little phone I'd gotten before we moved into the rental house, telling her I was going out with a few friends and would be back home later. It was as close to the truth as I felt like I could get.

And as we passed residential roads and drove into the industrial part of the city, I couldn't help but feel like I was getting myself into something... weird. Wrong side of the tracks was an understatement as the pavement became more and more potholed and the level of graffiti art on brick walled buildings elevated. I bit my lip as the wind blew in my hair and the music blared from the convertible's speakers—loud, but not loud enough to drown out Misael singing to it.

The warehouse Bishop brought us to was still standing despite the fact that it'd obviously been abandoned for years. Tall, dirty windows were broken, and portions of some of the walls were crumbling. Most of it was still intact though, and like the guys had said, there wasn't anyone around. No cops patrolled the area, and no one cared that a band of underage kids were running around a place they probably shouldn't be. On one hand, it meant that I could avoid the possibility of having to deal with police—something I'd been a little worried about, considering my dad was still in jail. Another family member in lockup would probably kill Mom, even if it was just for a day.

But on the other, having no cops in the area meant that once again, the Lost Boys were the ultimate authority. They made their own laws, and around here, those laws would be unbreakable.

Bishop pulled us close up to a broad steel door, and I peered out the window at it, surprised it was still in halfway decent condition. Rust gathered at the hinges, but otherwise, it looked sturdy.

He killed the gas and looked at me. "Help us unload."

I blinked. It was the first time a request from Bishop had actually sounded like a request. But that didn't make me any more anxious to comply.

Unload? Unload what?

I got out of the car nonetheless, walking around to the back with the others. Kace had the trunk popped, and my mouth dropped.

There was a whole cooler in the trunk, a few bags of chips and snacks, and then a smaller cooler. Kace reached in, grabbing the bags and handing them over to me. He grabbed the larger cooler, and Misael grabbed the smaller, as well as a boombox that I realized was tucked deeper into the back of the trunk.

Not knowing what all this was about, I just took what was given to me and headed over to meet Bishop near the front of the building. He was unlocking the deadbolt on the steel door, and when the lock clicked, he nudged the door open with his foot. He held it open for me, gesturing me through before him. When I stepped inside, my footsteps slowed, and he nudged my back to keep me moving.

Inside the empty warehouse, there were a couple of old couches, worn down and used, but kept up in decent condition. A large table sat off to the side, with a smaller coffee table between the couches and a couple of bean bag chairs too. It was obvious this was a frequent haunt; while the place overall was run down, this was kept up too much to not be a place where the Lost Boys spent a lot of their time.

This was... well, it was different.

I was used to country clubs, golf courses, warmed pools and soft instrumental music. I was used to pool boys with toned bodies taking "summer jobs" to make it seem like they were learning how to work, and the girls that went to the clubs with their mothers flirting when their fathers weren't looking.

I wasn't used to this, the concrete floor beneath my heels echoing with each of my steps, the raucous laughter that came from behind as Misael and Kace trailed in after us. I wasn't used to walking over debris and leaves and smudges of dirt, and I certainly wasn't used to the way Misael just flopped down on one of the couches as if it were perfectly natural to sit on furniture of such questionable origin. As I gaped around me, Bishop popped open one of the coolers, pulling out a beer and handing it over to Kace.

Out of my element? You could say that.

I didn't even think my element was recognizable in this situation, and I had no idea why they'd brought me here, why they *wanted* me here, in what was obviously a sort of haven for them. I set the bags of snacks down on the table and stood there awkwardly as Bishop and Kace pulled things out and Misael put on music.

They all moved with purpose, talking and joking as they settled in, as if this all made perfect sense to them. But I couldn't figure out the point of all this was.

"Um... so... what are we doing here?" The words came out low, only gaining volume as I spoke. Misael looked over to me.

"We come here to chill," he said simply. "You never chill before?"

"Not... like this," I admitted. "Not exactly."

"Well, we ain't got nothing to do tonight." Misael shrugged. "Not till later at least. We come here and hang out. Nice setup, eh?"

"Sure..."

"You don't have to lie if it's not nice enough for you, Princess," Kace grunted.

I looked over at him, surprised that he'd spoken to me again. Twice in one day was a lot for him. It felt sometimes like he went out of his way not to speak to me at all. Out of the three of them, he always felt the most hostile—more so than Bishop even. He didn't actually do or say anything threatening, but there was something about his heavy silence that made the fine hairs on the back of my neck prickle.

"It's not a lie," I said, straightening my spine. A thrill of nerves ran through me as I lifted my chin, standing up to Kace. It felt a little like passing my hand through fire and hoping I didn't get burned. "It's just... listen. You can't just expect me to *get it*, and get this, to get you guys, just because you tell me what to do and bring me random places." I folded my arms. "It's a nice set up for what it is. I just don't... get it. Why out here? Why not somewhere else? You know, one of your places or a park or something."

The three of them exchanged a look, then burst out laughing.

"Wow, Princess. A park or something? What are we? Five? You wanna ride the merry-go-round?"

I rolled my eyes and scoffed. "You know what I mean. I just... don't know what people here do for fun. That's all."

"It's alright. You can say you're out of the loop because we don't have fancy cocktail parties or whatever," Misael laughed.

"Maybe she thought we should hang out on a yacht," Kace put in blandly, the intensity of his light moss-green eyes belying the casual tone of his words.

I shook my head. No answer I gave would have been good enough for them—they all still thought I was nothing but a spoiled rich brat, and everything I said seemed to convince them they were right.

But, whatever. I was here, as they'd requested. Now it was just a matter of figuring out what they'd brought me for, and why they thought it was necessary.

"Fuck. You really do look like a little lost lamb."

Bishop came up and stood beside me, nudging me with his shoulder. He held out a bottle of opened beer to me, beads of sweat already gathering on the dark glass. I eyed it. Aside from a glass of champagne or wine at a gathering or event, I didn't really drink. Even at my parents' massive parties, the one thing that'd always kept things tame was the fact that personal image was everything—and ending up sloppily drunk did nothing for someone's image.

"Come on, Princess." Kace spoke up again. "There's no one here to go back and tell Daddy his little girl wasn't behaving herself."

I wasn't sure if he was talking so much because he was comfortable in this place, this little hideaway, or because he just really wanted me to loosen up. But whatever the reason, I found that I liked it. His gruff voice was equal parts scary and soothing, but something in me wanted to keep him talking, to hear more of what he had to say. To break open the facade and see what the boy beneath was really like.

Bishop tilted his head toward his friend in silent agreement, keeping the bottle held out to me.

I was apprehensive. But I was also curious. The two feelings clashed inside me just as strongly as I always seemed to with these boys. Right now, my carefully controlled upbringing was telling me that ladies shouldn't drink beer out of bottles in warehouses with strange boys they hardly knew.

But that wasn't the world I was living in anymore. That life was no longer mine. This new version of Cora *did* go to warehouses with strange boys, and no one cared enough to stop her.

So why shouldn't she try a drink? Why shouldn't she live while she still could?

"Come on." Bishop's voice dropped, the low tone dripping down my spine like honey. "Loosen up. That's why we're here, anyway."

I eyed him curiously. "Excuse me?"

"Uh uh." He shook his head, lifting the bottle a little higher. "You drink, we answer. That's the deal."

I gave a skeptical scoff; deals with the Lost Boys seemed to end with them coming out on top more often than not. Still, I took the beer from him, and after eyeing the bottle for another moment, I tipped it back.

Bottoms up.

FOURTEEN

THE TASTE WAS... different. Potent at the front end, sharp at the back. Swallowing burned, but I'd be damned if I was going to spit it out. I took the swallow and gasped a bit as I pulled the beer bottle away from my lips. My body felt warm. A weird tingle went down to the tips of my fingers.

"Took that like a champ." Misael whistled, lifting his own bottle in a sort of mock salute.

I flushed. "Deal's a deal," I said, looking up to Bishop. "Why am I here?"

"Because you agreed to it," he answered with a shrug.

That son of a...

I huffed.

"Okay. Better question. Why did you stop that guy the other day? Logan?" I asked, more boldly than I probably should have. "I'm still not really sure I get it, even if you guys say that I'm... yours. I know you hate me because of my dad, but then why wouldn't you want to see the whole school go after me? Wouldn't that be more satisfying?"

It was a dangerous question to ask—if they realized I was right, they could go back on our deal and let everyone at Slateview have at me. I doubted I'd last a week. But the question had been poking at my brain ever since they'd made their offer, and I felt like I needed to know.

I needed to know what they expected. What they wanted from me.

What they had planned for me.

The three boys exchanged a look, seeming to communicate without speaking.

"No. It wouldn't be," Bishop answered after a moment. "No one else at that school gets to have you. Not Logan, not any other motherfucker. Like we keep telling you, Princess. You're ours."

My thoughts instantly flashed to the other night. To how I was very much not *theirs*, and more like Bishop's. Did the other boys know what he'd done? Did they know that he'd broken into my room at all, much less what had happened after he crawled through the window?

Taking another swig from my bottle of beer, I crossed over and settled onto the couch. Then I looked him in the eye, my gaze almost challenging.

"I can't possibly 'belong' to all of you. There are three of you and one of me. It just doesn't make any sense."

"It only makes sense if you're not creative." There was something different in Kace's voice when he spoke, and the sound of it made my heart beat a little faster. "Come on, Princess. Think about it. I know all that high-priced schooling wasn't wasted on you."

I swallowed, glancing between the three of them as I processed his words. Before I could come up with a response, Bishop spoke again.

"You think I'm the only one with a claim on you? You think what happened between us the other night made you mine?"

My head whipped up to meet his gaze so fast I almost made myself dizzy. Furtively, I cast a glance out of the corner of my eye at the other two boys, trying to see if shock or surprise registered on their faces. But they were both watching me calmly, Misael with a wicked grin curving his lips and Kace with his usual inscrutable expression.

They knew.

They'd probably known since the day after it happened.

And what Bishop had just said...

When they'd told me that I was theirs, I'd never been entirely sure what that meant. To what extent they intended to claim me. That night with Bishop—no matter how short-lived it had been—had made me believe that, at least in the physical sense, he was the only one interested.

But I'd been wrong.

These boys were close like brothers. Closer than that even. And they didn't just share beers, rides to school, and years of history with each other.

They shared girls.

Or at least, they were willing to share me.

I caught Misael's gaze again as the realization hit me fully. Heat flooded my body, pooling low in my stomach, even as nerves made my skin chill. I was in so far over my head it wasn't even funny—I was miles below the surface, and with the way my lungs were suddenly burning, I wasn't sure I'd ever make it up for air.

The blush that crept up my face must've been bright red, because it felt like my cheeks were on fire. Misael smirked, catching my gaze and holding it. There was heat and something like possessiveness in his gaze, and I was torn between conflicting impulses to lean toward him on the couch and to run for my life.

I had agreed to their bargain, but I didn't—*shouldn't*— want this.

It shouldn't make my nipples peak, and it shouldn't make my breath stutter like this.

Breathe, Cora. Just breathe. Nothing's even happened yet. Maybe it won't ever.

The only one who had made any kind of move was Bishop, and even that had seemed to be almost against his will. The other two boys touched me like they owned me, but never in that way yet.

Did I want them to?

Could I handle it if they did? If *all* of them did?

"That clear enough for you, Princess?" Bishop asked, tilting his head as he watched me carefully. His tone suggested he was actually asking for once, that the question wasn't rhetorical.

"Yeah." I swallowed, ripping my gaze away from Misael's dark, hypnotic eyes. "Yeah, I get it."

Eye contact broken, I left the conversation at that, my heart still thudding hard in my chest.

I was a virgin, but I wasn't entirely inexperienced. I'd heard plenty of stories from the girls at Highland Park Prep who'd done a lot more than me, so it wasn't like I was some blushing wallflower. But I also wasn't sure I was ready to prod at the details of what happened when a girl was shared between three boys—and I definitely wasn't ready to examine why the thought of it made my clit throb, made my core clench with some nameless need.

We didn't speak any more about the idea of sharing.

Instead, we shared more beers.

Even though I was still freaking out on the inside, it felt like our little discussion had broken the ice between us in a way. Now that I knew exactly what our bargain entailed, it was actually easier to relax around them—possibly because I didn't have to second-guess what might be coming anymore. I knew.

But for the first time since losing the house, since coming to the "wrong side of the tracks", since meeting the Lost Boys and getting pulled into their strange, dark, questionable arrangement, I allowed myself to have fun.

Misael cranked up the music after deciding that we were all being too serious for his liking. I drank one beer, then another—that seemed to be the threshold of letting myself relax and let loose.

Bishop and Kace were easily the more reserved of the three boys, although in different ways and for different reasons. So it was Misael that finally hopped up from the couch, pulling me up and tugging me into his arms, getting my body to move to the music that played.

It was nothing like the elegant instrumental I'd grown up with, the only thing that'd been allowed in my house. This music was thick with bass and heavy with vocals; a rhythmic Latin rap that Misael moved his hips to with ease.

I tried to keep up with him, but the feel of his body so close to mine and the scent of cloves that always seemed to cling to him distracted me. My feet kept tripping over each other, and I felt gangly and awkward.

"Loosen up, Princess. It's just dancin'," he said with a crooked grin, pulling me tighter into his hold and swiveling his hips against me.

My breath caught in my throat, and I clung harder to his shoulders, practically wrapping myself around him as I let him guide our movements. I could feel every inch of him, the firmness and solidness of his body. He was a little leaner than Bishop and Kace, but still big compared to me. I fit perfectly in his hold, my hips in his large hands...

As I gave myself over to the music, I finally found the rhythm with him, "loosening up", as he called it. Following his movements was like moving through water, a liquid ease that rolled like the tide.

I loved it—and that was the most surprising part.

Even with my life turned upside down, even in this strange, often terrifying new world I found myself in, there were little parts of it that felt halfway normal. That felt *good*.

What would Dad think, I wondered, *if he knew this was my new normal? What would Mom think?*

But the honest truth was, in that moment, I didn't really care.

It was late by the time the Lost Boys dropped me off at home. It was dark, the night sky hanging over the city like a shroud. My old home was less than fifteen miles away, but it truly did feel like it belonged in a separate world sometimes. Here, the sky wasn't clear. You could barely see the stars glittering through the smog, but there was something endearing about that.

Or it was the alcohol. It might have been the alcohol.

We pulled up to the front of the house, laughing, more than a little tipsy. I was impressed that Bishop managed to drive steadily—but then I remembered he'd only had one beer, maybe part of a second one. I wondered if that was on purpose because he was the only one with a license, or if he just didn't drink a lot.

To my surprise, he got out of the car with me, taking my arm as I slid out. I was grateful for the gesture; between being tipsy and having to carry my backpack and books, I probably wouldn't have made it to the front door without going down in a heap.

"Try to stay outta trouble," he said lightly as I fumbled

with my key. He eventually took it from me after one, two, then three attempts to get it into the lock. I giggle-snorted.

"No trouble in my house," I said, and then added before I could stop myself, "Mom would have to care for there to be trouble."

His gaze flicked up to mine, and I suddenly wished he'd drunk a lot more beer at the warehouse. His hazel eyes were too clear, too perceptive as I scrambled to cover up my pain with a half-smile.

"Mm-hm. See, ya, Princess." He reached up to tuck a lock of hair behind my ear, his touch lingering for a fraction of a second. "It was... a good day with you."

I could have sworn he said it softly, like he actually meant it.

FIFTEEN

IN THE MENTAL list of firsts I was accumulating, I could add another alongside "going to public school", and "drinking beer".

Having a hangover.

I was grateful it was the weekend, because there was no way I would've been able to get through one period of class, let alone seven plus lunch, with the massive freight train that was chugging its way along through my brain. My skull felt like it was going to split open, and I spent most of the morning snuggled under the blankets so that the sunlight filtering through the dingy, dirty windows didn't make my headache worse.

Drinking, no matter how fun it was, had clearly been a mistake. Maybe next time I would need to take it slower. Or actually eat something beforehand.

It was around noon when I finally dragged myself out of

bed. Mom was in her room like usual, her television on—I could hear the soft drone of voices from some game show. I decided not to bother her. While I didn't think she would ask too many questions about where I'd been last night, I still didn't want to risk the possibility of having to explain to her that I'd taken the evening off to chill out in a warehouse with three boys and drink.

Still, I paused just outside her bedroom door. I felt shitty about how hard she was taking all of this. I'd found small moments of happiness and levity, little pockets of sunshine amidst the gray clouds, but Mom didn't have a school to go to —no way to meet new people, nothing to force her out of the house. I didn't think there was any chance of her getting to know the neighborhood mothers or foster mothers either.

Sighing, I shook my head. *Shower, water, food.*

I checked them off in that order, and with each item I checked off my list, I felt progressively more human. By mid-afternoon, I felt good enough to make an attempt at sprucing up the house a bit—starting with those grimy windows.

Ava had left cleaning supplies for us, which had so far been left completely untouched. I was out of my depth, but a quick look at the labels revealed she'd left us with window cleaner and bleach.

Soon, I had my hair tied back, rags in my hands, and was using a small step stool I'd found in the tiny pantry in the corner of the kitchen to reach the outside windows. They looked like they hadn't been cleaned in at least a decade; spiderwebs cluttered the corners of the window panes, and the grime I managed to scrub from the windows' surfaces couldn't be cleaned from the cracks that networked over the glass. It was an improvement though. It was better than nothing.

I had moved from the windows on the side of the house by the kitchen to the ones around the front when a voice behind me made me jump.

"Didn't expect to see you out here working like a normal person, Princess."

I paused, turning around. It was Kace.

"What are you doing here?" I asked, wiping off my hands on my rag. I glanced around, expecting the other Lost Boys to be with him, but he was alone.

He shrugged. "Bish thought you might have a hangover, but he had somethin' to do. A thing came up," he answered cryptically, holding up a greasy Burger King bag. "So I brought some hangover food."

I blinked.

"Burger King is hangover food?"

"Anything greasy is hangover food. Sops up all the alcohol. Settles your stomach. You want it or not?"

Well, I wasn't going to turn down Burger King. Not now that I knew it was so damn good. I took the bag, reaching in to find two of the same burgers I'd gotten last time, an order of regular fries, and an order of chicken fries.

"I'll make sure to pay you back for it—"

"Don't worry about it," he interrupted, already turning

around to head back toward his house. "Bish wanted you to have it."

"You... you want to stay here for a bit?"

I stepped off the stool, moving toward him before stopping myself. I wasn't quite sure why I'd asked, or why I really hoped he'd say yes. But it was the polite thing to offer, wasn't it? I remembered at least that much from the lessons Mom had taught me.

He hesitated, turning his head slightly as his moss-green gaze caught mine. Then he shook his head.

"Nah. Got shit to do. See you at school, Princess."

I HAD Kace's random appearance on my mind all day on Monday. I was picked up by the Lost Boys as usual, but there wasn't any hint of Kace's visit, the fact that Bishop had apparently sent him, or really any conversation about our Friday excursion at all. They all seemed a little subdued; I wondered if it had anything to do with that "thing" Kace had mentioned, but I decided not to ask. I was already way too involved in these three boys' lives.

The day started off fine. No one had forgotten over the weekend that I was under the protection of the Lost Boys, so the rest of the students left me alone as usual.

But I should've known that at Slateview, "fine" never lasted long.

It was just after lunch when shit hit the fan.

I was at my locker, swapping out my books. I had history next, with Mr. Tyson. He was by far my favorite teacher at Slateview, the only one who actually seemed to care about the students who walked through these doors. I liked his assignments, and I liked that he seemed to really enjoy history. It wasn't my favorite subject, but at least he made it an interesting class.

With my history textbook in my hand, I was just about to close my locker when a large body suddenly slammed into the locker beside mine. I jumped back, clutching my books to my chest as my heart tried to crawl up my throat. For a fear-filled moment, I thought that the Lost Boys' warning to the school had been for nothing. That Logan or someone even worse had decided to come for me after all.

But I wasn't the target of the fight.

Two boys threw angry fists at each other, slamming each other against the lockers in a brawl that rivaled a pro wrestling match. I shrank back against the bay of lockers, keeping my books in front of me like a shield, my eyes wide as other students started cheering and shouting, egging the boys on. The crowd in the hallway had parted around them as if by magic, and the two boys crashed around the space, yelling and cursing at each other.

I glanced around, adrenaline flooding my veins as one of the boys slammed the other into a locker again, feet away from where I was standing. Where were the teachers? The admins? Was no one going to step in and stop this? Maybe they were just as used to it as the students were and just couldn't be bothered to care anymore.

A door opened down the hallway, and I caught Mr. Tyson's gaze. But even he looked on, shook his head, and retreated into his classroom.

I was so distracted by the sight of Mr. Tyson that I forgot to watch out for the fight. There was a shout and a grunt, and before I could react, one of the boys stumbled backward, plowing into me. My shoulder caught the lockers painfully, and I let out a yelp as my books tumbled from my arms.

"Watch it—!"

"You motherfucker—!"

"Break this shit the fuck up."

The voice that spoke over the fighting boys was calm but cold. The shouts and taunts of the gathered students died out immediately, and I looked up, gripping my bruised shoulder with one hand.

It was Kace.

He pushed his way through the crowd without trouble, students parting for him quickly when they saw who it was. He grabbed one boy by the back of his shirt, pulling him off the other. But the guy obviously didn't realize who it was breaking up the fight—or maybe he was just pissed enough to be reckless. He swung his arm back, his fist catching Kace in the face with a glancing blow. Kace reacted like lightning, his own right hook flying through the air to smash the boy in the face.

It didn't knock him out, but it did knock him down.

Blood spurted from the boy's nose. He curled up on the floor, hands clawing at his face as he whimpered and groaned.

"I thought I said break this shit up." Kace said, standing over the downed boy's body and glaring at the other one. "We don't have a place for this dumb shit here. Now beat it before I beat you."

It wasn't just the two boys that followed his command, but the entire crowd. Someone darted forward to help the guy with the bloody face, and the hallway cleared out moments before the bell rang.

I blinked, staring around at the suddenly empty corridor. It was still a shock to me to see how much pull the Lost Boys had over the school. More than even the teachers, who did nothing to control their students' actions. Not even Mr. Tyson had been willing or able to step in and stop the fight.

Kace hadn't moved since he'd issued his order. He'd just stood still and silent, watching the other students scurry away, as if waiting for one to linger too long so he could pounce.

As the ringing of the bell faded, he glanced over at me. "You should get to class too."

I was about to obey just like every other student had—the impulse to follow Kace's commands was almost too strong to ignore, and I really did need to get to class. But as I bent to pick up my books, I glanced up at him. The kid who'd hit him hadn't gotten in a good shot, but a small line of blood dripped from Kace's nose anyway, and his knuckles were smeared with it.

Tugging my bottom lip between my teeth, I hesitated, warring with myself. *It's not your business, Cora. This isn't one of the stipulations of your agreement with them.*

But even as the rational voice in my head reminded me of that, I remembered the weekend and the food Kace had brought me to combat my hangover—something I was pretty sure Bishop hadn't actually told him to do.

He had taken care of me.

And although it was probably stupid of me, I wanted to take care of him too.

SIXTEEN

MAKING A SNAP DECISION, I shook my head and reached out, taking hold of the blond boy's un-bloodied hand to drag him along.

There was resistance, but he didn't actually stop me. I knew he could've if he'd wanted to, so I kept tugging, accepting that as a win.

"What are you doing?" He sounded honestly confused for the first time since I'd met him.

"Cleaning you up, Mr. I-Want-To-Be-A-UFC-Fighter."

"Do you even know what UFC is?" he asked. There was something almost like suspicion in his voice, though he let me pull him along to the bathroom. I chose the men's room, figuring it was better for me to invade that one than to invite Kace into the ladies' room.

"Yeah. My father actually liked watching it. Said it was

his trashy guilty pleasure," I explained with a shrug. "Although he never let me watch."

I set down my books and school bag just inside the bathroom door, went to the paper towel dispenser, and then crossed to the sink to soak them. When they were wet, I waved Kace over.

"Give me your hand," I instructed.

His brow quirked, his broad features registering surprise, but he said nothing. Shockingly, he did what I asked with no resistance, holding out his bloodied hand with his knuckles up. I took it, dabbing the blood from his skin where he'd punched the boy.

The sight of blood had never bothered me, thank goodness, although I did feel a little queasy when I remembered the loud crunch I'd heard as his fist had connected with the boy's nose and the spray of blood that had erupted like a geyser.

"Why did you do that?" I asked, keeping my gaze trained on the back of his hand as I worked.

"What?"

I rolled my eyes. "You know what. Stop the fight. You guys aren't exactly the Hardy Boys, but you're all very much about... I don't know, stepping in when something bad is about to happen. Or is in the process of happening. I just don't get it."

His knuckles were clean, but I lingered on them a little longer, noticing the weight of his hand in mine, the warmth of his skin.

As I moved on to his nose, he shrugged.

"There's nothing you need to get. We keep order in the school. Sometimes you need to use violence to keep order."

I'd studiously avoided his gaze as I worked on his knuckles, but now that I was cleaning up his bloodied nose, it was impossible. Against my will, my gaze trailed up, catching on his light, moss-green eyes.

"That doesn't make any sense," I murmured.

"Of course it does. You show that you're bigger and badder than the moron who's parading all over, waving his dick around, you get to come out on top. Bish, Misael, and I? We dominate. We just don't do it indiscriminately. There's a method. A reason. When people behave, we're fine with them. When they don't, they get what Caleb got."

Ah, so that's what that boy's name is.

Still, it was a little strange.

"How can you dominate and call it a good thing?" My curiosity was genuine as I pulled away, moving to pull more dry paper towels from the dispenser.

Kace laughed. "Domination ain't always a bad thing, Princess. You might actually enjoy it if you weren't so prim and proper."

I paused on my way back to him, my footsteps stuttering to a halt. That concept had never even occurred to me. And the way he said it, that I might enjoy it...

It sounded like...

Oh.

I blushed but resumed walking quickly, trying to hide the

thoughts racing through my mind, hoping Kace hadn't noticed my reaction to his words. Stepping close to him again, I dabbed at his face and knuckles with the dry paper towels, keeping my movements fast and barely daring to inhale.

He was so big, his presence so overwhelming, and I was standing so close to him that I felt tiny in comparison. He had a faintly spicy scent, an addictive aroma that seemed to cling to his skin. He was wearing a dark t-shirt today, its color a striking contrast to the light blond of his hair. It stretched across his chest as he shifted beneath my touch.

"You're curious," he murmured, his voice a soft rasp. "You want to know what it's like. I can see it in your eyes."

My gaze flicked to his, my heart rate picking up so fast it left me dizzy.

Oh God. He did notice. How does he always notice so much?

"I—I don't know what you mean." My voice was low as I moved to grab the collection of paper towels to throw them away. But before I could step away from him, Kace reached out and threaded his fingers through the hair at the back of my head, stopping me in place.

"Don't you?" he asked, looking me dead in the eyes.

This was the closest I'd been to Kace since my first encounter with the Lost Boys. He wasn't like Misael or Bishop, who invaded my space on a regular basis. He'd seemed to intentionally keep his distance... until now.

Now, his grip on my hair tightened, making a slight stinging sensation spread across my scalp. He used his hold on me to tilt my head back a little, and before I could speak, before I could even gasp, he pressed his lips to mine.

Fire ran through me, the same intense blaze that'd raged inside me when Bishop had kissed me, making liquid heat pool low in my core.

I shouldn't be doing this.

I shouldn't be allowing this to happen.

But Kace moved like a man possessed, and I couldn't stop him from kissing me—or stop myself from kissing him back. He controlled the movement of my head, taking what he wanted from between my parted lips as our kiss deepened. His tongue plunged into my mouth as his grip on my hair loosened, and then I was letting him push me back against the sink and hoist me up so he could settle between my legs.

I could feel the hard heat of his cock pressing against my core, and all the layers of fabric that separated us felt like nothing as he ground his hips against mine. It was thrilling in the same way it was frightening, and the tandem feelings beat through me with equal vengeance.

Without a conscious command from my brain, my legs lifted to wrap around Kace's waist, bringing him closer and securing him to me as I hooked my heels together. His answering groan filled my mouth, and that sound alone made a flood of wetness dampen my panties. He was controlling every bit of this, taking what he wanted without question or hesitation—but somehow, when he made that sound, *I* felt like the powerful one. As if I could bring this massive, broad-shouldered boy to his knees with a single touch.

Wanting more of that incredible feeling, I pressed harder against him, battling his tongue with my own, trying to draw another groan out of him.

But what I got this time was a sound almost like a growl as Kace grabbed my hair at the roots again, taking back control of our kiss.

I could feel my lips bruising, banging against my teeth as he kissed me so hard and deep it felt like we were at war. The hand that wasn't in my hair splayed across my lower back, holding me in place as his hips moved against mine, every thrust hitting a spot that made sparks dance in my vision. I was so close, my body hovering on the precipice of overwhelming pleasure.

I had touched myself sometimes in the darkness of my bedroom in my family's old mansion, in the quiet loneliness of the night. And Bishop had found my clit with unerring fingers the night he'd broken into my room, making me come harder than I ever had in my life.

But I had never come like this.

From just the feel of a boy's ravenous lips and the rhythmic press of his cock at the apex of my thighs. From just the sweet promise of what might happen if we weren't clothed, weren't separated by anything. My inner muscles clenched as my clit throbbed, and I had never felt so... empty in my life.

My heart was beating like a hummingbird's wings, fluttering in my chest, and when I let out a sound halfway between a whimper and a sob, Kace tore his lips away from mine, using his grip on me to hike me even closer to his body. His hips thrust against me hard and slow as he gazed down at me with green eyes that seemed even lighter than usual somehow.

"Come, Princess. Let me see what you look like when you come."

The words were barely out of his mouth when my body followed his command. The desperate ache building inside me released in a torrent, and I squeezed my legs around him as my clit throbbed. A noise I was sure I'd never made before in my life escaped my mouth, and I might've been embarrassed by the raw, wanton sound if I hadn't been distracted by the sensations crashing through me.

I tried to bury my face in Kace's neck, too overwhelmed by everything I was feeling, not wanting him to see it on my face, but he used his grip on my hair to stop me, watching me with glittering eyes as I trembled and shook in his grasp.

When the orgasm finally subsided, I sucked in a deep breath. My heartbeat had slowed from a rapid flutter to a heavy, dull thud against my ribs. I blinked at Kace, shocked and embarrassed that he'd made me come in the men's bathroom at school just from grinding against me like that. I half expected him to laugh at me, to mock me for being so easy, so desperate.

But there was no humor in his expression as he gazed back at me. Just an intense kind of hunger that made my stomach flip-flop.

"What's your favorite color?" he asked, narrowing his eyes.

The question surprised me so much that I blurted out the answer before I even thought about it.

"Blue."

He nodded. "If you want this to stop, say 'blue'."

I blinked at him, completely lost. Say 'blue'? What did that mean?

Before I could ask, he was sliding his hands under my thighs, lifting me from the sink. I yelped, clinging to his neck as he carried me toward the door. Was he going to take me out into the hall like this? Parade me around in front of everyone?

I opened my mouth, about to scream "blue", for all the good it would do, when he stopped directly in front of the door. He turned around, putting his back to it, and then set me on my feet. I staggered slightly, my legs still weak and my clit still throbbing from the orgasm that'd torn through me.

Two large hands came up to grasp my face, and Kace tilted my head up so he could look me in the eyes.

"I made you come, Princess. Now you're gonna suck my dick until I come."

My eyes flew open wide, and I almost choked on my next breath as I registered what he'd said. *Holy... holy shit.*

His words were dirty and crass, no sweetness or gentleness to them at all. So why did they turn me on so much?

I could say "blue". I could see if the magic word he'd

given me would really stop this in its tracks. But I couldn't get my mouth to utter that one simple syllable.

Because I didn't want this to stop.

As terrifying as it was, there was something in me that wanted this too. So when Kace gathered my hair in a loose ponytail before wrapping it around his fist, I said nothing. When he used his grip on me to force me to my knees, I said nothing. Only when he moved his free hand to his pants, flipping the button and unzipping the fly, did I finally speak.

"What if someone comes in—"

"They won't." He shook his head, his half-lidded eyes intense as they gazed down at me. "That's why we're standing here. They won't get inside."

I wasn't nearly as confident about that as he was, but when he reached into his pants and drew out his heavy, hard cock, I forgot all about the door, about other students, about the fact that it was the middle of sixth period. My gaze zeroed in on the thick piece of flesh gripped tightly in his hand, and I couldn't make myself look away.

It was almost exactly at my eye-level, and when he took a small step closer to me, my body tensed. I knew he could feel it, but he didn't stop. The hand in my hair brought my face closer to his cock, so close I could smell the tangy, musky scent of his arousal, and his voice was like sandpaper when he grated out one word.

"Lick."

I did. My tongue darted out, quick and tentative, as if I was tasting a flavor of lollipop I wasn't sure I would like.

The skin at the rounded tip was soft and smooth, and a little bead of liquid had gathered at the small slit. I ran my tongue over that, shivering at the saltiness, the unfamiliar taste. Kace shuddered too, his entire body quivering as he let out a low noise.

"Good. More. Put your mouth on me."

As if he wasn't sure I'd understand his command, he used the hand wrapped around my hair to guide my movements, bumping my lips against the head of his cock until I opened my mouth. When I did, he thrust his hips forward a little, sliding deeper inside.

I kept my lips wrapped around him, using my tongue to spread saliva all over his shaft, making sure to avoid scraping him with my teeth. I didn't have any idea what I was doing, but from conversations I'd overheard in the locker room at Highland Park, I knew that much.

And whatever I was doing, Kace seemed to approve, because more of those noises I liked so much were falling from his lips. He kept his thrusts shallow, but tears still gathered at the corners of my eyes as arousal clashed with panic every time he filled my mouth. There was just so much of him, and I was so much smaller than he was. Even my mouth felt small compared to the size of his cock, so I brought my hand up to help me, wrapping my fingers around his thick length and moving my hand as I worked my lips up and down his shaft.

"Fuck, Princess. Fucking hell."

His movements became rougher, his thrusts deeper, until

he was hitting the back of my throat. I made a noise and swallowed roughly, fighting down my gag reflex, and he groaned loudly as my throat undulated around his broad head.

My own arousal was building again as I gave up control entirely and let him use me however he liked, abandoning my grip on his cock and grabbing his thighs with both hands, holding on for balance as his movements became more jerky and erratic.

Then the door behind him started to open.

Panic flared inside me, like a shot of ice water injected into my veins.

But Kace didn't let me go. He didn't let me stop.

He lifted one foot and kicked the door hard, slamming it shut on whoever had been about to enter.

"Fuck off."

The words were harsh and ragged, and when the person on the other side tried again, Kace gave it another kick.

"I said fuck off!"

The reality of what we were doing hit me like a truck as I felt his cock thicken and swell inside my mouth. Another boy was on the other side of that door. Maybe even a teacher. Who knew how many other students were out in the hall, having stepped out of class or skipped it entirely.

And inside the bathroom, separated from them all only by the heavy metal door, I was giving Kace a blowjob.

That thought made me moan involuntarily, and Kace glanced down at me, his eyes flashing. His face contorted with something almost like determination, his nostrils flaring as he breathed heavily.

"Oh, shit. I'm gonna come," he grunted. "I'm gonna come in your pretty pink mouth. Paint your fuckin' lips with my cum."

My cheeks flushed hotly as embarrassment and arousal surged inside me. Those words shouldn't turn me on so much, shouldn't make me ache to move my hand between my own legs and come again when he did.

This was dirty and wrong.

So why did I like it so much?

Kace thrust into my mouth three more times, cursing softly under his breath, and then his cock jerked between my lips as he groaned out his release. Tangy, salty liquid exploded on my tongue, and I swallowed quickly, my throat working over and over as I tried to catch it all. When he pulled away, a bit of it escaped my lips, trailing down my chin.

Not wanting to risk getting it on my shirt, I quickly used my finger to gather it and slip it back inside my mouth, and when I looked up, I caught Kace staring down at me like he couldn't quite believe I was real.

His cock had hardly softened at all, and it glistened in the harsh florescent light, still wet with saliva.

"Jesus fuck, Princess," he muttered. "Your mouth is—" He broke off suddenly, his face growing still. "You ever done that before?"

I shook my head, craning my neck to look up at him. The

hard floor dug into my knees painfully, but I was only just now starting to notice it. And before I could really register the discomfort, Kace was hauling me to my feet, his large hand grasping my chin as he pulled me in for a kiss that nearly stopped my heart.

It started off bruising and intense, but by the time his lips broke away from mine, it had softened, becoming something else entirely.

Something sweeter and even more terrifying.

Moss-green eyes gazed back at me, and Kace gifted me with a rare smile as he released me, nodding in satisfaction.

"Good."

SEVENTEEN

MY ENTIRE BODY was still buzzing, wound up, and on edge when the Boys dropped me off at home. Kace said nothing about our encounter, and I was beginning to think this tendency toward silence, toward ignoring complicated feelings, was a trait all three of them shared despite being so different. All things considered, maybe it was a good thing. I didn't know how to begin to process the fact that all three of them were attracted to me on some level, or that I was attracted to them.

When I stepped inside and poked around the house, I realized Mom was gone. For a split second, panic fluttered in my chest, beating against my ribs like a trapped bird. Then I put a hand over my heart when I spotted the note on the fridge.

Your father's attorney got us a replacement car.

Went out.
Be back later.

I frowned. I hadn't realized Dad's attorney had that kind of pull, or that he would be interested in helping us by getting us a car. I almost felt a little worried that Mom was out on her own—it was the first time that'd happened in weeks. But this could only be a good thing, right? If she was leaving the house, then that meant she was doing something other than sitting in her room watching daytime television and getting no sun or human interaction.

Setting my backpack down, I decided to try my hand at cooking again. I couldn't live off Burger King all the time—though it was tempting—and rather than trying to sort through my feelings about the Lost Boys, I rummaged through the cabinets.

Spaghetti. That shouldn't be too hard to make.

We had frozen ground beef, a few cans of sauce, and packages of noodles. Water needed to be boiled to cook the noodles—but then I also needed to brown the beef. Should I put spices in the beef while it was cooking or after? Or when I put the sauce together after all of it was completely cooked?

I decided, as I'd done in most of my cooking endeavors, to wing it. Working quickly, I defrosted and started browning the beef while bringing water to a boil. While I was waiting on those two things, I pulled down a few of the spices Ava had left for us. I kept an ear out for Mom in the driveway, hoping she'd be back by the time I was done. It would be nice to have a sit down dinner with just the two of us. It wouldn't be a multi-course meal, we wouldn't be served and waited on, but it would be better than cold cereal.

I actually managed to brown the beef instead of burning it and got noodles in the water to cook without a single hitch —a feat that I would write on a calendar to celebrate later. I'd started adding the cans of sauce to the meat when there was a knock on the door.

My brows furrowed. Mom and I didn't have visitors here. Ever.

Foolishly, my heart leapt. Maybe it was Dad, or his lawyer with news about his trial. Maybe they'd finally found proof that Dad was innocent, and this whole mess was about to be over.

I raced to the front door and yanked it open—only to find Bishop standing on the other side. I stopped dead, mentally berating myself for still having such wild surges of hope. I needed to cut that shit out; my heart couldn't take it.

My face must have showed my stark disappointment, because Bishop smirked.

"Well, I didn't realize you hated me that much." There was humor in his voice, and even if he believed his own words, it didn't stop him from stepping into the house past me, looking around. He lifted his chin, sniffing experimentally. "Smells like food in here. I didn't know you cooked."

"I don't," I muttered, still holding onto the doorknob as I

watched him walk deeper into the house. "I was trying my hand at spaghetti."

"Hm."

He walked into the kitchen without asking if he could stay, but considering this was the same boy who'd broken into my room in the middle of the night, the fact that he had bothered to knock and use the front door was monumental in and of itself.

I followed him into the tiny kitchen, watching as he strode over to the stove, poking around the pots and breathing in.

"Actually smells good," he commented, lifting his eyebrows.

I frowned. "I don't know if I'm supposed to take that as a compliment or not."

"Take it however you want. It at least looks edible." He glanced over to me, and the glint in his hazel eyes told me he was teasing. I rolled my eyes.

"Whatever. What are you doing here?" I stepped forward, nudging him away from the pots so I could stir them myself. He leaned against the counter, the small space forcing us to stand way too close, and watched me as he answered.

"We're going to a party later tonight. Me and the guys. You're coming with us."

Not a question. A statement. I was starting to learn the difference between the times when Bish meant to give me a choice and when he didn't, and this was definitely the latter.

I glanced over to him. "It's a school night."

"Yeah. What's your point?"

"Well, I mean—isn't this a bit different than going to a random warehouse on a Friday after school? I don't even know what kind of parties people throw... here."

His brow quirked. "Well, they're usually lively as fuck, so I bet they're different than you're used to. There's booze, pot, gambling, sex." He shrugged. "We always go. Means things stay chill, and that's a good thing for the Slateview kids."

"Well, if you're just going to chaperone, then why do I need to come?"

"Because we want you to."

I stopped stirring the sauce for a moment, letting that statement linger in the air. *Because we want you to.* What a strange thought. Nothing about this arrangement the four of us were in really made sense to me, and every time I thought I'd found my footing, something came along to knock me off my axis again.

Going to a party actually sounded kind of fun. A little thrill of nerves and excitement skittered up my spine as I thought about it—about seeing what these kinds of parties were really like. Still, I hesitated. My thoughts went once more to the bathroom incident with Kace, dancing with Misael, and then the other night with Bishop.

Hadn't things gone far enough, gotten *confusing* enough, already? Wouldn't going to a party with all of them just be asking for trouble?

That's when it hit me.

Bishop and I were totally alone here.

My mom was out of the house and wouldn't be back till God only knew when. I was standing in my kitchen with one of the Lost Boys, and he was so close to me that his arm brushed against mine as I worked. I could feel the heat from his body, smell the woodsy scent of his cologne as it mixed with the aroma of the pasta sauce.

I flushed against my will and tightened my grip on the spoon as I resumed stirring.

God, could he tell I was breathing harder? Could he see the blush spreading across my cheeks?

I wished I could keep my reactions under control around these boys, but with every line we crossed, it seemed to be harder to control them, not easier.

"Fine," I conceded, partly just because I was desperate to say something. "But I'm finishing this and eating before we go. I want to at least make sure Mom has something to eat when she gets back—we haven't exactly had a lot of food in the house."

Bishop shrugged. "Sure. Whatever you want."

"You can have some too, if you want."

He actually looked surprised, drawing his head back as he straightened. "You're offering me a meal?"

"Well, it's the least I can do. You've given me food before and stuff."

He blinked at me, his brows drawing together over his intense hazel eyes. "You're so fucking weird for a rich girl."

"And you're weird for a not-rich boy, so I guess we're just

both weird. Shut up and get a plate; they're in the cabinet behind you. I think this is done. Probably."

Bishop laughed. "You don't even know if the food is done? You're makin' me nervous, Princess."

I scowled at him, narrowing my eyes. "I'm still learning. Be nice, or you can stand there and watch *me* eat."

"Okay, okay." He lifted his hands in mock innocence, a warm, deep laugh falling from his lips. "Chill out. Don't you know what a joke is?"

This was the loosest I'd seen Bishop—the most easy and relaxed. I wasn't sure what had brought about the shift in him, but I couldn't deny that I liked it.

He got down the plates as I made the final preparations with the food. The house didn't have a dining room, just a tiny table in one corner of the kitchen with two mismatched chairs. After serving up the pasta, we settled down across from each other, our knees brushing under the table.

I looked down at the plate. It wasn't the prettiest thing I'd ever seen, but I was beginning to learn that when it came to food, edibility was much more important than looks. Twirling my fork into the noodles, I took a bite.

My jaw froze halfway through chewing as a single flavor overwhelmed me.

Salt. Too much damn salt.

Bishop coughed, forcing down his own first bite.

"Well, it doesn't taste like arsenic, so I guess that's a plus." He pulled a face, clearing his throat.

I sighed, disappointment filling me. *Dammit. I was so close.* "Yeah... but it doesn't taste edible, either."

"Easy fix." His expression cleared, and he shrugged. "Let me show you."

To my surprise, he got up, going to the cupboards to rummage through them. I watched him with a curious gaze as he pulled out a bag of sugar. He spooned out a small helping onto my plate, and then onto his.

"Mix it." He jerked his chin toward the pasta and the little pile of sugar.

I couldn't see how it would possibly make anything better, but I did as he instructed, then took an experimental bite.

"Oh... oh, wow." My eyes widened. "That's actually... good. How the hell did you do that?"

Bishop shrugged, tucking into his own food. "When you're always broke, you learn how to make food edible no matter what. Sauce too salty? Add a little sugar. Sauce too sugary? Add some salt. Or some spice. It's all about balance. Honestly, Misael is a fucking wizard in the kitchen. Most of the stuff I know, I picked up from him. My foster mom can't cook for shit."

"Huh. I'll have to ask him for some tips then."

There were so many more questions I wanted to ask, so many more things I wanted to know about this boy's life. I'd discovered that all three of the Lost Boys lived with foster families, but I didn't know how they'd all ended up there.

But Bishop had never been this easy-going and open

before, and I was a little afraid that if I pushed too hard, he would realize he'd said too much and clam back up. So I didn't push for more, and we fell into silence as we ate—but it was a comfortable, enjoyable kind of silence.

Too soon, our food was finished. Bish stood up, taking our plates. "Get ready. I'll clean up."

I was surprised by his offer, but I nodded and headed to my room to change. My misguided attempt at making my wardrobe fit in at Slateview had left me with very few clothes that weren't distressed in some way, but I was actually starting to feel comfortable in them.

It didn't feel so much like a costume anymore.

After trying on a couple of outfits, I settled on something that seemed appropriate. I pulled my light blonde hair back into a ponytail, peering at my face in the tiny mirror on the dresser before deciding against any more makeup. Then I headed back out to meet Bishop.

Well, here goes nothing.

EIGHTEEN

I NEVER WOULD'VE THOUGHT I'd feel out of place when it came to a party. I'd been to so many with my parents that the concept of "social gathering" was probably ingrained in my DNA somewhere, to be honest.

Smiles, politics, and flattery. Cocktails, five to seven course meals, and glasses full of the finest champagne—those were all the things I was used to at the parties I'd attended.

But a party with Slateview students was nothing like the refined parties I was used to making appearances at with my parents. When we pulled up to the house a couple miles from where Mom and I lived, there were already dozens of cars out front, haphazardly parked alongside the worn-out sidewalk. Deep, pounding bass blared from within, and I got the distinct impression that most of the neighbors didn't care, since the central house on the block wasn't the only one where something was going on.

It did seem, however, that the central house was the main hub of entertainment. It was the one that the Lost Boys parked in front of in a space that felt suspiciously like it had been reserved for them.

As we walked inside, I recognized faces from school, kids everywhere holding red plastic cups and moving their bodies to the music that sounded even louder now.

The other thing I noticed quickly was how much skin was on display. It was everywhere.

I would've felt overdressed if it weren't for the fact that I had on a pair of cut-off shorts made from custom tailored jeans and a crop top that I'd fashioned out of one of my old shirts—my outfit was still tame compared to some girls, but at least I didn't stand out too badly.

When I'd stepped out of the bedroom, Bishop had said I had a surprisingly good figure for a little rich girl. I was still trying to figure out what that was supposed to mean as we made our way through the house, the Lost Boys flanking me as if they dared anyone to cross my path or even look at me funny.

No one did. It was almost comical—and maybe it was due to the copious amounts of alcohol being consumed—but people actually said hello to me. Jovial, red faces grinned or nodded in my direction, Solo cups were lifted up in cheers, and the Lost Boys were greeted with the respect I was sure they'd spent years earning.

I was grateful for the fact that we moved quickly through the main section of the house, not lingering too long. It was the loudest and most chaotic area, and honestly, we'd been at the party less than five minutes and my ears had already started hurting. Instead of mingling with the "common folk", as Misael playfully muttered into my ear, we headed toward the "VIP section".

I had no idea what that was supposed to mean, but I was pretty sure there wouldn't be champagne in crystal flutes in that section either.

The VIP section was downstairs, in the basement, away from the heated gyrating of half-naked girls on boys with lustful interest in their eyes. There was still music down here, but at least the volume was tolerable, and on the couch situated in front of an old-school, big-backed television, sat Liam and Jessica. They were locked in a make-out session to rival anything I had seen upstairs, Liam's hands at Jessica's hips as she sat straddling his waist. I had the decency to blush, but the shock kept me looking. The Lost Boys didn't even blink.

"Hey. You knew we were coming, you degenerates," Bishop said, giving the couch a kick as he laughed.

Misael gave a wolf whistle, plopping down onto the couch while Jessica climbed off Liam's lap. She rolled her eyes, adjusting her top back into place to cover her bra, but Liam actually looked a little embarrassed. I would be, too, if my friends had just burst in on... that.

I took the chair beside where Misael ended up, Bishop taking a chair opposite me. Kace didn't sit at all, instead choosing to stand off to Bishop's side. He looked the least affected by the scene; I wondered if he even cared about being at a party to begin with, with how bored he seemed to be about the whole thing.

Jessica leaned over toward me, smirking. The red lipstick she wore hadn't even smeared during her heavy make-out session. I was impressed.

"I see they dragged you out for this little shindig. Hope it's not too overwhelming. Somehow, I doubt uptown parties are like this."

"Uh... no, it's not overwhelming," I lied. "It's just... different? I'm not sure what I should be doing, to be honest."

"Whatever you want!" She laughed. "Aren't you used to doing that?"

I snorted softly. "No. Not like how you're thinking anyway. Most of the parties I've been to weren't for, you know, drinking and dancing and stuff. Most of the time it was for business."

Jessica groaned. "*Boooring.* What kinda people throw parties for business?"

"Rich people?" I offered. She cocked her head, eyeing me for a second before seeming to realize I was just joking. Then she laughed again.

"Fair enough. C'mon, loosen up! I'm glad the guys invited you. You gotta relax and let your hair down a little—show those fuckers up there you're not just some stuck up rich bitch."

She stood and walked across the room, and when she looked back at me expectantly, I realized she wanted me to follow her. I got up too, shooting a glance over my shoulder at the guys and Liam. They were already engrossed in a conversation, but Bishop looked up and gave a slight nod, which I took to mean I was allowed to go with Jessica.

I followed her to a little makeshift bar that consisted of a long length of plywood set on top of two kegs. A row of coolers sat underneath that setup, and Jessica reached inside one to grab two drinks—wine coolers, I was pretty sure they were called. They were more friendly looking than the beers I'd shared with the guys at the warehouse. The bright colors made them look more like punch than booze. She popped them open and handed me the electric green one, keeping the pink one for herself.

I eyed the label. *Green apple.* Sounded a lot better than a lager. My suspicions were confirmed when I tipped it back. Sourness hit my tongue first, followed by a strong, sweet apple taste that made me smack my lips.

"Good shit, huh?" Jessica asked with a smirk. "They're my go-to drink at these things. Takes longer to really get smashed. Means you enjoy more, ironically."

"I thought the point with these things was to get smashed?"

"Nah, 'cause then you can't remember anything. Where's the fun in that? Not like that'll stop the people upstairs from getting smashed. But whatever. They have fun, hopefully they don't break too much shit, they come back for more next time—as the hostess, it works out well for me."

I took another sip of the wine cooler, enjoyed the sweet fizz on my tongue. "Why is that so good for you?"

She arched a brow. "Oh, come on now. You of all people should understand the power of social standing. People know they can have a good time here. If people like you, like what you do for them, they're more likely to do things for you too."

"So... these aren't really your friends? Like everyone that's here?"

Jessica laughed. "Were all the people who attended your family's parties your friends?"

I almost answered in the affirmative but stopped myself. Because how could I answer "yes" when none of them had stuck around after my father got arrested?

The dark-haired girl smiled at me, almost sadly. "Hey, don't worry about it, Cordelia. If it makes you feel any better, I like that you're here—not for your social standing or whatever shit, but just 'cause I like you. You're pretty chill for a rich girl." She grinned, waggling her eyebrows. "And the boys inviting you over means a lot, sooo..."

I took another sip, wishing the drink could cool the flush rising in my cheeks. "What do you mean?"

"Well, it isn't like they just invite girls with them everywhere they go. I mean, I guess you're aware they share sometimes, but that doesn't mean every time—and it doesn't mean every girl gets the pleasure of being out in public with them. I don't know the extent of your arrangement, but they wouldn't drag you out here if they didn't want you here. You get it?"

Honestly? No, I didn't. But it didn't stop me from glancing their way, my gaze curious as I watched Bishop and Misael banter back and forth with each other. Even Kace seemed in a better mood now that there was a beer in his hand.

I shifted, turning back to face Jessica.

"So... they like me?"

I didn't see how on Earth that could possibly be true—especially when, as far as I knew, they still hated my father with a burning vengeance.

They all wanted me, were attracted to me. I was pretty sure of that. But it was entirely possible to be completely drawn to someone physically and still not be sure if you liked them at all, as evidenced by my own feelings about the Lost Boys.

Jessica tossed her hair over her shoulder, laughing.

"Who the fuck knows with those three? I just know they keep glancing over here when you're not looking at them. Maybe friend isn't a good word for it—but they're all interested in you."

Again, a little thrill went through me. I couldn't decide whether to be terrified by her statement or to lean into the mutual attraction that seemed to hang like a cloud over me and the Lost Boys, to throw myself into those feelings and indulge in them. To kill the last vestiges of the prim and proper Cora that still lived inside me.

God, when did my life get so damn confusing?

Jessica and I continued to talk, and I continued to steal glances at the Lost Boys now and then when I could. I thought I was discrete about it, but sometimes I would catch one of their gazes, and they'd always linger when I did.

I had to wonder if what Jessica said was true—that there was something indefinable drawing them to me and me to them. It wasn't like we hadn't crossed several lines already. All three of them had had their hands on me at one point or another.

About an hour into the night—and a couple of wine coolers that had me comfortably buzzed—Bishop got a call. He was in the middle of telling a story, talking animatedly as he glanced down to check the caller ID. As soon as he registered the name on the screen, his expression hardened and he answered, rising from the couch.

"Yeah, it's Bish. What do you need?"

He sounded surprisingly serious, like he was talking to someone that held authority. It was a strange change from how he usually was, namely because if anything, Bishop was *always* the authority in any situation. It sent a shiver down my spine to watch him listen silently to whoever was on the other end of the call. He nodded, gave an affirmation, and then hung up.

"Looks like we got a job," he said. I was surprised to see how weary he looked at the thought of it. But, a job? This late? And I'd never heard any of the Lost Boys talk about having work before.

Then again, I *had* seen them suspiciously leaning over into spooky black cars, so it was hard to say what kind of "work" it was that they might be doing.

Misael sighed, then quickly finished up his beer.

"Weak. Always when we're trying to have some damn fun." He wiped the back of his hand over his mouth.

"At least we get paid," Kace muttered, downing his beer too before chucking the empty bottle in a bin near the bar. He looked over to me. "Finish that up. You're coming with."

I stared at the three of them in confusion.

"What? To work?"

"Yeah. If we leave you here without us, you'll be a sitting duck. People will get too shit-faced to remember the rules, and even if we break their fuckin' knees for it tomorrow, it won't undo what they did."

"Jessica and Liam are here."

"Jessica and Liam will be boning in an hour. Come on. We don't have all night."

It would be stupid to argue. I could tell none of the guys were going to bend on this. And besides, I wasn't sure I wanted to argue—there'd been something in Kace's tone that made a shiver of fear pass down my spine. The Lost Boys' feelings for me might be growing murky and complex, but for a lot of kids at Slateview, things were still very black and white. They hated me, and if they got a chance to fuck with me, they might take it if they were drunk enough to forget the consequences.

Jessica gave me a wink, already crawling back on to Liam's lap. "Come back around sometime, Cordelia!"

"It's Cora—you can call me Cora," I corrected.

Before she could answer, I was following Bishop, Kace, and Misael out of the house.

NINETEEN

MISAEL DROVE THIS TIME—SOMETHING new, but I wasn't going to question it, even knowing that Bishop was the only one with a license. I was mostly interested in what we were doing. Or, rather, what the guys were doing.

After all, I was the only one out of the loop on this one, and being the only one out of the loop, I felt like I needed to sit back and observe until I knew exactly what I'd been brought along for. It couldn't be anything too bad, or they wouldn't have brought me. They didn't want me alone with kids from Slateview, so obviously they wouldn't bring me into something worse.

That's what I told myself anyway.

The drive wasn't long, but it was quiet. Misael didn't joke, Bishop didn't talk, and there was no music. The only sounds were the rush of air through the windows and the light strumming of Misael's fingers against the steering wheel.

I kept an eye on where we were going. Not too far away, along the same route the guys had driven when they took me to the old warehouse. We didn't get that far tonight though. Instead, Misael pulled off down an alley between an old brick building and a dark house that looked like it might be abandoned. I squinted; Misael had cut the headlights before pulling into the alley, but I realized a car was sitting at the other end, shrouded in darkness. I opened my mouth, ready to ask what was going on, but Misael shushed me before I could speak.

"Not right now," he muttered.

He sounded so serious that I took the direction and snapped my jaw shut.

Misael left the engine running as Bishop and Kace hopped out of the car, heading toward the other vehicle at the end of the alley. No one got out of that one, and Bishop leaned into the car while Kace stood beside him, looking like a bodyguard with his arms crossed over his chest.

They were only over there for a few moments. I couldn't see into the car to make out who was inside, and it was dark enough in the alley that it was hard to make out what was going on, but it looked like Bishop reached in through the car's open window and pocketed something given to him.

Then he and Kace strode quickly back, sliding into our car. The dark vehicle at the end of the alley flashed its lights, and, seemingly in response, Misael backed us up, pulling back onto the road.

"Flint wants us on a run," Bishop said. "'bout an hour, tops. VIP gets the whole load. Harrington on Lucifer."

I had no idea what the hell any of that was supposed to mean, but Misael seemed to. He nodded, turned the car music on low, and hummed to the beat as he turned down another dark, quiet road.

I was sure we must be headed to a not-so-nice part of Baltimore, until I realized that we were nearing and then entering a relatively upscale suburb. It wasn't as affluent as where I used to live—but it was certainly several steps up from the kind of life the kids of Slateview were living. It only made me even more curious. Questions buzzed under my skin like a swarm of bees. The Lost Boys ran the school with impunity, and I could respect that. They obviously had shady friends—and I could even understand that, considering where they grew up. It probably wasn't the best thing, but who was I to judge? My dad was in prison, for fuck's sake.

This, though... I couldn't help the uncomfortable feeling that settled into my stomach at the idea that there was something bigger at play here. What were they doing here? What kind of job would require them to be here? What was the meaning of that strange, cryptic phrase Bishop had uttered?

I held my tongue though. No one else was talking; in fact, they all seemed a little tense. For the moment, that was enough to keep me quiet too.

Misael brought us to an abandoned lot, a small, unlit

swath of concrete just behind a nice but closed gas station. I pulled my phone out and glanced at the time. Two AM. Much too late for anyone in a good neighborhood to be working. He cut the gas, and Bishop and Kace hopped out of the car.

"Back in a bit. Don't get into trouble." Bishop ducked his head to speak through the open driver's side window.

I had no idea what kind of trouble we could get into when there was no one around, except perhaps the odd stray cat or something, but I kept my mouth shut. We watched Kace and Bishop walk away until the darkness made it impossible for me to see them anymore, and then I slouched back in the seat.

"I actually would have taken that party over this," I said quietly.

Misael laughed.

"What, you don't like a night out on the town with some good lookin' guys?"

I raised a brow and looked at him. It was so dark I could barely see his face, even though he was sitting less than two feet from me.

"I think I'd like it more if said boys told me what was going on." I turned in the seat to face him more fully, fishing for a bit of information.

He shrugged evasively. "Just work, Princess. That's all it is."

Uh huh. Sure it was. But if he wasn't going to offer up information, I wasn't going to press. Not yet, at least. I'd ask again when the deed was done and Bishop and Kace were back. Then one of them would have to tell me something.

I sighed, leaning my head back against the seat. I looked up at the sky, and for the first time since moving, I saw the stars. It sent a strange, melancholy pang through my chest.

Misael reached over, resting a hand on my thigh, just above my knee. His palm was warm against my bare skin.

"Don't worry about it too much, Princess," he said, his voice surprisingly soft. "We got you, ya know?"

I looked down at the hand secure on my thigh. It was amazing how it wrapped around and dwarfed the limb, how it radiated heat against the growing chilliness of the night. A sudden rush of feeling rose inside me—a confusing mix of emotional and physical responses—and I sucked in a gasping breath before I could stop myself.

It was like we were both made of pure electricity, and when we touched, we closed a circuit, making high-voltage energy surge through my body.

The Lost Boys owned me.

They could do whatever they wanted to me.

But this wasn't about that.

This wasn't coercion or force. It was chemistry. Pure, untamable chemistry that scared me with its intensity.

It was a bad idea to indulge any of the feelings I had around these boys. But knowing that didn't make my body any less reactive to Misael's touch, nor did it stop the warmth his touch elicited in me from sinking low, low, low, deep down where it shouldn't—

I moved my leg, subtly pulling it from under his hand. I looked away, pretending the moment hadn't happened, trying to get my breath back under control.

But Misael, like the Lost Boy he was, took my chin in his hold. And then, against everything that should have been the trademark of a Lost Boy, he turned my head gently to face him, giving me time to look up at him when I did.

"Why do you always do that?" he asked curiously.

"What?"

"Hold back from what you want. I thought rich girls just did whatever they felt like, whenever they felt like it. You always hold back."

I didn't know what I was supposed to tell him. That despite what he knew of my father, or thought he knew, Gideon van Rensselaer hadn't raised me like that? That I really didn't and couldn't just do what I wanted? That there had always been an element of control to my life—parents who dictated what I could do, who I could befriend, even what I could wear? That the very act of sitting in a car with someone I was pretty sure did illegal, dangerous things, went against everything my father had raised me to be—even if it was the only way I could survive this new world his arrest had thrown me into, whether intentionally or not?

Of course I couldn't tell him any of that. It was far too intimate a confession to make, and one thing I was certain of was that I couldn't let the Lost Boys any deeper under my skin than they already were.

But Misael was looking at me so intently, with such

warmth and curiosity in his deep brown eyes, that I had to do something.

So I did.

I kissed him.

He tasted like bitter beer, and it clashed horribly with the wine cooler still sweetening my tongue, but I didn't care. He gripped my hair, keeping me close to him, but his lips moved with mine in a soft hunger that was different from the dominating way Kace had kissed me, or the deep, desperate way Bishop had. It was as tender as it was powerful, and I let him do it because... it felt good.

It felt amazing, *perfect*, even though I knew it shouldn't.

I gasped again as Misael's hands wandered, drifting softly up my thigh, fingers trailing up under the edge of my shorts. My skin dimpled with goosebumps, and I moaned softly.

"Goddamn. You make it hard to be good, Princess."

His words were quiet and teasing, and they made me smile against his lips. I had spent my life trying to be good, trying to be the best daughter and student and heir to my family name that I could be.

But at the moment, the very last thing in the world I wanted to be was *good*. Not when bad felt so much better.

I shifted toward him on the seat, trying to get closer in the awkward confines of the car. I wanted to feel my skin pressed against his, wanted to feel the taut strength of his muscles as he moved. I wanted to know if he was hard for me—to feel him pressing against my core like I'd felt Bishop and Kace.

There was no way to do that without crawling over the

console, and I wasn't quite sure I could manage it without ruining the moment, so I stayed where I was. But I didn't let that stop my hands from exploring, and when I brushed my fingertips up his thigh and then even higher, I could feel his stiffening cock twitch under my touch.

He let out a hissed breath, his own hand finding my leg again, and the feel of his palm on my bare skin made sparks dance through my entire body.

He'd been wrong.

Back in my old life, I had never done what I wanted just because I'd wanted to. My life had been tightly regulated and controlled, every decision made for me before I could even consider what I might want.

It was only since moving to the rental house, since meeting these three wild, dangerous, alluring boys, that I had started to listen to my instincts, to push aside the constraints of my upbringing and obey the urgings of my body.

Misael's hand slid up my leg as his lips moved against mine, devouring me, *feeding* me. He kissed the same way he did everything else, with an openness and unrestrained abandon that made it impossible not to give in.

When his hands met the frayed edges of my cutoffs and then slipped underneath them, traveling higher up my leg, I let out a gasp, rubbing his hardness through the material of his pants. A single fingertip found my core, drawing a line down my slit, slipping and sliding in the wetness already gathered there.

"Oh, shit!"

The curse fell from my mouth without thought, and I worked my hand harder against his cock as he found my clit. He kissed me over and over, making me breathless and dizzy, before breaking apart and resting his forehead against mine, letting our breath mingle in the fraction of space between our lips.

"Are you doing what you want now?" he asked, his voice warm and teasing.

"Yes." It was just a gasp. "Are you?"

"There's nothing else in the damn world I'd want to be doing."

He might've had more to say, but I never found out. I never gave him the chance. I tilted my head to capture his lips again, needing to get another dose of his taste, his softness, his sweet, sensual energy.

God, I need more.

I was just debating whether to say "screw it" and crawl into his lap despite the steering wheel and the console and the too-low ceiling—

When a noise from outside the car caught my ear.

Oh, shit.

TWENTY

WE HEARD the crunching of footsteps at the same time and pulled apart quickly. Maybe out of a bit of paranoia, I straightened myself up as much as I could, not wanting to look suspicious. What if it was a cop approaching? Were there laws against teenagers fooling around in empty parking lots?

Probably not, but I was sure we'd get busted for something anyway.

But instead of a cop or any of the even worse possibilities that were running wildly through my head, it was Bishop and Kace. They both slid into the back as though nothing was amiss, and Bishop tossed a handful of files into the front.

"Let's beat it," he said.

I blinked down at the files, but Misael just shot them a cursory glance before shoving them into the glove compartment. My brows furrowed as the glove compartment clicked shut. I hadn't gotten to see any of the documents contained inside the files—and it was too dark to read them even if I had—but the files themselves had looked a lot like the ones my father liked to keep important documents in, or the kind that he put his business agreements into.

Movement in the back seat drew my eye, and I craned my neck to look back at Kace and Bishop as they both pulled off black ski masks that had obscured their features. Bish ran a hand through his shaggy hair, tousling the strands as they dropped the masks to the floor of the car.

It wasn't hard to put two and two together.

Whatever was in those files in the glove box must be important—because the boys had stolen them.

Shock and fear flooded my body in a rush, followed almost immediately by burning anger.

What the fuck?

Jesus. I'd known the guys were doing something shady. I wasn't stupid enough to believe that they'd drive to a neighborhood miles out of their way in the dead of night for reasons that were totally above board. But... a robbery? That was a serious crime. One they could easily go to jail for if they were caught. And they'd brought me along with them like I was a damn accomplice or something.

Fury made my hands clench into fists, and I wanted to scream at the boys, to lean over and punch Misael before launching myself into the back seat with claws outstretched. I had agreed to a bargain I was still sure had been a bad idea, and I was slowly coming to terms with what it meant.

But maybe I hadn't even scratched the surface.

Was this what they'd been doing every time they had a "project" come up? Every time one or more of them disappeared for a while? And if they'd brought me with them tonight, how long would it be before they started dragging me deeper into all this bullshit?

As Misael pulled out of the gas station parking lot, I turned around, my jaw clenched tight. Kace was stuffing something into a small bag—a set of lock picks, maybe—and he and Bishop both looked up.

"What were you guys doing?" I asked, my voice blunt and hard, without any hint of the hesitation I'd had earlier with Misael. "And why the hell did you decide to bring me along for whatever it was?"

"Told you. A job. We didn't have time to drop you off anywhere, and we weren't gonna leave you behind with a bunch of drunk people that hate you. Don't think I need to explain to you the type of shit that happens at parties like that to people who aren't liked."

His smooth, matter-of-fact answer just pissed me off even more.

Of course, Bishop never missed a beat, did he? Well, neither would I. Not this time.

"No. Fuck that! I want an actual answer," I pressed. "You *robbed* someone. What the hell were you thinking? And I know it was because they're rich! You went to a nice neighborhood, and I know those kinds of files. They're probably trade agreements or business arrangements or something. Did you even think about the kind of harm you could be doing to someone by breaking into their house to steal what doesn't belong to you? Do you even care? God, you aren't any better than the rich people you say do terrible things! Doing terrible things right back doesn't make you any better, you know. It just puts you on the exact same level as the people you hate! Well, fuck you for doing this, and fuck you for bringing me along on your stupid little illegal adventure. I want out. I didn't sign up for this."

The boys were quiet as I ranted. None of them interrupted me or cut me off, and that fact surprised me so much that I ran out of steam before I wanted to, the wind ebbing from my sails.

I broke off, breathing hard. I was still furious, but I couldn't figure out what their game was, why they were all just watching me in silence. Kace's face was unreadable in the flash of streetlamps, and Bishop's brows were drawn together, his lips pressed into a line. I wondered for a moment if I had angered them.

For the first time since I'd met them, I honestly didn't care if I had. There might be consequences for this later. But right now, I just wanted answers.

After a moment, Bish spoke.

"Hey, Misael. Pull in up there."

He didn't point anywhere, but Misael seemed to know what he was talking about. A few blocks ahead of us, a little twenty-four-hour food shack stood on a street corner, its blinking, yellowed lights making it look like the perfect setting for a horror film, but Misael didn't seem bothered as he pulled into the cracked cement lot and parked.

"Stay in the car." It was the only thing Bishop said before he, Kace, and Misael got out of the convertible, heading up to the kiosk on one side of the small shack.

I stayed. My stomach churned with anger at having to obey them once again, but it wasn't like I had much choice. Even if I figured out how to get home from here, there was still a decent stretch of city between me and the house, and I wasn't dumb enough to go marching off down dark, unknown streets by myself just to prove a point to these boys. Besides, I'd already learned they weren't above tailing me in a car from point A to point B, and that was an embarrassment I was keen to avoid.

After several long minutes, the boys returned to the car with their arms laden with food. Misael handed me what I discovered were two huge coney dogs with chili and cheese and a rather large sack of tater tots.

"Eat," Bishop ordered. "Then we'll talk. I think your little attitude comes out when you've got alcohol in your system."

I scoffed. "It comes out when I'm forced to play around with criminals."

"I thought you were used to criminals. Y'know, given your daddy and all."

Kace's words cut deep, and I almost threw a bitter comment back to him before deciding it wasn't worth it. Let them think what they wanted about my father. What I was concerned with right now was the three of them. What they were doing. Why they were doing it.

Then we could talk about who deserved more condemnation.

Under better circumstances, I think I would've actually enjoyed the coney dogs. They were surprisingly delicious for a having come from a shack in the middle of a run-down neighborhood, and while I was pretty sure there was nothing remotely healthy or nutritious about them, I could see why the Lost Boys liked them. Then again, the Lost Boys were down to eat anything that was greasy, fatty, and covered in something saucy and salty. About halfway through my first coney, I looked over to Bishop.

"Well, I've eaten."

He raised a brow. "You sure are pushy tonight."

"Yeah, well, I think I've earned it," I said sharply, my anger spiking again. "I think I've earned the courtesy of an explanation, even if I can't do anything about it. You should've given me one before dragging me out on this excursion blind. I might *belong* to you, but that doesn't mean I'm not a fucking person."

I'd never cursed so much in my life, but I was shaking with lingering adrenaline and anger, and the polite words I'd been raised to use just didn't seem to cut it right now.

Bishop shrugged. "Fair enough."

He shoved a fry in his mouth, as if this conversation wasn't anything that bothered him. I wished I could be like that, totally unbothered with things that should definitely, one hundred percent upset me.

"You wanna know what we were doing tonight, and why. You wanna know like it's an easy answer, like you already know the ins and outs of shit. But you don't. Because despite what you've seen of Slateview and the wrong side of the tracks, you still don't fuckin' get it, Princess," he said, his voice cool and blunt. "Yeah, we broke into a place, and yeah we stole, and yeah we didn't fuckin' tell you. Because you know why? It's our damn job. We've been doin' this for years, Princess, and you suddenly plopping yourself into the middle of our lives isn't gonna change that. You ever heard of Nathaniel Ward?"

Blinking slowly, I shook my head.

"Yeah, well, of course you wouldn't. He's a bit of a crime lord around here. Leverages information. Sometimes drugs. Got his hands in a lot of shit, actually. He's powerful and connected enough to do pretty much whatever he wants without the cops gettin' involved. The three of us have been working for him forever, because it's the only viable option for three guys with no families and a need to take care of themselves."

His voice hardened, and he leaned forward in his seat, bringing his face closer to mine.

"You think any of the people whose houses we hit are *innocent*? After everything you've seen? Get fuckin' real, Princess. Nobody makes it to a certain position in the world without sacrificing something. You can just call what we do 'karma'. And when it comes down to it, if you were in our positions, you'd do the same damn thing if it meant putting food on your table, or clothes on your back, or taking care of your family. You got no right to judge. None. And you ain't learned a fucking thing since coming to Slateview if the first thing you do when you find out about our business is go on a tirade about 'well, what about the rich people'. Fuck rich people. Those cocksuckers are the reason we're even doing this shit to begin with."

There was something in Bishop's voice I'd never heard before. Even on the night when he'd broken into my bedroom —an action that was a lot less surprising now—he hadn't sounded so bitter. There was a deep, hard anger in his tone that brought me up short.

I honestly hadn't considered that this was something they were doing out of necessity. I'd always been taught that every criminal had a choice: they could either choose to break the law, or they could do the right thing. Circumstances were never an excuse.

But I knew Bishop had been on his own for years, with no parents and a foster family that barely registered his existence. What about Kace? And Misael? Why did they need to break into people's houses and do shady jobs at all the hours of the night just to make ends meet?

Why was I even wondering if it justified anything they were doing?

I breathed through my nose, sitting on all of those questions. Earlier in the evening, before the party and before the break-in, I'd thought about how badly I wanted to know more about these boys. Then, it'd been about simple curiosity, a burning desire to understand these boys who drew me in against my will. Now there was an element of self-preservation to it—a need to know what exactly I'd gotten myself into.

For several long moments, Bishop and I faced off in silence. I'd been the subject of his ire before and had caved every one of those times, but this time I refused to back down, and anger crackled between us like lightning.

Then Misael spoke up.

"Maybe... we should explain a little more about where we come from? All of us?" He turned in his seat, looking back pointedly at Bishop. "Might help Princess understand more, since she's still got a chip on her shoulder." He looked to me. "Y'know. No offence."

Kace scoffed. "Bit heavy for a coney night."

Misael shrugged. "So? Better than nothing, if you ask me."

"We didn't," Bishop deadpanned. Misael threw a tater tot into the back seat.

"Don't be a smart ass, Bish. I'm just sayin' this whole thing might go smoother if we laid it out there."

I tore my gaze away from the brown-haired boy in the back seat, flicking a glance over to the driver's side.

Misael was openly offering up information to me? Really?

Then again, maybe I shouldn't be so surprised by it. The

boy with caramel skin and laughing brown eyes was the least reserved out of the three of them. He was the shockingly open ray of sunshine that somehow penetrated the hardness of Kace and the stoicism of Bishop.

It did make me curious about how the three of them all worked so well as a unit—how their pieces had ended up coming together and fitting into the little puzzle that they were. I already knew a bit about Bishop's history, that his parents had both died in quick succession and that he was convinced it was because of my father... an accusation I was still trying to come to terms with.

I sucked in a deep breath, setting down my half-eaten coney dog on the console beside me.

"I'll listen. Whatever it is you have to say... I'll listen." I looked to Bishop, my gaze a silent reminder that I'd listened to him before. That he could talk to me and trust me to keep his confidence.

Shockingly, the harsh lines of his face relaxed. Then he sighed and nodded.

"Fine. But I'm not rehashing any of the shit Princess and I already talked about."

Misael blinked at him, obviously surprised that Bishop had even explained a tiny bit of his past to me. Bish said nothing, however, sitting back with his coney and a quietly assessing look on his face. Misael shrugged and looked back to me.

"Well, we've all been in the system for years," he said with that same lightness that always followed him. "Where

I'm at now? That's my eighth foster home. My mom passed when I was young. Like *young*, young. My dad was never in the picture, but that was fine by me. According to Mom, he was an asshole anyway." He smiled a little. "I ended up in foster care when I was six. Been bouncing around from place to place ever since. That's where I met Bish and Reaper; we all lived in the same house for about a year." He nodded over to Kace like he was passing the ball over to him. "Go on."

Kace's gaze trailed over to my face. He almost could've looked bored if not for the glimmer of something in his eyes that I'd never seen before. A hint of real vulnerability. He was hesitant.

"You don't have to tell me if you don't want to—"

"My mom's a junkie," he said with a shrug. "She's not dead like Bish and Misael's, but the courts obviously don't think a woman high off her ass all the time on ice has it in her to be a good parent. They took me away from her when I was thirteen."

He said nothing of his father. Something about that omission seemed very intentional though, and I didn't press for more details. I was still trying to process what they'd told me already.

What were you supposed to say to revelations like those?

My chest ached as if my heart had suddenly forgotten how to beat, as if it sat between my ribs like a useless lump of clay. These three boys who were closer than brothers had all met each other in foster care, and the circumstances that'd put them all into that system were terrible. There had been drugs, shady dealings, violence. Dead parents, absent parents. It was all so horribly... unfair.

"I can see the wheels churnin' in your head." Bishop spoke up, his voice softer than it had been before. "I don't think it's anything to try to wrap your head around. Bad shit happens all the time, Princess. You've just been living outside of the fucked up bubble long enough to avoid it."

"So, tracking back to your question about why... That's why we do what we do. Because boss man might be a little skeevy, but the things he does knock down people who need to get knocked down a peg or two. Granted, he don't do it because he has a kind heart or whatever." Misael waved his hand dismissively. "But that doesn't matter. Still gets done. So if we gotta break into a house to steal some files that proves an exec is swindling people who aren't privileged enough to fend for themselves, then so be it. And if it means sometimes doing shit we don't really want to do because it's what keeps us afloat, then that's cool too."

I let that sink in, chewing on my lip. The anger that had burned through me like an inferno was gone, its fuel dried up.

Because even though I could never truly comprehend what their lives had been like, the shit they'd had to deal with while I'd been learning how to play piano and greet guests properly at cocktail parties, I *understood*.

Our lives had been vastly different, not because I deserved any better than the lost Boys or anyone else, but simply because we'd been born into different circumstances.

And up until recently, my family had had the power and wealth to be able to shield me from the harshness of life.

Because the truth was, no one was truly innocent. No one was purely good. The world was full of terrible people and awful things, and only the strongest survived.

The Lost Boys might not have the money and privilege I had for so long, but they *were* strong. They might've been three of the strongest people I'd ever met.

"I..." My gaze shifted to each of them, tracking from Misael's earnest eyes to Bishop's pursed lips to Kace's clenched jaw. "I didn't know. I'm sorry—"

"Don't be." Kace's voice wasn't angry. It wasn't anything. It was purposefully blank, as if he refused to waste more precious emotions on the things he couldn't change. "We don't need your pity. Don't want it. We just need you to get where we come from and understand that your world isn't how it is for the rest of us."

I nodded silently, not offering another useless apology, even though the words pressed against my lips.

Bishop had told me it wasn't worth trying to wrap my head around. And he was probably right, in a way. How could it be possible to comprehend a world that was full of such chaos and violence, where so many things—both good and bad—were based entirely on chance?

But that didn't stop the thoughts from spinning over and over in my mind the entire drive home.

TWENTY-ONE

MY WORLD FELT like it was reeling out of my control. It felt like I'd lived my whole life with blinders on, and now that they'd finally been removed, I could barely see through the harsh, bright glare of the truth that shone down on me. I couldn't stop thinking about where the Lost Boys had come from, and how it'd made them into the people they were today. And what about all the other students at Slateview High, who probably had similar stories? Because I couldn't assume that the Lost Boys were the exception and not the rule. Not with what I saw of the world I now lived in.

In the two weeks after the ill-fated party, I saw it more than I had when I first arrived. How many of the pregnant girls that roamed the halls with their rounded bellies had fathers like Misael's who just weren't around? The students that sported track marks—how many of them got their drugs from their parents, and how many of those parents were locked in a cycle of dealer-user?

It had me hyper-focused on my surroundings, wondering how many of my perceptions were negatively colored by the fact that I simply didn't know what life on this side of the tracks was like, and I would never truly know because I simply hadn't grown up in it.

It was a sobering experience. I think the Lost Boys recognized it. We didn't have another warehouse day or attend another house party, and although I still saw all three boys every day, still drove to school with them, I could feel them pulling away a little—keeping some distance between us. I wasn't entirely sure if it was for my benefit or for theirs. Maybe a little of both.

But either way, I was grateful for it.

Since the moment Mom and I had pulled up in front of the squat little rental house, everything in my life had seemed to move like a whirlwind, sucking me up, tossing me around, and spitting me out in an unknown landscape where I could barely tell up from down.

I needed a moment to just... breathe.

On top of my attempts to sort through my broadening understanding of the world, and compounding my confusion about everything I knew and thought I knew, were the lingering questions about my dad.

My first trip to visit him at the prison was scheduled for a Friday afternoon in late October, and I boarded the city bus with some trepidation. I'd been excited when Mom had finally agreed to let me visit, but now I wasn't sure how to feel; although part of me couldn't wait to see him, another part of me almost didn't want to go.

Mom had been uncomfortably secretive about my father since his first call. She still remained in her room most of the time, only going out sparingly in the new—well, *newish*—car that Isaac had gotten for us. I wondered where she went on these excursions, but I didn't ask. If she wanted to tell me, she would. Besides, secrets seemed to be the recurring theme of our relationship lately. She didn't tell me what she did when she left the house, and I never spoke to her about the Lost Boys.

I wonder what that conversation would be like.

A laugh got caught in my throat at the thought, and I dropped my head, staring at a piece of gum stuck to the floor of the bus. I couldn't even begin to imagine what that conversation would be like, because Mom and I didn't actually speak to each other enough for me to predict how it would go. It was almost sad; the only conversations I could picture clearly in my head were ones I might have with one of the Lost Boys, not even with my mother. I'd known them for less than three months, and in some ways, it felt like I knew them better than my own flesh and blood

That notion lingered in my mind as I transferred to a new bus that took me to the outskirts of Baltimore. Soon, city streets gave way to a large expanse of road, and the looming, concrete building of the prison came into view. I wasn't the only person getting off at the stop just outside its gates; I wondered how many other passengers were going to visit a friend or family member like I was. How many of them were having doubts and second thoughts as to whether that person actually deserved to be behind bars?

My nerves buzzed under my skin as I checked in and waited. They took us back in small groups, and a guard checked us to make sure we weren't bringing in anything we weren't supposed to. The sensation of having a stranger pat me down and stare at me with eyes that seemed to penetrate sent a prickle of discomfort down my spine, but I tried not to show it. I hadn't done anything wrong, so I shouldn't have anything to fear. What was I going to smuggle into a prison anyway?

As I was ushered through to the visitation area, I almost wished I had someone with me. Not my mother though. She was too fragile for a place like prison, and I needed someone strong with me, to help *me* be strong.

Against my will, my thoughts flitted to Bishop, who I knew would be stoic in the face of leering prisoners and their salacious grins. Or maybe Kace, who would give them a cold stare right back to make them rethink ever looking at me wrong. The one who'd make it the happiest would be Misael. He'd probably just stride right on through, not giving a shit about who was watching or what they thought. He'd probably crack jokes, maybe even make me laugh.

But there were no jokes as I sat at a booth separate from the general visitation area. There were round tables where families sat and where pairs conversed with each other, but my father wasn't allowed that. Instead, when I sat on the uncomfortable plastic chair across from him, there was a thick pane of plexiglass separating us from each other.

I picked up the receiver on my side of the glass, and he did the same.

For a long time, we were silent.

He looked tired. Deep bags hung under his eyes, like he hadn't been sleeping properly. His hair, usually slick and styled to perfection, not a single strand out of place, looked lackluster without his usual pomades and products. Even his skin seemed sallow, like he wasn't going outside regularly. Now that I thought about it, did men in prison get to go outside? I figured they must, but I didn't know that for sure. Until this year, it never would've occurred to me to wonder.

I made a soft noise. The silence was growing uncomfortable, but I couldn't speak around the sudden lump in my throat. It broke my heart to see my dad like this, more than I ever could've imagined. I wasn't the only one who had changed so much in the relatively short amount of time he'd been in prison.

"Hi, Dad. It's good to see you."

"You as well. You look... different."

Self consciously, I looked down. Dad had a way of saying simple, mundane things and filling them with heavy meaning —and that had definitely been a loaded statement. His scrutinizing gaze continued to take me in as I shifted on the hard seat. This morning, I'd put on a pair of ripped jeans, thinking those would be better than the cutoff shorts I'd made, along with a shirt that was less cropped than most of my others. Compared to what I wore to school most of the time, this outfit was conservative, but it was nothing like what my father was used to seeing me in.

I glanced up, straightening my spine a little.

"You look different too."

He shifted. I couldn't get a read on him, and it was a strange feeling. I could almost always read my father—or at least, I'd thought I could. Usually, I didn't have to guess whether he was happy or angry about something, confused, annoyed, or disappointed. I wondered if it was because he was in prison, out of his element. It felt like I was sitting across from a stranger. Then again, considering what I'd learned since he'd been brought here, maybe that wasn't so far off. How well had I ever really known my father?

I didn't want to talk about that right now though.

"How've you been, Dad?" I asked instead, attempting to strike up a normal conversation. Well, as normal as one could have in prison.

"Food is terrible," he answered, gazing at me through the glass as he held the phone to his ear. *God, this is all so awkward.* "Sleep is terrible. I'm alive. Waiting for this damn sham of a trial to be over."

I nodded. There was a pause in the conversation before he continued on.

"How are you? Studies going well? Your mother?"

There was a momentary pause as I tried to formulate an answer. "How are you" was such a simple question, but given the state of my life right now, it was hard to think of what to say. What the hell was I supposed to tell him?

Oh, I'm great, Dad. I'm being shared between three criminal boys that I'm drawn to in a way that scares me, and Mom never leaves the house unless she's going off someplace that she doesn't talk to me about.

"Good. School is good. I have some friends. Mom is taking things in stride."

What a sanitized answer.

Dad nodded though, as if it were a satisfying enough response. I wondered what a regular conversation between a normal father and daughter would be in this situation. And then I wondered if there even *was* such a thing.

"How long do you think you'll still be in here?" I asked, deciding to springboard off something he said earlier. "You said that... the trial was a sham?" *What would make him think that?*

He waved his hand.

"Not much longer. Not if my lawyer does his job. Someone planted evidence in my office, I'm sure of it. Fool ass criminals..."

He muttered the last part, shaking his head.

My thoughts went back to the Lost Boys—their pasts, their accusations, and the accusations of almost every student in Slateview High against my father.

I didn't know if it should bring any of that up on this visit. I was desperate to know how much of what I'd learned from the Lost Boys and other kids was true, how much of it was just bitter gossip, and how much of it was rumor and speculation. But a part of me knew that the answers—the real, unvarnished truth—probably wouldn't be found by talking to my father. I'd lived with him my whole life and had only just learned of his possible underhanded dealings. He either wouldn't admit or didn't believe that he'd done anything wrong.

And in all honesty, it was entirely possible that he could've done some shitty things and still been completely within the law. His guilt or innocence as far as a jury was concerned was a separate issue from the question of whether he'd built his empire by taking advantage of people who couldn't defend themselves.

I allowed our conversation to meander, drifting from one boring topic to another like a slow-moving stream until our allotted time was up. It never got less awkward, and although I'd been glad to see my father in person, I was just as glad to leave.

TWENTY-TWO

THE RIDE HOME took over an hour. Finally, I transferred onto the final bus, which brought me back to the decrepit little neighborhood my father's actions—real or not—had forced Mom and me into. I didn't expect the bitterness to settle in, acrid in my core, but it was there.

I had spent weeks rolling with the punches, adjusting and readjusting and making the best of a shitty situation, but something about seeing my dad had seemed to put everything back to square one. He seemed utterly convinced that the trial was a sham, that he'd been set up by someone, intentionally sabotaged, but his reassurances that he'd be out soon rang false somehow. Even if he really was innocent, even if evidence had been manufactured against him, he obviously hadn't found a way to prove that or he would've been released before his case even went to trial.

The bus trundled away after I stepped off in my

neighborhood, and I dragged my feet as I headed toward the house. Tears welled in my eyes as I walked, and I blinked them back over and over again until my eyes stung. I didn't know what to do about any of this, but I couldn't bare to force myself through the front door of our new home, to fix another badly prepared hot meal, and then go to bed just to do it all again the next day.

The car was in the driveway when I got back.

At least Mom's home.

I didn't go inside though. I stared up at the rundown little house, then turned to look across the street. Bishop's house was just across the way, and I was pretty sure his foster parents weren't home.

My feet moved before my brain made any kind of conscious decision. I didn't even know what propelled me forward. Just a sense that I needed to do *something*—and I knew Bishop was a person who could get things done or at least point me in the right direction. When I reached his sagging front stoop, I knocked on the door, three hard raps that I knew would get his attention.

"Who the fuck—"

He yanked open the door, irritation clear in his voice, then paused when he saw it was me. I must've caught him in the middle of changing clothes, or maybe he'd been working out. He didn't have a shirt on, and his hair was disheveled. I'd seen him shirtless a few times before, but the sight of it still caught me by surprise. All of the Lost Boys were so purely, darkly masculine. His skin was lightly tanned, and it covered muscles that bunched and flexed as he moved, reaching up to run a hand through his slightly damp mess of hair. A little water droplet ran down his neck and over the broad plane of his pec, and I had the most insane urge to dart forward and lick it off.

Shit. Get it together, Cora.

My heart thudded hard as I pulled my gaze from his torso to look him in the eye, a slight flush to my face.

"Hey, Bishop. Can—can we talk?"

He stared down at me for a moment, his head cocked slightly to one side and his hazel eyes narrowed, as if wondering what I was doing here, what I could possibly have come to bother him with.

This wasn't part of our arrangement, I knew that. Our deal gave them control over my life, the right to step into my house uninvited at any time, the ability to demand what they wanted from me and get it. But the opposite wasn't true—it wasn't a two-way street, so I was out-of-bounds asking him for this.

I was bracing for the door to slam in my face when Bishop surprised me by stepping aside without question, leading me deeper into the house.

It was a dimly lit space, clean in a sparse way—there was just enough furniture that it didn't look like the house had been completely abandoned. I was pretty sure his foster parents were barely ever home, and I wondered if he knew where they went but figured it was better not to ask.

We could compare absentee parent stories later. That

wasn't what I'd come for today, and I didn't want to waste the hospitality he was showing me.

He led me into this bedroom, and I tried not to breathe too deeply as we passed through the door. Not because the room smelled bad, but because it smelled like Bishop, and I liked that aroma way too much. The faint, woodsy scent of his cologne teased my nostrils, bringing with it an almost instantaneous reaction in my body.

I cleared my throat, stepping forward quickly to sit on his bed as he lingered in the doorframe, crossing his arms over his chest and staring at me with an expectant gaze.

God, I wish he'd put a shirt on.

Between trying not to look at him and trying not to smell him, I was likely to pass out before I could even voice the questions I'd come here to ask.

"Didn't expect you'd be coming over here," he said. He fidgeted a little, the muscles of his biceps flexing as he shoved his hands in his pockets. Was he nervous too?

No. Of course he isn't.

"Yeah. I, uh, just came back from seeing my father. In prison." *Ugh. Why did I feel the need to tack that little bit on at the end? He already knows my father's in prison...*

"Yeah? How'd that go?" He leaned forward a little, asking the question so earnestly that I almost forgot to answer. I hadn't expected that tone in his voice, something almost like sympathy.

"It... went." I sighed, lifting my shoulders in a small shrug. "To be honest, I almost don't know why I went. We'd had this visitation day set up for a long time, and I hadn't seen him since he was taken away. But, I mean, it isn't like we had a lot to talk about."

"Well, he's your dad." Bishop shrugged too, still watching me carefully. "Didn't you talk about how school was going or check in on each other or your mom or something?"

"Sort of." I bit my lip. "It was very barebones."

He nodded. "Guess you and your pops don't talk a lot to begin with."

"Not really." I cleared my throat. "But that's not what I came over here for. I wanted to ask you a question."

"Sure. Ask away."

"I wanted to know if there was some sort of... connection between the kind of people you work for and people like my father." I asked, forward. "I know you guys report to Flint, and then he reports to Nathaniel. But what does Nathaniel do? Are there other people like him in the city? Other people as powerful as him?"

Bishop squinted at me, gauging my question.

"Is there a hierarchy? Is that what you're asking me?"

I nodded.

He shifted, brushing a hand over his chin as he considered his answer. I was quiet, patient, letting him mull it. When he spoke, he chose his words carefully.

"There's people in a 'network', I suppose. But the people at the top are the real big fish. There's people like Flint, who run small-time operations at a high frequency. Then there's people—like Nathaniel—who have as much power as the wealthy upperclass like your dad. They sit at the top and play the long game and pull the real strings. I guess you'd call them the closest thing to kingpins this neck of the woods has." His eyes narrowed. "Why do you want to know all this?"

I bit my lip, glancing down at the faded and worn floorboards.

"Because I'm not sure my father is guilty of what he was arrested for, and I don't think it's too crazy to consider that someone set him up."

A heavy silence met those words, and my stomach pitched sideways.

Bishop must know what I was thinking. My question had made it obvious.

My father had insisted since the day he was arrested that he'd been set up, sabotaged, framed. And just a couple weeks ago, I'd seen Bish and Kace come out of someone's house in a wealthy neighborhood bearing stolen files—evidence to be used for blackmail or a setup, probably.

I wasn't stupid, and although I may have been sheltered from the harsh realities of the world for much of my life, I was learning on a fast curve these days. Nathaniel had sent the Lost Boys to steal something from a wealthy businessman he had a grudge against, so was it really that far-fetched to think someone out there—whether Nathaniel or another man like him—might've done something similar to my dad?

Maybe it was naïve to think my father really might be innocent of fraud, but it was something I had to at least consider.

Because if it's true... maybe I can do something about it. Maybe I can fix this, and we can all go home.

"Do you really think he's innocent?" Bishop's voice was hard. "Do you really think, after everything we've told you—"

"You don't know my father like I do," I interrupted. "You didn't grow up with him, he didn't raise you. You keep telling me I'm not allowed to judge you or anyone here, but all you do is judge me and my father and my family!" My stomach knotted and twisted, and I rose from the bed, stepping toward him. "Why is it so hard to think that maybe he's innocent of this one thing? That maybe it was 'karma' or something, and this is the one thing he *didn't* do, even if he is guilty of everything else you've said he's done."

"And have you considered that even if that's true, maybe he doesn't deserve to be proven innocent?"

A loud *crack* filled the quiet room, the sound a sharp and piercing as a gunshot. I heard it before I felt the prickle in my palm, a tingling pain from the impact of hitting Bishop's cheek. And then I saw it—the bloom of red across his skin and the pure shock in his bright hazel eyes.

I breathed in. Breathed out.

He did the same, his nostrils flaring as he gazed at me, unblinking.

We were both still, *so still*, staring at each other in a room that felt like it had no oxygen left.

Then my body lurched into motion again, darting forward and bolting out the door on shaky legs. I practically threw myself down his front steps and ran across the street without even checking for cars in the road.

My entire body felt jittery and numb at the same time, and pain still radiated out from my hand—I could only imagine what Bishop's cheek felt like.

The strange thing was, I wasn't afraid of Bishop. I didn't think he would hit me—there'd been too much shock and not enough anger in his eyes for that. What scared the actual fuck out of me was the fact that I'd been so angry that I had lashed out and hurt someone. That my reaction to my pain and confusion had been violence. That wasn't me. That wasn't who I was. Was it?

How much had I changed since coming here? And was I changing for the better or worse?

I had hit Bishop. And that was so fucked up—especially when, on some level, I knew he could be right.

What if my father was innocent of this one crime? If he'd done everything else Bish had accused him of, did it even matter? One count of innocence wouldn't exonerate him from all the guilt he may truly carry.

I burst through my front door, slamming it behind me like I was shutting out everything ugly and vile in the world with it. I leaned my back against it, panting for breath as my heart raced. My anger beat in tandem with my sadness, and a lingering loss made my chest ache. I laughed bitterly.

It wasn't even like Dad and I had a great relationship. Where was the warmth? Where was the tenderness? Those things didn't exist between us, and although that fact was more obvious now that he was in prison, the truth was, they never had.

So why did I care so much?

After a few moments passed and Bishop didn't come knock on the door—or break it down—my heartbeat slowly began to calm. Blowing out a breath, I looked up.

"Mom?"

Pushing away from the door, I stepped forward. She and I never spoke a lot, but I needed her right now, in a way I'd never needed a mother before. I felt the sting of tears in my eyes and the childish desire to curl up tight in her arms and bawl my eyes out, to sob and tell her everything that was wrong with the world. Ava used to be that person, but Ava was long gone, and I had no way to contact her. Even if I did, I couldn't find it in myself to force her to deal with my family's ugly baggage.

"Mom?" I repeated, louder this time.

She didn't answer, and I called to her again as I went to her door. The car was outside, so she had to be home.

I knocked on her door at the same time I pushed it open a little, poking my head inside.

"Hey, mom. Are you—"

The words died in my throat.

And then a scream poured from my lips instead.

TWENTY-THREE

MOM LAY ON HER BACK, arms splayed, body limp. I might've thought that she was sleeping if it weren't for the bile built up at the corners of her mouth. My scream cut off with a guttural, choked noise as I noticed the bottle of pills beside her bed.

The ones she always took to go to sleep.

What am I supposed to do? Who do I call? Is she alive? Oh God. God. Is she alive?

It felt like bees were buzzing through my skull, the droning hum making it impossible to think. My fingertips tingled and my skin felt numb. I moved like a robot, crossing to her bedside and putting my hand to her neck to feel the faintest of pulses thudding through her veins. Tears slipped down my cheeks, but there was only the smallest moment of relief because she still wasn't moving, and her heart wasn't beating hard enough, and then she started to convulse—

"Cora?"

A voice called my name from the other side of the house, but I didn't respond. I couldn't. I kept trying to feel her heartbeat again, but I couldn't find it this time. Her body was jerking on the mattress, and I couldn't find her pulse, dammit, *dammit*! Panic consumed me like an untamed fire, eating me alive and leaving nothing but ash.

"*Cora?*"

The voice came again, closer, and then someone was at my side, moving me away from my mother. My vision was unfocused, blurred with tears, but I recognized the mop of shaggy brown hair.

Bishop.

It was Bishop. He stood over my mother, his hands on her chest, pushing up and down, up and down. The movement was hypnotic, and I wrapped my arms around my stomach like I was trying to keep myself from flying apart and watched, unblinking, numb.

I'd known she was despondent, known she missed our old life, known she had spent too many hours curled up in bed. But she'd been better lately. She'd been getting up, at least. Going out.

Was this my fault?

Had I missed important signs?

Please, Mom. Please.

Don't die.

THERE ARE realizations that hit you at inopportune times. They're almost funny, even though they really aren't.

Mine came as I slowly blinked my eyes open to find myself propped up in a bed in the ER with an IV drip in my arm—and it suddenly struck me that I had never been in a public hospital before. Back in our old life, we'd had a private family doctor who made house calls. Even for my birth, my mother had been at home, comfortable in her bed, with what amounted to a fully staffed and stocked hospital room around her.

This too bright, sterile environment, where I could hear the person in the room beside mine vomiting up everything in their stomach and another down the hall yelling that they wanted pain medications or else they'd sue the hospital, was the farthest thing imaginable from every other encounter with doctors I'd ever had. Those visits had always been calm and serene, even the one after I'd broken my arm running down the large spiral stairs when I was six.

I let my eyes drift closed again. My throat felt scratchy and dry, my tongue like sandpaper.

Most of the last several hours felt like a blur, but as I sorted through the chaotic thoughts and images in my head, everything began to solidify. My father. My talk with Bishop. My mother—

Oh God. Mom!

Mom had overdosed.

Fuck. Why was I the one laid up in the hospital bed? Where was she?

I blinked up at the fluorescent lights, eyes hurting a little as I tried to sit up. A firm hand settled on my shoulder, pushing me back down onto the bed.

"Easy, tiger. I don't think you're ready to move all that much right now."

Bishop.

A dozen emotions clogged my throat as if they were all trying to escape me at once. Tears pricked my eyes. I wanted to be angry with him, because I *had* been angry with him, but I couldn't find any of that inside myself anymore.

"My mom—"

"Is fine," he said. "She's recovering right now. Pumped her stomach, put her on a drip, and she's not gonna be left alone, not until the doctors can be sure that she's not gonna try something, and not till they understand what happened."

Wasn't it obvious? She'd tried to kill herself...

I sniffled, swallowing against the lump in my throat.

"You're here..." I muttered. I looked over to where he sat next to my bed. He'd thrown a shirt on, and he looked tired. The mesmerizing hazel of his eyes was a little dull, and there were circles under his eyes. "You're here. You helped."

"Yeah. Of course I did, Cora." He shook his head, looking almost insulted even as concern still darkened his features. "The fuck kinda person would I be if I didn't?"

He had called me Cora when he'd called for me in my house too. Had he heard my scream from all the way across the street? Impossible. He must've already been close to the house when I yelled.

"Why... why did you—"

"Because I was an asshole, and I shouldn't have said that shit to you about your dad." He ducked his head to avoid my gaze, looking almost uncomfortable. "But don't worry about that right now. You kinda went into shock. So don't strain yourself too hard."

Bishop withdrew his hand from my shoulder, and part of me wanted to ask him to put it back. To let me feel the weight of him touching me, the comforting, grounding warmth of his hand. To put it back where it belonged.

I kept silent though. He had already done so much for me. Helping to save my mother. Getting us to the hospital. Staying with me. It was more than any stranger should be asked to do for another.

Then again, we really aren't strangers anymore, are we?

I knew him better than I knew my own parents. The thought was sobering, yet somehow comforting. I had fought with this boy, I had kissed him, I had hated and desired him. We had both confessed fucked up things about our lives to each other, and somehow, no matter how messed up the situation was, it was something that gave us a connection.

At this point, I wasn't going to question it. I just wanted to hold on to the feeling of having someone beside me for once. I hadn't even realized how alone I'd been for so long until he and the other Lost Boys had stepped in to fill that empty space in my life.

My gaze caught Bishop's, and even as he pulled his hand back, he scooted his chair a little closer.

It wasn't close enough, but I'd take it.

"Princess..."

He licked his lips, like he was trying to taste the words before he spoke them, and I lifted my head off the pillow a little, leaning toward him. But before he could finish his thought, his phone buzzed. He frowned, glancing down at the screen, and my stomach clenched.

My immediate assumption was that it would be another call like the one he'd gotten the night I found out just what it was the Lost Boys did for a living. He didn't swipe to answer though, just read something that flashed across the screen. Then he snorted, sounding both resigned and amused.

"We're gonna have company."

That was all he said before the hospital room door burst open.

"Yo, came over as fast as we could. Buses to the hospital take forever. Good thing we ain't fuckin' dyin'."

Despite his crass words, I couldn't help but smile at the way Misael entered the room, followed closely—but quietly—by Kace. The blond boy nodded to me and leaned against the wall, arms folded over his chest. I glanced between the three of them, even more surprised at the arrival of the other two than I had been to discover Bishop had stayed. He, at least, had already been here because he'd come with us, but Kace and Misael had just... showed up.

"What are you guys doing here?" I asked, looking between them.

"Well, Bish texted us that something went down and that

both of you were at the hospital. Shit, I'm sorry your mom's in here," Misael said, sitting down on the edge of the hospital bed.

"I also said not to come and crowd her up," Bishop added flatly, looking at the caramel-skinned boy with a raised brow.

"Well, you weren't giving us any real details, and with the way the ambulance peeled out of the neighborhood, and you driving off like a bat out of hell..." Misael shook his head, waving Bish off. "You're not the only one who gives a shit, you stone-faced brick-man."

I blinked. "Stone-faced... brick-man..."

"Good description, huh?"

I laughed a little. It felt surprisingly good to laugh. And it felt good to feel *good*. Like levity was okay for now.

It felt like a reminder that even with the darkness that loomed over our heads, there was something to be happy about. I... had people around me that cared for me. Even if it was in a strange, insanely possessive kind of way. Even if it was in a way I didn't fully understand.

Even if it had started from a place of darkness, possession, and vengeance.

"Thank you... for coming by and checking on me," I whispered softly. "Just... really. Thank you. I don't know what I'd do if..."

I don't know what I'd do if I had to go through this alone.

TWENTY-FOUR

MOM HAD to stay in the hospital overnight, but I was free to go after it became clear I didn't need any extra care.

The doctors let me see her when I was back on my feet, but the reunion was a short-lived one. She just lay in bed, still asleep and unmoving. Somehow, even in the harsh white lights of the hospital room and against the bleached bed sheets, she managed to look more peaceful than she had in a long time. I didn't want to think about why that might be; did her unconscious mind think she'd succeeded in what she'd set out to do? Were her dreams filled with heavenly choirs and angel trumpets?

She would be sent home when they were sure she wasn't going to be a danger to herself, but in the meantime, I was told to go home and get some rest myself. I wanted to stay overnight, but the doctor said it would be best if I didn't, although I was free to come back and visit.

It was close to eleven PM when I was finally released. I could've taken the bus—I had cash since Bish had grabbed my backpack on the way out the door—but the Lost Boys were more than willing to drive me home.

I was still trying to wrap my head around the fact that they'd all come to the hospital to be with me as we pulled up to the house. I hadn't been prepared for the looming, uncomfortable feeling that filled me as I looked up at the house with its dirty paint and broken shutters and the cracked walkway that led to the door. I hesitated with my hand on the car door handle, delaying the inevitable for a few more seconds.

The little house had never felt welcoming, but now, something about it felt downright threatening.

"Something wrong, Princess?" Bishop looked over to me, his head tilted.

"No." I swallowed, forcing my expression to clear. "Just feels weird to be going back in there, that's all."

He glanced at the rearview mirror, exchanging a look with the other two through the reflection before turning back to me.

"Well, we'll keep you company."

With that, Bish killed the car's engine and slid on out himself, followed by Misael and Kace. I looked at them disbelievingly, but said nothing else as I got out too. I trailed behind them as all three marched purposefully to the front door, turning to wait for me on the stoop.

Their habit of just doing things as they felt necessary was

still a little jarring; they were so confident in their ability to do whatever they pleased, as if they were the kings of whatever pocket of the world they happened to be occupying at any given time. Maybe I should have been used to it, but it still took me by surprise more often than not.

It was one of the things I'd hated most about them when I'd first met them. But now?

I liked it.

Unlocking the door, I let them in. The lights were still on, and the TV in Mom's room was still on, spilling sound out into the hallway. I looked down the hall with a measure of trepidation, but again, it was Bishop who took the lead and made sure things were taken care of.

"I'll clean up back there for you," he said, his tone leaving no room for argument. "Misael and Kace can help with dinner. You definitely need it."

And, to my shock, he actually smirked and winked at me.

I watched Bish stride down the hallway, my disbelief mounting as Kace and Misael headed into the kitchen without a moment's hesitation. Was I in some kind of liminal space? Was I still at the hospital and just dreaming all of this? I couldn't tell, but I wasn't going to discount the possibility. I was tired. Mentally, physically, and emotionally exhausted. And there were three boys in my house that were... taking care of me.

Trailing into the kitchen behind Misael and Kace, I watched them dig through my pantry. A small stab of embarrassment tightened my stomach; there wasn't really much in there to speak of that looked like it would make a decent meal.

But instead of judging or giving me shit for it, they hummed to themselves, seemingly to expertly pull out ingredients as though they were chefs in a fancy restaurant and not wayward boys in a run-down kitchen, looking after a girl who should have been able to look after herself.

"Y'know, this is pretty good shit," Misael said, surveying the ingredients they'd found. "How's lasagna sound?"

"That's the least Mexican thing you could suggest," Kace teased.

That's right. *Teased*. Kace, of all people, cracked a smile and made a joke.

The black-haired boy shrugged. "Hey, man, even across the border we won't say no to some good pasta."

I laughed. Misael looked over his shoulder and grinned at me.

"See. Princess thinks I'm funny."

Kace grunted. "Only because she feels sorry for what a dumbass you are."

They went back and forth like this as they maneuvered around each other, throwing together an improvised lasagna. It felt nice, relaxed. It was just what I needed, and I was positive that if I'd ended coming home alone, there was no way I would have done anything but eaten cold cereal by the light of the television.

I sat and watched them—because every time I tried to help, they made me sit back down—and eventually, Bishop came out of the back and joined us. He settled down across from me at the little table, watching Kace and Misael work their magic. A serene look fell over his face, and I couldn't help but smile.

"Thanks for staying with me," I murmured softly. "I really needed it, and I probably wouldn't have ended up asking you guys to."

Bishop chuckled.

"I know you wouldn't have. You're a stubborn little thing. I still haven't figured out if it's 'cause you're rich, or just 'cause you're you."

"Well, I'm not exactly rich anymore, am I?"

"You know what I mean." Bishop reached across the table, flicking me on the nose. "Don't split hairs. Dinner's almost done."

I didn't know what dinner being done had to do with splitting hairs, but I didn't comment on it. He was right. Dinner was almost done, and I didn't realize until a plateful of homemade lasagna was put in front of me just how terribly hungry I was. My stomach growled, and even as Kace and Misael grabbed their own plates and leaned against the kitchen counter near the table, I was already tucking in.

It should have been embarrassing, the way I shoveled my food into my mouth, but I wasn't bothered with keeping up appearances. What did appearances matter anymore, anyway?

All that stuff—the careful attention to every move, every gesture, every word—was the currency of my old world. It was a made up game the wealthy played because at some point, it wasn't enough just to have more money than others.

I didn't have to play that game anymore. I didn't have to worry about it.

There was a small beat of silence as I ate greedily, and then all three boys laughed. I looked up to find them all gazing at me, various degrees of amusement on their faces as I forked layers of pasta, sauce, and meat into my mouth.

"What?" I asked, holding a hand over my mouth.

None of them said anything, shaking their heads and turning to their own meals, still chuckling softly.

After dinner, Misael and I did the dishes. What started out as the two of us working peacefully side-by-side ended with me splashing water at him when he insinuated that I'd probably never washed a dish in my life—lies; I'd recently begun washing dishes, a fact I was stupidly proud of—and we ended up getting suds and water all over each other and the floor. It was an otherwise quick cleanup, and Misael had me laughing despite the gloom that had hung over me earlier.

When we were finished, we joined the other two, who were sprawled on the lumpy couch in the living room watching what looked like an old action movie. Misael and I took the floor in front of the couch, and we all settled into silence as we watched, occasionally yelling commentary or warnings at the screen.

It was a little thing: dinner and a movie. But it felt so good.

I wanted things around here to feel like this all the time.

Like there was a possibility for a bit of levity in our darkened lives. Like there may be a bit of light at the end of the impossibly long tunnel we were currently navigating. Tiny moments like this helped me hold on to the little bubble of hope in my chest, to keep it from blipping out entirely.

Dad would be alright.

Mom would be alright.

And, for now at least, I was alright.

"I think I'm gonna shower and head to bed," I said, standing up and stretching once the movie was done. "You guys don't have to stay the night. I mean, I have a few extra blankets, and I can get the living room set up for you if you want—"

Before I could finish, Misael reached up and caught my wrist in his hand.

"Stay out here a bit?" he asked.

There was a sincerity in his tone that made warmth pool in my belly. Unlike when Bish or Kace asked a question, this one actually *sounded* like a question. Like I had a choice, and he really hoped I'd say "yes".

I bit my lip. "Stay... out here?"

He grinned, flashing his teeth. "Yeah. Out here. With us. Y'know... let us take care of you. You deserve it. You need to relax and all that."

My brow rose. I had the sneaking suspicion that their idea of "relax" was very different than what I was used to.

I also couldn't find an ounce of willpower in me to say no.

A little thrill of excitement moved up my spine as I

crossed back around the couch, sinking back down onto the floor next to Misael. The credits were still rolling in the corner of the TV screen as another movie started to play, but none of us were paying much attention to that anymore.

A hand tangled in my hair, tugging gently to tilt my head back, and when I looked up, I saw Kace's glittering eyes staring down at me. Keeping his grip on my thick blond locks, he bent his head to kiss me. Our lips met upside down, and the strangeness of that made everything feel new, as if I'd never kissed this boy before in my life. I could feel his lips in a whole new way, and it sparked a little fire inside my belly that burned low and hot.

A half-second later, hands landed on my shoulder before moving down to massage my breasts, palming them and pinching my nipples, making little shocks of sensation jolt through me as pleasure mingled with a bite of pain.

My breath was already coming faster, my heart rate picking up, when I felt Misael's hands on the button of my jeans. As he worked the zipper down and tugged them off, I shifted my weight to make it easier for him. Only once he'd pulled them off entirely did nervousness rise up in me as I felt cool air hit the skin of my legs.

I'd been touched and kissed by each of these boys before, but never like this. Never all at once.

It was an overload of sensations that threatened to drag me under and drown me.

Misael's hot breath trailed up my leg as Bish slipped his hands beneath my shirt, resuming his torture of my breasts on my bare skin. Kace tightened his grip on my hair as he kissed me, making a soft grunting noise low in his throat.

Then my arms were being lifted, and the shirt was dragged up and over my head, leaving me in just my bra and panties. We were in the living room, and even though I knew there was no chance Mom would be back tonight, it still felt risky and rebellious somehow, to do this out in the open, not hidden behind closed doors.

"Fuck. Switch."

Bishop's voice was raspy, and a second later, his mouth replaced Kace's on mine. New hands roamed over me, their touch rougher and more demanding, and when Misael buried his face in the space between my legs, I arched my back, asking without words for more.

"God, you're so wet already, Cora," he muttered, and I swore I could *feel* his words against my core just as much as I heard them.

He wasn't lying. I could feel it, the slick wetness soaking my panties as my inner muscles clenched tightly, demanding something I had never had yet. Something I was a little afraid of but craved with my entire being.

To be full. To be filled up.

To be made whole.

Part of me wanted Misael to tear his own clothes off, to line himself up and slide inside me, to steal my virginity and give me something so much better in return.

But he didn't. Instead, gentle fingers tugged the fabric of my panties aside, and his mouth closed around my clit, his tongue lashing back and forth in a pattern that made me writhe on the floor.

Kace's grip on me tightened, holding me still, and he flicked one of my nipples roughly, sending sensation zinging straight down to my core.

"Oh God!"

My arms flailed as I searched for something to hold on to. One hand latched onto Kace's short hair, gripping the strands as hard as he was gripping mine, and the other hooked around Bishop's neck, pulling him deeper into our kiss.

"Good girl," Bish murmured, his lips barely separating from mine to speak. "Come for us."

Then his hands cupped the sides of my face, holding me still while his tongue delved into my mouth over and over. At the same time, Misael stiffened his tongue, thrusting it inside me just like I'd imagined he might do with his cock.

And it was all too much.

A loud, naked cry tore from my lips as I came hard, twisting and jerking as I rode Misael's face unabashedly, chasing every last bit of pleasure that rippled through my body.

"Jesus fuck, that's hot," Kace muttered, his voice strained.

Bishop's kiss slowed a little, then he broke away, and before I knew what was happening, I was being pulled up onto the couch and wrapped in his arms.

I was still in my bra and panties, although my bra was a little twisted and my panties were soaked through. Kace grabbed a blanket off the back of the couch and draped it over me as Bish sat back, arranging my body so I was draped partially over him and partially over Kace.

Misael gave a satisfied smirk as he rose up on his knees and leaned in to kiss me thoroughly. He was hard—I could see his cock straining against his pants. And judging from what I felt beneath me, the other two boys were too.

But when I tried to roll over, reaching for them, Bishop grabbed my wrist in a firm hold.

"Not tonight, Princess. Misael was right, you're exhausted. Get some sleep."

I wanted to argue, wanted to show him I wasn't tired at all. But before I could even form a thought on exactly how to do that, sleep was already creeping up on me, stealing me away.

All the events of the day finally caught up to me, piling on top of me like a mountain of bricks.

And I slept.

TWENTY-FIVE

THERE WAS a pep in my step as I waited for Mom to be released from the hospital on Sunday. I leaned against the wall, humming to myself.

Giddiness was a new feeling. It was probably wildly inappropriate, given the reason why my mother was in the hospital to begin with. At the moment, I couldn't say that I cared.

No, it wasn't that I didn't care. It was that I felt so good that the feeling inside me couldn't be contained, so I didn't try. I was still worried about her, still concerned. I still cared. But there were other feelings clamoring for attention inside my chest now too, strong feelings that I was still trying to process. The Lost Boys had stayed with me for most of the weekend, and it was as if having them around so much, having them in my home, in my space, had ingrained them in my skin.

As if they'd slipped inside my heart somehow.

Finally, Mom came out, accompanied by a doctor I didn't recognize. The sight of her sobered me up in a rush. She still looked frail, almost fragile, like a glass doll that would break if I touched her too suddenly.

"Here we are." The man beamed at me, his smile surprisingly bright—but I wasn't going to shun a good attitude. Then his gaze flicked to my mom. "This is your daughter, you said?"

She nodded stiffly. "Yes."

"Good." He stuck out his hand to me. "I'm Dr. Paulson. I don't want to bore you too much on the details, but I briefed your mother about aftercare, as well as a few resources for some long-term treatment." Just from his tone, I could tell Mom hadn't taken the suggestion of "long-term treatment" well. Mental illnesses weren't something the elite had to worry about, as far as she and my father were concerned.

Or maybe they do, but no one ever talks about it.

I didn't voice that thought out loud though. Instead, I nodded at the doctor. "Of course. Is there anything I need to be aware of—"

"I'd just like to get home," Mom interjected. "As soon as possible."

She strode past me, and I frowned. Before I turned to follow her, the doctor took my arm, a little line appearing between his brows as he bent his head toward me.

"I sent a packet along with her," he said in a low voice. "It's in her bag, so take care and read through it, even if she has no interest. I don't believe we'll be seeing a return, but with things like this, you can never be too certain. She seems to be a woman very much... out of her element right now."

God. He didn't know the half of it.

I thanked the doctor and dealt with Mom's discharge paperwork, since she'd already left the building and didn't look like she had any plans at all to come back in. When I met her outside, she stood beneath the entry canopy of the hospital with a look of trepidation. I could barely reconcile this woman with the one who had thrown elaborate parties for hundreds of guests and played the perfect hostess to them all. *How is this the same person?*

I slid my arm into hers, leading her out to the car. We were quiet, but I figured that was probably for the best. I had no idea what to say.

How do people come back from things like that? Is it better to act like nothing at all happened? Or to talk about it?

To my surprise, when we slid into the car, it was Mom who spoke up first.

"Don't tell your father," was all she said. "Don't you ever tell your father."

MOM SAID nothing else about the incident, and neither did I.

Her flippant demeanor about it was almost jarring. Aside from the cool way she had told me not to tell Dad, she snapped back into place like a rubber band. She was still far from the radiant, put-together woman of high society that I had come to know her as, but she also didn't remain shut up in her room either. She was up before I was every morning, up and about, asking me about school and how things were going—I'd taken a few days off to stay with her and make sure she was okay.

It was a confusing switch, especially considering the fact that aside from knowing whether I was making good grades, Mom never showed an interest in my schooling before. She'd never had to; I'd been the perfect student, juggling strategic extracurriculars with a challenging course load and never letting anything fall behind.

Despite my trepidation about what this change in her meant, I tried to embrace it. If she was ready to try to make the best of our situation, that could only be good for both of us, and even though her energy often seemed forced, at least she was trying to accept things the way they were now.

Or at least, I thought she was.

The day before I was due to return to school, there was a knock at the door in the late afternoon. I was sitting at the kitchen table working on a paper I wanted to knock out so I wouldn't be too behind when I got back to school. I glanced up when I heard the sound, but before I could stand, I heard Mom answer the door.

"Who... are you?"

Disdain and discomfort were apparent in her voice even

from where I sat in the next room. And the sound of Bishop's voice made me sit up straighter.

"We were wondering if Cora was in?"

It was the most politely I'd ever heard him speak. *Ever.* I hadn't thought politeness was in his repertoire, but he sounded subdued and respectful. I stayed where I was, ears perked as I heard my mother make a sound somewhere between a grumble and a scoff.

"And who are you?"

"A friend from school."

"Cora hasn't mentioned any... friends from school."

"To be fair, she's a little shy."

I snorted. I definitely wasn't that when it came to school and the boys. Not even in the early days—but I supposed that wasn't the actual point Bishop was trying to make. I closed up my textbook and stood, going to the door. I slipped in beside Mom, giving Bishop a smile.

"Hey, Bish."

"You know this young man?" Mom asked me, not bothering to look down at me. Her gaze stayed keenly trained on Bishop, suspicious, like he was going to slither in here like a viper and bite something.

"Yeah. Of course I do, Mom. He's a boy in my class." I glanced to Bishop. "You can come in—"

"Aren't you doing homework, Cordelia?" Mom interjected stiffly.

"Yes, but—"

"Then you need to make this quick and get back to it. Education is important, after all. It gets you places."

I didn't like the snooty tone Mom's voice took on. Even when we were living at home, she'd never spoken like that to anyone I'd gone to school with, even people she didn't necessarily like—usually because of their parents. I knew instantly why she wasn't giving Bishop the respect she would have given them: because she thought he was beneath her.

I opened my mouth to say something, but Bishop spoke up.

"I actually just came by to drop off some homework for Cora." He reached into his backpack and handed me a few packets of paper. "You know. So you don't fall behind on your education."

He hit the last word a little extra hard, and I saw something glint in his hazel eyes as his gaze flicked to my face quickly, but otherwise, he gave no indication that he'd heard or been bothered by the snobby undertones in my mom's voice.

"See you at school, Cora."

With a dip of his chin, Bishop turned and left.

Mom stood there and watched him walk all the way down the cracked front path and all the way across the street to his house. I thought the entire display was a little much, and *more* than a little uncalled for. When Bishop was gone and out of sight, and Mom had securely closed—and obnoxiously locked—the door, I turned to her with an angry glare.

"Mom, what the hell? That was uncalled for."

Her eyebrows shot up, and a surprised little noise fell from her lips. Now that I thought about it, I didn't think I'd ever truly talked back to her or Dad. Not once.

There had always been "yes, sirs" and "no, ma'ams" and even when I had pushed back a little, the words had never come out harshly. But she'd just insulted and run off someone I considered a friend... or a... something.

That was unacceptable. Especially when Bishop was the one who'd probably saved her life.

"Excuse me?" Mom's voice was soft.

"That was uncalled for," I repeated. "He's a friend from school, and he was just coming by to drop off homework. He's *helping* me. He wasn't doing anything wrong."

"He looks like trouble."

I had never seen my mother turn her nose up at someone before, but I definitely saw the upturn in the way she looked away from me and back to the door—like she expected Bishop to just barrel on through it and wreak havoc. I openly rolled my eyes. He *was* trouble, but she didn't know that, and she definitely didn't know why or how.

"He is also the reason you were able to get to the hospital so fast after your accident," I said bluntly, my voice growing hard. "So maybe next time he comes around, you should *thank* him."

Mom's eyes flashed with surprise and something like shame. But instead of softening, her expression just grew harder.

"I don't want a boy like that around here or around you, Cordelia. I mean it."

———

I HAD NEVER SNUCK out of my house before.

Not when we were still living on the "good side" of Baltimore; not even when I was invited to college parties by guys at my school who were looking to get an in and a head start on mingling.

But there was a first time for everything.

In the few months since I'd started at Slateview, I had experienced more firsts than I had in the entire year before that. And tonight was another one as I opened up my bedroom window and slipped out of it.

Mom was safely asleep; all the sleeping pills we'd had in the house had been flushed down the toilet by Bishop when he'd cleaned up that first night while she was still in the hospital. It made me a little wary about sneaking out—we were closer to each other's rooms in this house than in our old, sprawling mansion, and that meant that without sleep aids, she could very easily hear me.

On second thought, I don't care if she hears me.

Landing smoothly on my feet below my window, I carefully closed it enough so that no animals or anything would be able to get in, but it wouldn't be hard for me to slip back through when the time came. For a split second, I wondered what it would be like if I just stayed out all night and didn't come back until morning, striding in through the front door to a mother who thought her daughter was comfortably still in bed.

Pushing those thoughts away, I crept across the street to Bishop's house. His foster father was gone again—the man was seriously never home.

The streetlamps flickered above, casting a faded yellow over the cracked sidewalk as I stepped on it. A few moments later, I was knocking on Bishop's door. As I waited, I had a vivid recollection of the last time I had popped over to his place unexpectedly, and I chewed on my lip, glad as hell that things were better this time around.

He answered the door—a beer in his hand. I raised a brow as he raised his.

"Well, well. Hello, Princess."

I smirked, pushing inside.

"Hey. Can I crash here for a little?"

"Can you crash here? Picking up the lingo, I see."

"Hey, Cora! S'up!"

In the living room, Misael lifted his chin from where he sat sprawled on the sofa next to Kace. They both seemed surprised but not unhappy to see me.

I smiled and gave a wave before turning to face Bishop as he closed the door.

"I just wanted to come over here and apologize for how my mom was earlier."

Bishop waved it off and shrugged.

"It's whatever. I figure it's a plus that she didn't call the

police on me and only gave me a stern talking to." His grin
was sinful.

"Ooh, Bish got a talking to from our girl's mooooom."
Misael cackled. Then he patted the sofa seat beside him.
"But I guess that's good? Means she's up and about and stuff
after everything, right? She's okay?"

"I think she is," I said, plopping onto the couch. The
spicy scent of cloves and the warmth of his body made me
unconsciously scoot a little closer to him, like I was trying to
soak up his essence through my skin. "She has a little more...
pep? I suppose. Enough that she was totally rude earlier."

Bishop's eyes glittered as he gazed down at me. He'd
followed me into the living room but hadn't sat down yet.
"It's nice to see you care, Princess."

His voice had a teasing lilt, and I rolled my eyes at him.

"You should be so lucky that I care."

"I never said I wasn't."

A deep blush crept up my cheeks, and I cleared my throat
as Bishop arched a brow slightly and then turned to head for
the kitchen. It wasn't fair that sometimes, just sometimes, he
was the weirdest, most alluring balance of dangerous and
soft. It put me completely off balance and left me thinking
about things I had no business even considering.

Like what it would be like to really be with these boys.
Not just owned by them, not just in an arrangement that
ensured my protection, not just... whatever this was.

But *with* them.

I settled more comfortably into the couch, and Misael put

his arm over my shoulders, tugging me a little closer into his side. He pressed a kiss to my temple.

"Seriously though. Don't tell me the only reason you came over here was to make sure Bish's feelings weren't hurt." He chuckled. "That would be boring as fuck. And also a little lame. We all know Bish doesn't have feelings."

As soon as the words were out of his mouth, he yelped loudly. Bishop had come behind the couch and pressed a fresh, cold beer to the back of his neck. There was a faint smirk on Bishop's lips, and he winked at me when our gazes met. I was sure my blush deepened, which only made him grin wider.

"Hey, why don't we cut out of here?" he suggested. "We weren't going to stay in tonight anyway. Since you're here, might as well make it a party."

We ended up all the way across town again, back at the warehouse we'd gone to the first time I'd "chilled" with the Lost Boys. It was a lot more relaxed this time. After all, we knew each other a lot better by now, and the darkness of the night and the whooping laughter of three boys with nothing better to do on a school night than hang out in abandoned buildings was actually... comforting.

I didn't want to hang out around the rental house, having one-word conversations with my mother, or worse, having to listen to her trash people who had made it possible for me to survive in this world and even feel a little bit happy.

Of course, the excitement of hanging out was short lived.

We'd only been there for about an hour when Bishop got a message. He groaned.

"What is it?" I glanced over, peeling absently at the label on my beer.

The warehouse was chilly and dimly lit, but there were enough missing chunks and holes in the walls to let light filter in from the street. It'd taken my eyes a little while to adjust, but now I could see the boys' features easily through the shadows.

Bishop looked over to Kace and Misael. "Work," he grumbled.

The other two frowned.

"Maaan, that sucks balls. Ask if he can meet us here? We got company." Misael jerked his chin at me.

For the first time, I saw Bishop hesitate. He looked to me with an actual measure of concern.

"What?" Misael's gaze darted between the two of us.

"I don't think we need to have Flint around her like that..."

I rolled my eyes. "Come on. I won't be a bother. I won't even speak. I'll stay out of the way."

Bishop looked skeptical. "I don't know..."

"Come on, just tell him to come on over." Misael rested one hand on my knee while the other lifted his beer to his lips. "He hates being kept waiting, and it means that we'll have to make one less trip around town tonight. Maybe it's not even a job that needs doing tonight. Then we can partay."

He waggled his eyebrows at me on the last word, and I snorted a giggle.

Bishop still looked unhappy, but nodded. He sent a message, and a few moments later, another one came in.

"Says he'll be here in about ten minutes," he reported. "Cora, when he comes, we're gonna talk to him out front. Stay here. You don't have to be quiet, but don't make it obvious you're around either."

I raised a brow. "Is this Flint person a bad guy?"

Bishop deadpanned me. "What kinda question is that."

"I know he's a 'bad guy' but is he a bad guy?" I tilted my head. "You know. Do I like... worry about him being creepy, or something?"

"I dunno." Bish ran a hand through his hair, his relaxed demeanor from earlier shifting to a sort of tense agitation. "He's fine. I mean, I don't trust him farther than I can throw him, but I'd say the same about a lot of people. I just don't want him to know you're here and tell Nathaniel or anything. So just... keep your head down, alright?"

I had so many questions, but Bishop's tone signaled that now wasn't the time for them. That was fine. I could see the tension blanketing over him, an uncomfortable shroud. He didn't like whatever this situation was going to be, and instead of being a nuisance, I decided to follow orders.

Besides.

Bishop never said I couldn't listen in.

TWENTY-SIX

TRUE TO MY WORD, I stayed in the "inside" space of the warehouse when Flint showed up. Bishop, Kace, and Misael went out front. The warehouse walls had damage to them, some places where the bricks had been knocked down and others where the glass of the windows was broken. Their voices weren't loud, but I could still hear as Bishop spoke to Misael and Kace outside.

"I don't like this." He spoke low. I had to strain to hear him properly, and I got up from the couch to move a little closer to the wall. I chose each of my steps carefully, not wanting to give away that I was listening, let alone that I had gotten up from the spot Bishop had commanded me to stay, deeming it a "safe space".

"Yeah, well, it was either meet here or go somewhere else, and I didn't want my whole night taken up with this shit," Misael said. "The princess will be fine. You worry too much."

I was inclined to agree with the easy-going boy on that one, though I couldn't help the feeling of butterflies in my stomach at the fact that Bishop seemed genuinely worried, and despite his nonchalant tone and words, even Misael seemed cautious.

"Hey. He's here." Kace spoke up, his voice slightly louder than the other two. "Let's go."

But to my dismay, they moved away from the immediate front of the warehouse as they went to meet Flint. I peeked out one of the broken windows, watching as they walked over to the same black car with the tinted windows that I'd seen the first time I'd been brought around for one of their jobs. I squinted through the hole in the wall, trying to get a good look at the man named Flint, but their bodies blocked my view.

"Oh, goddamn it," I muttered.

I huffed a frustrated breath but stayed where I was, intent on listening in. Snooping wasn't usually my MO, but this was the first time that they had actively tried to keep me out of the things they got themselves into, and I was beyond curious. Bishop and I hadn't revisited our conversation in his room the day I'd slapped him, but I hadn't forgotten it. I knew Flint was higher up on the food chain in this underground hierarchy than the Lost Boys were, and he seemed to be the guy who doled out jobs to others at the behest of Nathaniel Ward.

From the way the guys talked, I got the sense they'd met Nathaniel in person at least a few times, but I'd probably never have a reason or opportunity to meet that man, which was fine by me. Bish had said he was pretty ruthless and powerful—and if he was the criminal underground equivalent of men like my father and his business associates, I was sure he was absolutely terrifying.

Everything about this world scared me a little, but it filled me with a dark, morbid curiosity too. And it was that curiosity that had me pressing myself closer to the wall, turning my head to angle my ear toward the sounds of low voices.

I picked up things here and there as they spoke to each other in hushed tones. Flint greeted them with some throwaway comment about the guys being hard to track down lately. A flare of regret burned through me; I knew they'd turned down a couple of jobs while they were staying with me after Mom's accident. Had it caused a lot of problems for them?

"Had a little emergency," Bishop explained smoothly. "No big deal."

A wheezing laugh followed. "No big deal. Uh huh. Don't tell me you've got your heads all wrapped up in some piece a' pussy these days, eh?"

Silence.

There was another wheezing laugh. From where I peeked, it looked like this Flint person clapped Bishop on the shoulder—a display of playfulness and camaraderie that didn't seem to match the tone of the situation at all.

"Hey, I'm just fuckin' with you all. Loosen up. Now... to business."

They ran over details from a previous job, one that seemed to tie in with whatever assignment they were being given tonight. I caught bits and pieces, but most of what I heard was stuff I already knew as far as what kind of work the Lost Boys did.

It all sounded pretty straightforward—if breaking and entering could ever be considered straightforward—so I wasn't quite sure why Bishop had seemed so on edge.

Flint finished laying out the final details of the upcoming job, and then the guys fell back into shooting the shit. I could tell Bish was trying to wrap it up, but apparently Flint was a bit of a talker. I was about to press away from the wall and return to the couch when I caught two words from raspy-voiced man that sent a chill down my spine.

"...Abraham Shaw. Nathaniel doesn't want to..."

My back straightened. *Abraham Shaw?*

That man knew my father.

"What was that?" Flint's voice came again, sharp and alert.

Oh, shit.

Quietly, I moved from my place near the warehouse wall and sat back on the couch. I didn't hear what came after that, but it was at least ten minutes of talking back and forth between the four of them.

All I could think of while I waited for the boys to return was the name I'd heard Flint drop. Abraham Shaw. He was a business associate of my father's. I wasn't sure what exactly it was that he did, but he'd been instrumental in securing a lot of Dad's deals, as well as deals for other people in my father's circles. He was well known within the upper echelon of Baltimore's wealthy.

So what the hell was his name doing coming out of Flint's mouth?

I kept my questions to myself as the Lost Boys came back inside. They weren't carrying anything with them, and none of them seemed to be in a bad mood. Misael plopped down beside me.

"See, aren't you glad we didn't have to drive all the way across town to talk to him? Ain't even going anywhere tonight." He grinned. "Which is good. Means more time with our girl."

My smile only reached my eyes halfway.

"Good for me, huh?"

Gears turned in my head. If Flint knew Abraham, then maybe Flint knew other things—like what had happened with my father. Maybe, if I played my cards right, I could find out if he had any information about Dad. About Dad's arrest.

But the boys would never let me get close to Flint. Their reluctance to let him know about my existence or even my presence in the building told me that they'd have a serious problem with me wanting to ask him about my father. What's more, with the way Bishop felt about my dad—hell, with the way *all* of them felt about him—going through them to get to Flint would be out of the question.

"Cora? You alright?" Bishop's voice pulled me out of my thoughts, and when I glanced up, the bright hazel of his eyes glinted in the dim light.

"Yeah. No worries." This time, I made sure my smile really did reach my eyes. "I'm fine."

TWENTY-SEVEN

WE GOT HOME WELL PAST "REASONABLE" hours. The street was uncommonly still—not even a wayward teen from school or an obvious out-in-the-open drug deal to remind me that peace was only as constant as the people in the neighborhood allowed it to be.

"You want us to come in?" Bishop asked as his car idled on the street between our two houses.

I seriously considered it, but for the moment, I actually wanted to be alone. Besides, there was the whole issue of my mom being a lighter sleeper these days. The part of me that was still pissed at her thought it would serve her right to wake up and find not just one, but *three* delinquents sleeping over at her house.

But that would probably only make things worse for the guys in the long run. My mom had a good memory, and she could hold on to a grudge forever. If I secured their spot on her shit list, I was afraid she might actually take real steps to stop me from hanging out with them.

And I couldn't let that happen.

Not just because they protected me at school, but for so many other reasons I didn't dare dwell on them all.

"Nah." I shook my head. "Thanks for the offer, but I think I might actually go to bed soon."

He looked at me skeptically, and I couldn't blame him. In all honesty, I did *want* them to come in. It just wasn't a great idea right now.

I thought he might press the issue—half the time his questions or requests were really just statements and commands—but he just dipped his chin in a nod, reaching over to tuck a small strand of blond hair behind my ear.

"See you tomorrow, Coralee."

My heart gave a little flutter at the new nickname.

I'd gotten used to all of them calling me "Princess", but even though it'd shifted over time to sound more like a pet name and less like an insult, it'd still originated during a time when they all hated me with a vengeance.

But this new name rolled off Bish's tongue in an entirely different way.

It sounded sweet.

Almost... tender.

I swallowed, turning my head a little to chase his touch. When he finally withdrew his hand, I reached for the door handle. "Bye."

"'Night," Misael called from the back seat, and Kace

leaned his head out through the window to watch me, making sure I got back into the house without incident.

Despite what I'd said to Bishop though, I didn't think I'd be able to sleep. Mom was still tucked safely away in bed when I went to go check on her to make sure everything was okay. I might still be pissed at her, but that didn't mean I wanted her to end up back in the hospital or something.

Instead of forcing myself to lie awake in bed, staring up at the ceiling, I decided to make something to eat and mull over what I had learned.

It wasn't much, really. It was just a name. I wasn't even sure what context Flint had mentioned Abraham in, and I couldn't really ask the guys about that either—I was too afraid those kinds of probing questions would just make it obvious I was after information about my dad.

To most people, I imagined it might not even seem worth pursuing. It was just a name. A loose connection. A shot in the dark. But Dad had always said that the smallest possibilities could lead to the biggest outcomes, and at the moment, I was a firm believer in that.

I couldn't rely on the boys to lead me to Flint.

That just meant I had to lead myself to him.

THE MAN with the raspy voice was still on my mind as the weekend came and went and a new school week started.

On the plus side, concerns about my dad and whether

he'd been set up were the most pressing things I had to worry about. With mom out of the hospital, the rest of my life had settled into relative calm.

I never would've seen it coming, but school had actually become a place I was excited to go to. That had largely to do with my deal with the Lost Boys. Their claim over me and protection of me were still in place, and once people stopped trying to come after me for what they thought my father had done, they actually treated me... decently.

In fact, some people even went so far as to start sucking up to me, probably trying to use me to get in good with the Lost Boys. My association and clear connection with the three of them gave me what Jessica laughingly referred to as "a fuckton of social clout".

It was weird to feel *comfortable* at Slateview, but that was the point I was reaching.

I liked being able to walk the halls and have people say hello to me without vitriol behind their words. Even Serena didn't bother me anymore, though I couldn't say she went out of her way to be friends with me either. We were comfortably out of each other's hair, and that was good enough for me.

The only person at school who seemed to have an issue with me hanging out with Lost Boys was the last one I would've expected: Mr. Tyson.

Over the course of the semester, Mr. Tyson had solidified his standing as my favorite teacher. He had this air about him —a little overworked and tired, but focused on ensuring that whatever he was teaching was quality, even if what he taught ultimately ended up falling on deaf ears. Mr. Tyson had never spoken to me directly outside of class, although he called on me all the time in History.

After class one day in the middle of the week, he caught my eye before I could leave the classroom at the end of sixth period.

"Cordelia. Can you stay behind for a minute?"

I was surprised by the request, but he was a teacher, so who was I to refuse? I nodded, gathering up my books and putting them away in my bag before I walked to the front of the classroom. A few gossip-hungry kids lingered, looking back with the hope of catching the conversation. Mr. Tyson very obviously walked over and closed the door, making sure people wouldn't be able to eavesdrop. I watched him curiously.

"Is something wrong?" I asked, sure my confusion was obvious in my expression. "I'm caught up on all my homework assignments, right?"

It was virtually unheard of, having a teacher hold a student back after class. That kind of thing had happened all the time at Highland Park, but most of the teachers at Slateview just didn't care enough to bother meeting with students one-on-one.

Mr. Tyson shook his head. "Nothing is wrong. Nothing with school, at least."

Well, then. That's not cryptic at all.

"Oh. Okay. What's up?"

"You've been spending a lot of time with the Lost Boys,"

he said, the words coming out more like a statement than a question. I had gotten used to even the teachers referring to the trio as the "Lost Boys". Even in classes, they ended up being a package deal in everything that they did. This was no different.

But why Mr. Tyson cared, and why he cared about my ties to the boys themselves, made me a little apprehensive.

"Um. Yes." I rocked on the balls of my feet. "They've helped me adjust here well."

He squinted slightly. "Is that what they're doing? Helping you adjust?"

His keen interest was unnerving. I shifted where I stood, uncomfortable with the way he'd worded it. As if he knew every detail of our arrangement—maybe even that what existed between us had spiraled far beyond the original agreement.

"Yup. That's what they're doing," I insisted, keeping my voice firm. "They're my friends. Mr. Tyson, what is the point of these questions—"

"You shouldn't be associating with them."

My jaw dropped open slightly. His previous comment about them helping me "adjust" had given me the distinct impression that he disapproved, but I hadn't expected him to just come right out and say it so bluntly.

"You're a smart girl, Cordelia," he continued, gazing at me from across his desk. He had ash-brown hair and a slightly long face; he was probably in his early or mid-thirties, although it looked like this job had aged him a little quicker than maybe another career would have. "I don't need to explain to you why those boys aren't the kind of people a girl like you needs to be hanging out with."

My cheeks heated with a sudden flash of anger. "A girl like me?"

He gave me an indulgent look, tipping his head to one side.

"Yes. A bright girl who has a future ahead of her. The Lost Boys run Slateview; I'm sure you know that already. But it doesn't mean they're on their way to doing anything good with the rest of their lives. Just promise me you'll think about it, and please be smart. I know you know what's truly best for you, and I know you know that their interest in you hardly started out with pure intentions."

I couldn't think of a single damn thing to say to that. How much did he know? *How* did he know?

With a small, satisfied nod, Mr. Tyson dismissed me, leaving our conversation at that. I still couldn't speak to protest, and even if I did, what was I supposed to say to a declaration like that?

I DIDN'T TELL the guys about my conversation with Mr. Tyson, though it stayed with me the whole day.

Why would he pull me aside to tell me to stay away from the boys when the most he'd ever spoken to me before was to tell me I had done well on a test?

Whatever the reason, it had left me feeling off-balance. I trusted the Lost Boys, but Mr. Tyson's warning had been a reminder that, no matter how hard I kept treading water, I was in over my head. But between dealing with Mom, Dad, and figuring out what I needed to do about Flint, I didn't have time to mull over his strange proclamation too much.

Just keep swimming. Just keep moving.

By the end of eighth period, I had finally shoved my strange conversation with the teacher to the back of my mind. I grabbed my backpack and swung it over my shoulder, nodding to Mrs. Hall as I left the classroom. At least *she* didn't pull me aside and issue dire warnings about the guys I was hanging out with—although that might've been partly because she looked like she was half-asleep. She was a nice woman, but she always seemed dazed and exhausted, and her class was so poorly run it was basically like having a free period.

Ever since the day they'd picked me up and stopped at Burger King for breakfast, it'd become habit for me to ride with the Lost Boys to and from school. They were all waiting for me as I approached the beat-up convertible, which was parked in its usual spot. But something was different.

The three boys were lounging in a row against the side of the car, their gazes trained on me as I approached—as if they'd been waiting for me for some other reason than to just give me a ride. The conversation with Mr. Tyson popped back to the surface of my mind suddenly, and a small ripple of fear moved through me.

What's going on? What's changed?

But the guys didn't look mad or upset. In fact, Misael was smiling broadly, and he held out a small box to me when I approached. It was black, just bigger than a ring box, with a small satin ribbon wrapped around it. I raised a brow as I glanced at it.

"What's this?" I asked, taking the box. It wasn't heavy, but I could feel the light weight of something inside. I held it, turning it over in my hands.

"Open it up. You'll see. It's from all of us." Misael was practically bouncing on his toes with excitement, and even Kace and Bishop were watching me with keen interest.

Oh my God. They got me a gift.

The worry that'd been twisting my stomach evaporated. Screw Mr. Tyson. He didn't have a right to get in my head about stuff he didn't understand. I knew that from the outside, this thing between the four of us probably looked strange and messed up. But I was happier now than I'd been since I came to Slateview, and maybe even since before that. The Lost Boys made me happy, and I wasn't going to let go of that just because a too-observant teacher with a need to fix his student's lives had poked his nose into mine.

Smiling softly at Misael, I pulled the satin ribbon off and opened it. My jaw dropped slightly, and a small breath escaped my lips.

Inside was a beautiful silver bracelet. It was one of those kinds that had a hinge, letting you open it to put it on, and then snap it shut to keep it safely on your wrist. I was almost afraid to touch it, like touching it would make it stop being real. It wasn't overly jeweled or fancy—it couldn't have cost even a fraction of some of the jewelry I'd worn to parties back home—but it meant more to me in that moment than anything my parents had ever gotten me.

"Oh my god... I don't know what to say..."

"If you don't like it we can get you a different one—"

"No!" I shook my head emphatically, pulling the bracelet from the box's velvet bed. I pulled it apart, and the metal glinting in the November sunlight as I snapped it into place. I smiled at how it fit against my wrist. The coolness chilled my skin pleasantly.

"I love it." The grin that stretched my face was so wide it almost hurt. Then it dimmed a little as I shook my head. "But why—"

"Just because." Bishop shrugged, but the intensity of his hazel eyes didn't match his casual tone. "We figured it'd be a good present. Princesses like jewelry, right?"

I rolled my eyes but stepped closer to press a kiss to his cheek. My hand rested on his chest as I rose up onto my tiptoes, and I swore I could feel his heart jump beneath my palm. His body stiffened slightly, and when I pulled away, I hesitated, our faces still so close together that I would've barely had to move to kiss him on the lips.

We'd done far more than kiss before. He had put his mouth on the most intimate part of me, had touched every inch of my skin.

But this felt different, somehow.

Like the small space between us was full of possibility, and like the whole world would change if our lips met.

I didn't kiss him. And he didn't kiss me. But we stayed like that for another heartbeat, letting the possibility echo between us.

When I finally pulled away, I realized the other two boys were watching us—and so were the crowds of students pouring out of the school. But for once in my life, I didn't second-guess or worry about what anyone else thought. I kissed Misael and then Kace on the cheek, their breath caressing the side of my face as they held almost perfectly still.

"This princess loves it." I smiled at the three of them, running my fingertips over the cool metal of the bracelet. "I just... wasn't expecting it. Thank you."

Bishop nodded, clearing his throat and pressing away from the car. "Besides. We got the perfect place you can show it off. We're going to another party this weekend." He cocked his head, looking down at me with a grin that made my heart skip. "You're invited. Obviously."

I chuckled.

"Obviously."

TWENTY-EIGHT

I WORE the bracelet almost religiously for the rest of the week, taking it off only when I needed to take a shower. Mom had seen it, eyed it, and said nothing about it. We had gone back to essentially ignoring each other since the day she'd been so rude to Bishop—she was going out more and more often, and I was generally left to my own devices.

It was fine with me. It meant I didn't even have to bother sneaking out the window when the boys picked me up for the party on Friday. It was in a neighborhood a few miles away, and we drove with the top up. Bishop had resisted for as long as he could, but the temperatures were dropping now, especially at night, and the last few drives to school had been freezing.

The party was at a house I'd never been to before—Jessica wasn't playing hostess this time, although I was still hoping she'd be there. She and Liam ate lunch with us almost every day, and although I doubted our paths would've ever crossed if I hadn't fallen in with the Lost Boys, I considered her a real friend by now.

Just like last time, loud music assaulted my ears as we approached the house. The place looked packed to capacity, and people were spilling out into the front lawn, laughter and loud shouts filling the air. Bish had told me it would be a mix of upperclassmen from Slateview and another high school on the same side of the wrong side of the tracks as ours. That was part of why the Lost Boys had decided to go to the party —trouble was more likely to break out when kids from rival schools got together.

And that explained why the place was so crowded. There were as many familiar faces as there were unfamiliar, and I instinctively pressed closer to the Lost Boys, feeling Kace's arm slip around my waist as Misael's hand ran through the hair at the back of my neck.

The music pulsed loudly through the two-story row-house the party was being held in. The bass-heavy hip-hop I was used to hearing at Jessica's parties was replaced by rift-heavy metal. It was strangely appealing—raw and primal somehow.

"Gonna get us drinks," Bishop called over the blaring music. "Mingle and stay out of trouble." He looked specifically to Misael when he said that part. The boy beside me laughed and flipped him off.

"Come on! I'm always on my best behavior!"

"Yeah, sure you are."

Bishop went off toward the kitchen with Kace at his side, and the crowd parted for them like a wave. Misael jerked his head toward the far side of the room where Jessica and Liam stood, and I nodded in answer to his unspoken question. He grinned, then threaded his fingers through mine, lifting my hand to his mouth to kiss my knuckles before leading me across the room.

The crowd parted for us too, and I squeezed his hand a little tighter as we walked, still feeling the imprint of his lips on my skin.

That sort of thing had been happening more and more often in the few days since they'd given me the bracelet. I wasn't sure if it was the gift or my reaction to it—or maybe a bit of both—but it felt like something had shifted between us. Deepened, somehow. Little gestures of affection were becoming common among all of us, and it made me feel both giddy and warm to think about it.

"Hey, girl! Nice to see you out and about and fitting in all the way," Jessica said, giving me a wink as she made a show of checking me out from head to toe, taking in my outfit for the evening—a skirt I had cut short and a cropped top.

I grinned, striking a little pose.

"I'm a chameleon."

Misael and I hung out with Liam and Jessica for a while, all of us talking and moving to the music at the same time. But when several minutes had gone by and Bishop and Kace still hadn't returned with drinks, I grabbed Misael's arm, leaning up to shout over the music.

"Let's go see if Bish and Kace need help!"

He nodded and made a gesture to Liam and Jessica that we'd be right back. They nodded and kept dancing, arms wrapped around each other and bodies pressed close together.

I laughed as we made our way through the crowd, keeping a firm grip on Misael's hand. "They'll forget we were even there in a second."

He glanced over his shoulder at them, grinning and rolling his eyes. "Yup."

We headed downstairs, since I was pretty sure that was where the kitchen was. We found the entrance off a long hallway, and when we stepped inside, I spotted Bishop and Kace by the collection of kegs that served as the party's source of booze. They were talking to a couple of guys I didn't recognize, probably students from the other school. A few obviously drunk girls hovered around the kegs, and one of them had wrapped her arms around one of the boys I didn't know, rubbing her body against him and kissing his neck.

I pulled a face as Misael and I moved through the crowd toward them. *God, if I ever act that desperate, I hope—*

Before I even had time to finish the thought, another one of the girls who'd been hovering around the drink station sauntered forward, wrapping her arms around Bishop. A third made a move on Kace, running her fingers over his chest as she stalked toward him like a predator.

And something inside me just... snapped.

I didn't know what propelled me forward. Bish was already pushing the girl away from him, but that hardly even mattered to me anymore. The way she'd looked at him, the way she'd touched him...

No. You don't get to touch what's mine.

I was across the room before I'd even realized I was moving. My hands connected with the girl's upper chest, shoving her backward in a forceful blow.

"Back the fuck off!"

She stumbled slightly, shock contorting her features as she caught sight of me. Then her lip curled in a snarl, and she moved to shove me back. I was ready for her though, and when her hands connected with my shoulders, I grabbed her wrists, yanking her off-balance.

I wasn't a skilled fighter, and I had no idea what I was doing.

But it didn't matter. Because I knew what I wanted.

This bitch needed to learn to keep her hands to herself.

As she spun to the side, losing her balance, I grabbed a handful of her hair. She shrieked in pain and anger, and I heard several shouts and yells around us. I barely registered the audience we'd drawn though—my focus had narrowed down to only what was in front of me, as if I had blinders on to the entire rest of the world.

Using my grip on the girl's hair, I yanked her closer to me, forcing her to look over at Bishop. When I spoke, my voice sounded harsh and ragged, completely unrecognizable.

Jesus. Who the fuck am I?

"Do you see that boy over there?" I tightened my grip, forcing her a little closer as she lashed out, her hands contorted into claws. "Do you see him? He's *mine*."

"Get off me, you fucking psycho!" the girl shrieked, twisting in my grasp.

I gave a sharp tug on her hair, turning her head toward Kace. The girl who'd been running her fingers down his chest had backed away from the fight, her eyes wide in drunken shock.

"Do you see that boy? With the blond hair?" I was breathing hard now, so hard it was almost impossible to get the words out. It felt a little like I was outside of my own body, like I was watching some other girl do this, not me. "He's mine too."

With that, I wrenched her around, surprised to see that Misael was right behind us—it looked like he'd frozen mid-run, as if he'd darted after me to stop the fight but then had decided maybe I could handle it myself after all. Some emotion I couldn't identify glinted in his eyes, and his nostrils flared as I used both hands in the girl's hair to tilt her head up toward him.

"And this boy. He's mine too."

I finally released my grip on her hair, shoving her away from me. She stumbled, almost losing her balance in her high heels, but righted herself at the last second. Her hair was wild, and her face was flushed as she turned around to stare at me with eyes like saucers.

"What the fuck is wrong with you?" she hissed.

I shrugged, standing my ground as my chest rose and fell heavily.

"Nothing. And nothing will be wrong with *you* if you keep your hands off what's mine." My gaze flicked to Bishop, who was standing stock-still, observing everything, then to the other two boys. "I belong to them. And they belong to me."

Someone in the crowd whistled, and a few other whoops and catcalls rose up. The girl flushed red, anger warring with fear as her gaze darted from me to the boys and back again. I stayed poised and ready for a fight, and each one of the Lost Boys met her look with a stony glare. Even the two boys Bish and Kace had been talking too had backed away, refusing to have this girl's back.

She held up her hands, grimacing as she let out a scoffing sound. "Ugh. Fine. Whatever."

"Yeah, whatever." I pointed toward the kitchen door, ignoring the fact that my hand shook from the torrent of adrenaline crashing through me. "Now get the fuck out."

The girl straightened, tossing her red-brown hair over her shoulder in an attempt to reclaim whatever dignity she could. Her gaze flicked to the boys again. "I hope you all like crazy."

With that, she limped unevenly toward the door—one of her heels had broken in the fight, I realized. Taunts and laughter following her, but once she was gone and the spectacle was over, the buzz of loud conversation resumed around us.

But for several long moments, I didn't move, and neither

did any of the Lost Boys. They were all staring at me as though they had no idea who I was, and I brushed my fingertips over the smooth metal of my bracelet, letting the feel of it sooth me.

Then, without warning, Bishop stepped forward and gripped my upper arm.

"Let's get the fuck out of here."

His voice was hard, his entire body vibrating with tension, and it was the only thing he said before he turned and dragged me through the crowd.

Shit.

Did I do something wrong?

Nerves made my heart beat harder as he pulled me along through the press of bodies, which parted to let us through. A few curious gazes landed on me, but I was too distracted to shrink under the scrutiny. I had a sudden horrifying certainty that I'd just done something monumentally stupid. That I'd crossed some invisible line I never should've breached, and that I had angered my three protectors by doing so.

These weren't supposed to be the terms of the deal, after all.

I had agreed to belong to the Lost Boys in exchange for their protection.

But they had never agreed to belong to me.

Things had felt different between us all lately. So many things had happened, and so much seemed to have changed, but maybe I'd misread the signals. Maybe the emotions I was feeling were entirely one-sided.

Hurt and defensive anger built up in my chest as Bishop dragged me upstairs, the other two boys so close behind us I could feel the heat of them at my back.

Dammit. Would they take back their offer? Would they claim I'd violated our agreement somehow? Would they abandon me, leave me to fend for myself in the halls of Slateview from here on out?

My heart seized with fear at that thought—but it wasn't so much fear at what the other students might do to me. It was fear of what losing these three boys would do to me.

Tears burned the backs of my eyes, and when Bishop pulled me into an empty bedroom at the end of the hall that ran through the long row house, I yanked my arm out of his grasp, stepping away and turning on him as Kace and Misael entered, slamming the door shut behind them.

"You can blame me if you want, but I don't—"

I didn't even get a chance to finish my half-formed, angry excuse.

Before I could say another word, Bishop reached me in a single long stride and wrapped his arms around me, kissing me like he might never come up for air.

TWENTY-NINE

I WAS SO STARTLED, my legs almost gave out.

My knees wobbled, and I stumbled backward a little—but there was no chance of falling over. Not with Bishop's strong arms banded around me like a vise, holding me up as his lips devoured mine.

The other two boys grabbed me too, sweeping my hair out of the way to trail kisses over my neck and shoulders, hands groping and massaging my ass, sliding up my shirt to skate over my bare skin.

"Fucking Christ, Coralee. Do you have any idea how goddamn sexy that was?" Bishop groaned, and Kace and Misael made similar noises of approval as our heavy breaths filled the air.

My shocked brain was still trying to grasp the fact that they weren't angry at what I'd done—that they *liked* it—as I was spun in their arms. Without hesitation, Misael's lips claimed mine, leaving the other two to explore my body with their hands and mouths.

My shirt was lifted, and I raised my arms to let them tug it over my head before I turned again, finding Kace's hot, demanding lips this time. The ferocity of his kiss made me certain he approved of my violent, public claiming of the three of them, and a shot of adrenaline and pride flared inside me, even though maybe it shouldn't have.

I should've been ashamed of what I'd done, but in this moment, it was hard to be.

Because it had gotten me what I wanted.

The three boys whose souls had infiltrated mine.

Kace gripped my arms tightly and walked me backward, and when we were about halfway across the small room, the backs of my legs hit the edge of a mattress. With a hungry, feral smile, the blond boy gave my shoulders a push, letting me collapse back onto the bed, which gave a little squeak as I landed.

I was vaguely aware of Misael locking the door as Bishop made quick work of my skirt.

The last time I'd been this naked with all three of them, it had stopped there. Misael had made me come on his tongue while the other two kissed and caressed me, but all of their clothes had stayed on.

I wouldn't let that happen tonight.

Maybe he saw the determined look in my eyes as I

scrambled up to my knees on the mattress, because Kace laughed, grabbing the hem of his shirt with one hand and yanking it over his head. The others did the same, and I swallowed as I took in the sight of all three of them side by side.

They were truly stunning—all solid muscle and wild, rugged beauty.

When I reached behind me and unhooked my bra, their eyes darkened. Keeping my gaze on the three of them, I let the small piece of silky fabric fall away.

The three boys moved so fast, and in such perfect synchronicity, that I lost track of who was where as they converged on me, pushing me back down to the mattress again.

Bishop kissed me again, his lips just as hungry as before, and Misael brushed kisses up my arm toward my shoulder. I could guess where Kace was headed, and I shivered with anticipation. The other two had put their mouths on me before, but I knew Kace would be nothing like either one of them.

And he wasn't.

Rather than pulling my panties off, he ripped them from my body, tearing the delicate fabric before delving between my legs like a starving man.

"God, please! Kace!"

I arched off the bed as he licked me with the flat of his tongue, reaching down to grab his head and press it closer to my core. Bish and Misael groaned as they watched him devour me, the heat of their gazes burning into my skin. Knowing that they were watching, that they could see me laid out, spread open before Kace, made fire burn through my veins.

The part of me from my old life, the one who was proper and poised and did only what she was told, felt a rush of shame. But that feeling only enhanced the pleasure crashing through my body, the thrill of the taboo making me feel wild and reckless.

And when I came on Kace's tongue, I screamed loud enough that even people downstairs at the party probably heard me over the heavy thump of the music.

His fingers dug into my thighs so hard I was sure he'd leave marks as his moss-green gaze flicked up to meet mine. His eyes glinted with desire and satisfaction, and he held my stare as he slowly slid one long, thick finger inside me. My inner walls were still contracting as the aftershocks of my orgasm quaked through me, and his nostrils flared at the feel of it.

I saw the moment he hit the resistance he'd been expecting. His gaze darkened, his expression becoming almost angry as he fought to keep himself in check.

"Fucking hell, Cora. No one's ever had you like this? No one's ever been inside this tight hole?"

My chest heaved as I tried to force oxygen into rebellious lungs. My core clenched around his thick finger, and I knew he could feel—not just see—my reaction to his question. How did he turn me on so much with such dirty, vulgar words?

"No," I gasped. "I want you—all of you—to be my firsts."

Even as I said it, I had a momentary flash of panic. I wanted all three of the Lost Boys. From the moment I'd met them, when I couldn't decide who I hated more, to right now, when I could finally admit I was starting to fall for all of them, I had always seen the three boys as parts of a whole. They were distinct people, and I felt differently about each of them, but I could never choose just one above the others.

I wanted them all.

But I also had no idea how that would even work. This was all new territory for me, and the fact that I was taking this step with three boys instead of one only added to the confusion I felt.

Fortunately, as they had with so many other things, the Lost Boys immediately took the lead, saving me from attempting to navigate this on my own.

Misael swooped in to kiss me, sliding his tongue against mine before nipping at my bottom lip. By the time he broke away, the other two boys were completely naked, kneeling on the bed beside me. Kace had his fist wrapped around the base of his thick cock, and Bishop was jerking himself off in long, even strokes.

The sight of it made my breath hitch in my throat, a strange combination of fear and longing filling me as I blinked at them.

I wanted them inside me—so, so much. But how would they possibly fit?

Warm, gentle fingers turned my head away from Bishop

and Kace, and Misael met my gaze. He knelt on my other side, and while I'd been distracted, he had removed the last of his clothes too. We were all naked, not a scrap of clothing left on us.

"It's okay, Coralee," he murmured, his dark eyes warm in the dim light filtering in through the window. "We've got ya. You trust us?"

My head was already moving up and down before I realized it was true. Entirely true.

Somewhere along the way, the boys I'd despised and doubted had become the only people in my messed up world that I truly trusted.

"Fuck," Bishop muttered, his voice sounding almost agonized. "I got no damn condom."

"It doesn't matter!" I gasped, "I'm on the pill."

Ava had taken me to the doctor for a birth control prescription when I was fifteen—not because I had expected to be having sex, but because it helped regulate my periods. The pill I'd been prescribed had actually helped a lot, and I was thankful as hell for Ava, because I knew my mom would never have taken me to the doctor for something like that, no matter how necessary it was.

Bish's face split into a wide, wicked smile, and he leaned over me, partially draping his body over me as he kissed me hard.

"Thank Christ." He licked his lips as he pulled back. "Now close your eyes."

My brows pulled together even as I did what he

commanded, turning my head slightly to try to track their movements through sound. "Why? Why can't I look?"

"Because one of us is going to take your virginity, and I don't want to make you choose who. I don't want you to know who. Because you belong to all of us. It's not about who claims you first."

Gratitude and arousal infused my body as he finished speaking. It was like he'd crawled inside my head and read my thoughts, had seen that I couldn't decide between them. And so they'd make sure I didn't have to.

"It's not," I agreed. "I don't care who claims me first or last or anything. Just so long as you all do."

Three voices groaned above me.

"Yeah, I don't think you need to worry about that. You're so damn gorgeous, only a fool wouldn't want you," Misael said, his voice slightly teasing.

And then the boys stopped speaking at all. Hands and mouths were on me again, seeming to be everywhere at once, licking and nipping and kissing. I stopped thinking and just let myself soak up each touch as it came.

Then, just like Bishop had promised, I felt the broad head of a cock nudge at my entrance. I honestly couldn't tell who it was—the overload of sensations had shorted out my brain, making it harder to sort through who each touch belonged to.

But that was okay. I didn't need to know who it was to know it felt right.

I had planned on graduating high school a virgin.

I had planned on giving my future husband my virginity on our wedding night.

Now, I didn't want either of those things. I just wanted this.

Whoever was braced above me hesitated for a moment, and I reached for him, pulling him closer and shifting my hips to urge him onward. He didn't make me beg, and he didn't draw out the intrusion, sliding into me instead in a single, hard stroke.

It hurt.

Like being shattered and remade, like being broken and reformed, the cock spearing me seemed to split me in two—and when the pieces came back together again, I wasn't the same person I had been a moment ago.

My chest rose and fell as the boy above me paused, stilling inside me, giving me time to adjust to his size. He stroked in and out of me twice more, letting my body acclimate to the sensation. Then, slowly, he pulled out.

I had never known what true emptiness felt like until then. I cried out in frustration, reaching out blindly with my eyes still shut, needing someone to fill me up again, to drive into me like that again.

Low noises reached my ears as the boys around me all groaned, and then Kace's voice reached me in the darkness.

"Open your eyes, Princess. Watch us while we fuck you."

My eyelids flew open, and I blinked at the three of them. They'd pulled back slightly, all still gathered around me. One of them had just been inside me, and I hoped I never knew who it was.

Biting down hard on my bottom lip, I reached out for Kace, pulling him toward me. He moved willingly at my insistence, but as soon as his body was poised over mine, he took back all control. His calloused hands pinned my wrists to the bed, holding me still as he slid smoothly inside me. It hurt a little as my inner walls stretched around him, but the pain was nowhere near as sharp as it had been with the first intrusion.

I couldn't use my hands to urge him on, but I used my legs and feet, wrapping them around his waist as I rubbed my body against his.

"Oh shit, you're tight," he grunted, baring his teeth as he withdrew and thrust in again.

When he bottomed out inside me, the base of his cock rubbed against my clit, and I moaned, squeezing around him. He picked up the pace a little, driving into me so hard our bodies rocked together. Pleasure built inside me like a slow-moving wave, but before it could crest, he kissed me with bruising force and then pulled away.

I whined in protest, and he chuckled darkly. "Someday we'll all finish inside you. Stuff you so full of our cum you'll feel us all for days afterward. But not tonight."

My body quivered at his words, and when Bishop draped himself over me and thrust inside, I was sure he could feel how close I was to coming again. My hips rose off the bed to meet him, and he braced himself on his arms as he drove into me, fucking me the same way he'd kissed me the first time—with desperation and fierce need, like he could never, ever get enough.

I was so close—*so* close—my body balancing on a knife's edge as I clung to his shoulders, nails digging into his muscled back.

But he didn't let me come.

It felt like he was torturing us both as he slowly, reluctantly withdrew from me.

Misael was there to take his place in an instant, and the moment he slid inside me, it was like something clicked into place. I had wanted all three of them. And now I'd gotten my wish.

My body felt exhausted and used in the best possible way, and I knew I would be sore tomorrow.

But it would be so worth it.

"Please," I gasped, looking up into Misael's beautiful, dark eyes. "Please—make me come!"

His expression shifted, determination hardening his features, and I knew I had chosen the right boy to beg. Kace would control me, Bishop would torture me, but Misael?

He would do whatever he could to give me what I wanted.

Draping his body over mine, he kissed me slowly and deeply as he began to thrust, slipping one hand between us to work my clit in tight circles.

As the orgasm that had been threatening began to build in my core, I became aware of new sounds around me and glanced at Bish and Kace. The two of them were stroking themselves in time to the rhythm of Misael's thrusts, and the sight drove me crazy. The looks on their faces, which mirrored Misael's, made me groan with wanton satisfaction. They might not be inside me, but they knew what it felt like, and watching their friend fuck me was turning them on, driving them toward the same precipice I was racing for.

Misael rose up suddenly, hooking his arms under my knees and lifting my ass off the bed as he continued to drive into me. At this angle, his cock hit an incredible new spot inside me, and it was the thing that finally pushed me over the edge.

I clamped down hard around him, swirling my hips against his as I sobbed out my release.

"Oh... God!"

"Fuck, Cora. So good."

He pulsed and thickened inside me, and the two boys kneeling on either side of me made strangled noises, their fists moving faster.

Then all three boys came at once. Misael drove into me hard before freezing inside me, cursing and groaning as Bishop and Kace spattered ropes of cum across my stomach and breasts.

We all grew still, breathing heavily into the quiet of the room as the tension slowly drained from our bodies. As Misael withdrew slowly, I felt a gush of wetness as cum spilled out of me, and the skin of my torso glistened with it in the semi-darkness.

A giddy feeling filled me like a rush of blood to the head.

These three boys had marked me.

Claimed me.

But I had claimed them right back.

I SPENT the night in a stranger's house, on a stranger's bed, wrapped up in a tangle of limbs with the Lost Boys.

We all fell asleep on the bed together, and while I felt a little bad for commandeering someone's bedroom like that, it was impossible to regret anything that'd happened the previous night, even in the harsh light of morning.

The four of us rose slowly, taking our time getting up and getting dressed. By late morning, we ended up at a Denny's— one of two in the area. According to Bishop, this one had the best breakfasts in all of Baltimore. And honestly? I couldn't disagree with him. I had a whole hamburger, fries on the side, and a giant chocolate shake to go with it. It was hearty and greasy and perfectly bad for me, and I was one hundred percent okay with that.

I was running on high octane. And I had a feeling I wasn't the only one. The four of us drew stares from the other patrons—mostly older people—as we laughed and joked around. Every once in a while, one of the guys would haul me toward him and kiss the breath out of me, and that *definitely* got the attention of the other patrons.

But I didn't care.

Maybe I shouldn't have felt the happiest I'd ever been after a night of doing everything I had been raised not to do... but I *was* happy. More than happy.

And I wasn't going to fight it or feel bad about it.

I wasn't going to feel one ounce of guilt for it.

"Ah, shit."

As we were finishing breakfast, Bishop spoke up, looking around.

"What?" Kace glanced over at him.

"Left my phone in the car. Let me out, Coralee."

He poked at my side to get me to move out of the booth, and I squirmed under his touch as it tickled my ribs. "Ah!" Then I held out my hand. "Gimme your keys. I can get it."

"Oh. You sure?"

"Yeah. It's not like it's that far away." I chuckled, the giddy feeling still infusing my body. "I may be a princess, but I can handle myself okay."

"Oh, believe me, we know." Misael's gaze heated as he winked at me.

I kicked his feet lightly under the table, then stood up, Bishop's keys in my hand. "Be right back."

I headed for the door, ignoring the looks that came my way and straightening out my skirt as I trotted outside. I didn't even have the decency to feel shame for the fact that I was still wearing my clothes from the night before, the scent of cigarette smoke clinging to the fabric. Hell, even my hair had that "just woke up" feel and look to it. It was comfortable. I liked it.

Outside, I made my way quickly to the convertible. I hopped in and started looking for Bishop's phone, but he hadn't left it someplace obvious like the dash or the console. Where the hell could it have gone?

As I was scanning the cup holders and door compartments, I heard a deep buzzing sound from somewhere beneath me. *Ah ha!* His cell must've fallen beneath the driver's seat, and Bishop hadn't noticed it. As it continued to buzz, I patted around under the seat until my fingers closed around a cool piece of metal and glass. I pulled it out... but paused when I saw the name of the person calling.

Flint.

I almost impulsively answered it. My fingers itched to hit the little green button that would connect the call. I'd been hoping for a chance to talk to the man anyway, to see if he knew anything about my father being set up. If I answered, maybe I could finally get answers to questions that'd haunted me for months—

But how the hell would I explain that to Bishop?

Bzzz... Bzzz... Bzzz...

The vibrating buzz stopped for a few seconds and then started again. He must've called back to leave a message—or maybe he was trying to see if Bish was screening his calls.

My grip on the phone tightened, and I stared down at the display as if it was the only thing left in the world.

As if it was the key to redemption. Salvation. Freedom.

Bzzz... Bzzz... Bzzz...

Guilt twisted my stomach, but I ignored it as I repeated the number that displayed under Flint's name over and over in my head until the phone finally stopped ringing.

Then I took in a breath, steeled myself, and went back inside.

THIRTY

I DIDN'T EAT that night.

If Mom noticed that I hadn't been home since the previous evening, or that I didn't arrive back to the rental house until mid-afternoon, she didn't say anything. Given the way she had acted toward Bish, I had a feeling she would've lectured me if she had any idea where I'd been. But she really didn't know. Although she wasn't as listless as she'd been before her overdose, she was still massively checked out in a lot of ways.

Maybe as an attempt at a peace offering, she ordered delivery for dinner, something we could only afford to do once every several weeks. Whether I was prepared to accept her peace offering or not hardly mattered, because I didn't have an appetite.

I couldn't get Flint's number out of my head. I couldn't

stop thinking about the fact that I was close, so *close* to getting answers.

And yet... something held me back from typing the number into my phone, from calling him and begging him to speak with me.

I should've been thrilled to have found his number and to have a way to get in touch with him. It was an in, and I was grateful for it, but the seed of guilt I'd felt earlier in Bishop's car hadn't died. Instead, it was growing and growing. What did it say about me that I was so desperate to make my life "normal" again when there were things about this new life that I liked? All day, my mind had been filled with thoughts of how the Lost Boys had looked after me while I was here. How much things between us had changed since our first meeting. How important they all were to me.

Was it selfish to still be thinking of my father? Of a life I was coming to realize was stifling in a way I hadn't known until it was taken away from me?

Mom finally gave up trying to get me to eat the food she'd ordered, and we both retreated to our rooms. I heard the TV in her bedroom turn off at around eleven, but even after I turned off the lights and crawled into bed, sleep wouldn't come.

As I stared up at the ceiling, dozens of thoughts whirling in my head, there was a soft tap at my window. At one point in my life, it would've made me jump. Now, it didn't even phase me. I assumed it was Bishop, and a grin tugged at my lips as I had the ridiculous thought that he was becoming more polite—actually knocking on my window before breaking in. But when I slipped out of bed and crossed toward the small window, I drew up short, blinking in surprise.

It wasn't Bish.

It was Kace.

"Hey—hey, what's up?" I opened the window for him since it was easier to do from the inside and instinctively went to my bedroom door, clicking the lock to it. At least if Mother heard something, she wouldn't be able to just burst in without a bit of warning beforehand.

Kace climbed in, and I padded back over to sit on the edge of my bed. He stepped forward from the window, coming to stand almost directly in front of me, and with him so close, I had to crane my neck to meet his gaze. He looked down at me, head tilted, muscled arms crossed. His white-blond hair shone in the faint street light that penetrated the grungy window, and he looked beautiful and dangerous—and completely out of his element.

I was about to ask him if he was okay when he opened his mouth and spoke.

"Is something wrong?" he asked bluntly.

I blinked. *I was about to ask you that.*

"Um. What?"

He sighed, the taut lines of his shoulders softening a little.

"Earlier today. When you came back from bringing Bishop his phone. You seemed off. You alright?"

My jaw dropped open slightly, and I let out a short breath. *That* was why he looked so unsure and stiff—he'd come to check on me. I didn't think this kind of thing was really in his wheelhouse. Touchy-feely wasn't a word anyone would ever use to describe this boy. The fact that he'd not only noticed the difference in my behavior but had decided to come make sure I was okay made something warm and sweet expand in my chest.

Kace shifted awkwardly from one foot to the other. I bit my lip, patting the space beside me on the mattress. He looked at it for a moment, then sank down to sit next to me, his large, solid body so close that his shoulder brushed against mine.

"I was just thinking a lot about my father today," I said. It wasn't a lie. I had been thinking about him a lot. "It just hit me suddenly and kind of... hasn't left me since. That's all. I'll probably get over it."

Kace was quiet. When I looked to him, he was staring down at his hands, his splayed fingers pressed together. He was thinking hard about something, but I couldn't begin to guess what.

"Do you miss him?" he asked suddenly.

"Do I miss my father? Of course I do." Then, as soon as the words were out of my mouth, a sigh followed. "I mean, I think I do. Sometimes I'm not sure what my feelings are, really. I think... I don't know. Yeah, I miss him. I do."

"You sound like you're trying to convince yourself."

That observation struck too close to home, and I said nothing. When I remained silent, Kace went on.

"Listen... I ain't a person to tell anyone how they should feel about their father. I'm not going to. Just... I don't know. You just had a look. That's all. Wanted to make sure you were... you know."

It wasn't poetry. It wasn't even particularly articulate. But his presence said more than his words ever could, and I felt a sudden rush of gratitude for the silent, observant boy. I leaned into him, resting my head on his shoulder and inhaling the sweet, earthy scent of sage that was all Kace.

"Thank you," I murmured. "I'm okay. Now."

He leaned down and pressed a kiss to my hair, and when he drew in a deep breath, I wondered if he was inhaling my scent too. I wondered what I smelled like to him, and whether the scent instantly relaxed him, like his did me.

When I finally drew away and sat up straighter, he stood. I watched him go to the window and slip on out. I leaned my forehead against the window, craning my neck to watch him as he headed down the sidewalk toward his foster parents' house. I wanted so badly to call to him and ask him to stay. I wanted—maybe even needed—him to stay, but on some level, that wouldn't solve anything.

Even if he stayed with me all night, my head would still be swimming with thoughts about what I was going to do. I'd still be wondering if it was even the right thing to do, and I'd still be questioning whether it was even fair of me to be thinking about my old life when I was settling so deeply into the new one here.

FOR A SOLID WEEK, I grappled with what the hell I was going to do.

I was distracted all the time, my mind clogged with too many conflicting thoughts. I'd programmed Flint's number into my phone in case I forgot it. The man with the raspy voice and access to possible answers about my father was just a phone call away, and even though I was desperate to call him, I found myself tensing up with anxiety every time I thought about it. My conversation with Kace kept playing over in my head, and the fact that I was still considering going behind the Lost Boys' backs to call Flint felt like a slap in the face to the genuine concern Kace had shown the night he snuck into my bedroom.

Finals were just a few short weeks away, and our more ambitious teachers were starting to make threats about difficult exams and final projects that would be worth a high percentage of our grade—but I couldn't focus on any of that.

Every day was a blur, and by the time the weekend rolled around, I'd realized I had to do something, if for no other reason than that I was going to drive myself crazy if I didn't.

I was a confused mess about everything having to do with my father, but a big part of why I was such a mess was the fact that I didn't *know* anything. I had heard so many conflicting stories about who my father was—from the kids at Slateview, from the Lost Boys, from his friends and acquaintances, from federal agents, and even from my dad himself. But I needed to form my own opinion of him. And to do that, I needed to know the truth.

If he'd been framed for the fraud he'd been arrested for, it wouldn't automatically mean my father was blameless. But at least I would know what I should and shouldn't be blaming him for. And if he was released from behind bars, maybe he could make up for some of the hurts he had caused undeserving people. He certainly couldn't do that while in prison.

On Saturday night, I finally couldn't take it anymore. I had nothing to do—no homework, and the boys were busy on a job.

I picked up my phone, scrolled through the contacts, and pressed the button to dial the number I'd found on Bishop's phone. And then... I waited.

"Yo."

The voice on the other end was raspy and gruff, like the person it belonged to had spent a few too many years smoking cigarettes.

"Uh, hello."

There was a pause. "Who the fuck is this?"

"Um—" I drew in a breath. *Come on, keep it together, Cora.* "My name is Cordelia. I'm a friend of the Lost Boys?"

Flint snorted. "Ah. Friend, eh? How'd you get my number? I'm not a fucking go-between for them and their women, so talk to them yourself if you have somethin' to say to them."

I grimaced.

"No. I'm—I'm actually calling for you. I'd like to speak to you. You see, I'm Cordelia van Rensselaer. I want to talk to you about my father."

Silence followed. I thought for a moment that he may have hung up on me, and my heart lurched. *Oh God, please, no.* If he cut me off before I even had a chance to make my case, I'd be stuck at square zero, trying to figure out how to explain this to the Lost Boys before Flint went and told them I'd called him.

"Hello?" I asked, tugging the phone away from my ear for a second to make sure the call hadn't disconnected.

"Rensselaer, you said?"

There it was. What I was looking for.

Recognition.

"Yes." I nodded as I spoke, my tone growing a little more confident. "Will you speak with me?"

"About what?"

"My—" I swallowed. "My father is in prison, being tried for—"

"Yeah, I know."

My heart jumped, and I stood up from the bed to pace restlessly around my room. Gideon van Rensselaer was a big enough name that several papers had covered the story of his arrest, and a few were running updates periodically about his case.

"Well, I..." I spoke slowly, choosing my words with deliberate care. I didn't want to get the Lost Boys in trouble by admitting how much I knew about what they did for Nathaniel Ward. They were already going to hate me enough for this—for trying to defend my father after everything. "I think there's a possibility he might've been set up. Had documents stolen or had evidence planted. I'm not totally sure. But I thought... you seem to know a lot about a lot of things, and I thought maybe you'd have an idea whether that's true or not. Or at least, you might know someone who knows. Could I ask you a few questions?"

There was another drawn out pause, and I held the phone tighter to stop my hand from shaking. I'd done what I could. I'd finally bitten the bullet and made my choice and laid it all out there.

Now it was time to see if my gamble would pay off at all.

Finally, Flint cleared his throat. "Yeah, sure. There's a diner on Flannery and Milton. Carrigan's. Meet me there. An hour."

My footsteps slowed as my stomach churned. "Can't we just talk over the phone?"

"You wanna ask me questions or not, little girl? The least you can do is buy me a damn burger while you do."

I flushed angrily at his patronizing tone but didn't protest. He had agreed, and if I pushed too hard, I was afraid he'd take it back. Besides, a diner was a public place. There would be witnesses around, and it was a far cry better than some abandoned alley like the ones the Lost Boys usually met him in.

"Okay. I'll meet you there."

"Yup."

That was all he said before the line went dead.

THIRTY-ONE

I WAS able to take the bus to Flannery and Milton. It turned out to be about thirty minutes from the rental house, in a slightly nicer neighborhood than the one mom and I lived in.

I had to fight down anxiety and guilt the whole way there. I didn't like going behind the Lost Boys' backs to do this. I hated feeling like I was betraying them somehow, repaying everything they'd done for me by sneaking around behind their backs.

But wouldn't they of all people understand that I was just doing what I had to for the people I loved? I might not always get along well with Mom and Dad, but they were all the family I had.

I shoved those thoughts out of my mind as I pushed into the diner. *Focus, Cora. Worry about the nuclear fallout later.*

Carrigan's was a run-down little place, but it was brightly lit and looked relatively clean for a greasy-spoon diner. As I

walked alongside the counter fronted by several stools with
cracked leather seats, I scanned the booths looking for Flint.

I knew who he was the moment I saw him. I'd never
gotten a good look at him when I'd seen him meeting with the
Lost Boys, but it didn't matter. There was no doubt in my
mind this was the man I'd come to meet. He didn't look like
any of the other diner patrons—who are a mix of high school
kids and blue-hairs. He was an older man, maybe in his
forties, who still looked good for his age. Shiny black hair was
slicked back from his face, and he lounged casually in a booth
near the corner, his eyes drooping and half-lidded, as if being
here was the biggest bore imaginable.

"Flint?" I asked softly as I approached his booth. He
looked up, brows rising toward his hairline.

"Cordelia?" He tilted his head, his gaze scanning up at
down my body as he took in my appearance. "You don't look
like a millionaire's daughter."

I glanced down at the clothes I was wearing. I'd gotten
used to my new wardrobe, and I liked how comfortable it all
felt—but the man wasn't wrong. I definitely didn't look like a
millionaire's daughter.

Don't really feel like one so much anymore ether.

Still, I tilted my head at a perfect angle, giving off what I
hoped was a confident, imperious air. Even when I *had* felt
like the daughter of a millionaire, I'd never taken delight in
ordering the house staff around. I wasn't really that kind of
person. But something about Flint put me on edge, and the

snobby princess act was like an armor I wrapped around myself.

"I see you know who I am."

"I don't think there's a person in Baltimore who don't know." He waved to the booth. "Sit."

I did so, and a moment later when the tired-looking waitress came over, I ordered a water while he ordered a burger. When she was gone, I looked to Flint.

"So, what do you want?" he asked me, picking at his teeth.

Okay. Time to put all my cards on the table.

"I'm trying to help my father," I said. "You know he's in jail... you know what for. But I think there's more to it."

Flint chuckled, obviously not taking me too seriously.

"Is that so?"

"Yeah. I mean, my father's a good man. But more than that, he's a smart businessman. He wouldn't risk his entire future to just make a quick buck in the short term—he thinks long-term, he strategizes."

"You might be barkin' up the wrong tree. You might be thinking a little too highly of your old man, if ya ask me."

"I don't think so, though." I bit my lip. "It's why I wanted to talk to you. I know you must hear things..."

Flint's brow rose more. "Must I?"

"Yeah... You know, in your line of work. Have you heard anything about my father?"

There was a slight pause as he regarded me across the

small table of the booth, drumming his fingers lightly on its surface. Then he shook his head.

"Can't say I have, cupcake."

Liar.

But I forced a smile to my face, moving on smoothly. I wasn't going to let this go so fast. "Okay. That's okay. What... what about an Abraham? An Abraham Shaw? I've heard some things—"

Flint's back straightened. He sat up a little straighter, opening his mouth like he was about to say something. Then he stopped, and a second later, he settled back against the faded leather of the booth seat, affecting a lazy, nonchalant attitude again.

"Can't say I've heard of him either."

Liar!

Dammit. He was making shit up, refusing to answer now that we were face-to-face. But as much as I hadn't wanted to come to the diner, I was glad I'd agreed to an in-person meeting. Because if I hadn't been staring into his eyes as he spoke, maybe I would've missed the lie.

But I hadn't.

He knew Abraham Shaw. And he knew at least something about my father.

I had to get him to tell me something. I scooted forward, leaning against the table that separated us.

"Please. Surely someone like you—"

"Not here." He cut me off.

His burger hadn't even been delivered by the waitress

yet, but he didn't hesitate before standing up. I glanced up at him, confusion and worry making my chest feel too tight.

"I said, not here," Flint repeated, his voice sharp as his gaze darted around the diner.

Shifting in my seat, I glanced around at the other patrons, nervousness flooding me. Was Flint afraid someone could be listening? What did he have to say that he didn't want anyone to overhear?

Before I could ask him any other questions, he turned, walking toward the diner's front door. He didn't pause to make sure I was following him, and I was certain that if I didn't follow, he'd keep going, disappearing into the night like a ghost. And that would be it. My last chance would be gone.

Follow, or get none of the answers you need.

Before I could think, I was sliding out of the booth, rising to my feet. The waitress was returning with Flint's burger, and I nearly plowed into her as I made a beeline for the door.

"Hey, hon, you want this to go or somethin'?" she asked, arching a brow.

"No. No thanks," I muttered, slipping around her, my gaze scanning the dimly lit street outside the large glass windows. Had I missed him? Was he gone already?

"Well, you still gotta pay for this!" she called, holding up the plate with the burger and fries. But I didn't answer, and I didn't stop.

Shoving open the door, I glanced around quickly, my heart thudding hard in my chest. My breath fogged before my face, little puffs of air in the cool, dark night.

There!

I'd been right. Flint wasn't bluffing, and he wasn't waiting around for me to make up my mind. I caught sight of his dark hair and leather jacket as he slid into a car halfway down the block.

"Wait!"

He glanced up, and the look on his face suggested he was hoping I would've just stayed in the diner, maybe eaten his burger as a consolation prize, and gone home.

But I couldn't.

He knew something. I was sure of it.

And I needed to find out what it was.

I half expected Flint to jump into his car and speed away before I could reach him, but he actually waited, leaning against his open car door and watching me with an annoyed look as I hurried up to him.

His car was the same black sedan with tinted windows that I'd seen him driving before. When I neared it, my footsteps slowed.

"Will you tell me about my dad?" I asked, eyeing him across the top of the car.

His eyes narrowed, something like pity glinting in his dark irises. "You really think you can handle the truth, little girl? You really wanna know what dear old daddy was up to?"

I swallowed, my blood turning to water at his words. No, I honestly wasn't sure I did want to know, but I *had* to. I needed to know if my entire life had been built on lies.

"I can handle it," I finally said, my voice low.

"Then get in." He shook his head resignedly before he dropped out of my view, sliding into the driver's seat opposite me.

There was one moment of hesitation as I stood outside the dark car. *Fuck. I wish I could text the Lost Boys and let them know where I am. Just in case.*

But of course, if they knew where I was, they'd also know what I was doing.

Shoving down my fear, I reached for the door handle, pulled it open, and slid into the sedan. The interior of the car smelled strongly of stale cigarette smoke, and I tried to keep the grimace off my face as I inhaled shallowly through my nose.

The silence was beyond awkward as Flint pulled away from the curb, but I kept my cool.

"Where are we going?" I asked, keeping my gaze trained out the windshield.

"Someplace we can talk without bein' overheard. You're askin' me for some information I really shouldn't be blabbing to anybody."

He shook his head, as if he really couldn't believe he was doing this. We drove in silence for a few minutes, through the dimly lit streets of Baltimore, and I tried to find a landmark I recognized—since I'd started running with the Lost Boys, I'd seen a lot more of the city than I ever had before, but I didn't know this neighborhood at all.

As he turned down a less busy street, I glanced over

toward him, taking in his profile. His nose had a little bump halfway down it from what I assumed was a previous break.

"Can we—I mean, do you want to talk in here? Seems as private as anything. Why do we have to go somewhere else?"

He dropped his head for a second, a huff of laughter falling from his lips. When he glanced back over at me, his expression was harder than it had been earlier. "That's a damn good question. Took you long enough to ask it."

"What—what do you mean?"

One corner of his mouth lifted in a smile that didn't reach his eyes. "I mean, who says we're going to be talkin', Princess?"

I'd gotten used to the Lost Boys calling me *princess*, and even though the tone of the word had been harsh and bitter at first, it'd changed over time. But the way it sounded coming from Flint was unsettling. What's more—

"You did. I thought we were going to talk? About... about my father?"

He chuckled again. "You just get into strange men's cars to talk? Come on. Don't play fuckin' dumb."

My heartbeat surged in my chest as my breath caught in my throat. On instinct, my hand flew to the handle of the car door. Locked.

Shit.

Shit, shit, shit.

How could I have been so fucking stupid? My desperation for answers about my father had made me rash and reckless, and maybe Flint had seen that. Maybe he'd known that if he just dangled the carrot of answers before my face, I would abandon safety and reason and follow him wherever he went.

We began to crawl to a slower pace, and the car turned down an alley. It was narrow and poorly lit, lined with a few large dumpsters that looked like hulking monsters in the darkness.

Oh, God. Nothing good ever happened in dark alleys.

My fingers shook as I pulled my phone from my coat pocket, turning away from Flint and swiping desperately to Bishop's name in my text messages. But I had only managed to type out two words to him before rough hands grabbed my shoulders. Flint grappled the phone from my grip and threw it down to the floor of the car.

"Oh, no you don't, you little bitch."

Then his hands were on my shoulders again, pulling at the coat I wore, yanking the zipper down, sliding inside to cup my breasts. I thrashed in his hold, and when he moved one hand up to grab my chin in a bruising grip, I pulled my head back and bit him. Hard.

The nails of his other hand dug into the soft, tender flesh of my breast, making me gasp in pain.

"You bitch!" he snapped, swearing as he jerked his hand away from me. Red blood was smeared across his skin, and I could taste the coppery tang of it in my mouth.

Pure instinct drove me. In the few seconds it took him to recover, I turned away again, yanking at the old-fashioned pop-up lock and kicking the door open. I tumbled out, rocks and gravel digging into my knees through my leggings. The corners of my eyes stung as pain radiated out from the wounds. I pushed myself up, scrambling to get to my feet as the car's other door slammed open.

This had been a mistake. A huge, monumental mistake. The reality of that chilled my blood even as my heart pounded heavily in my ears.

Run, Cora. Run. Run.

I needed to get away from Flint. I had no idea where I was or how to get back home, but I could figure all of that out if I could just get away from the large man with the unreadable eyes and the raspy voice.

As he rounded the car, I bolted. Flint had parked all the way at the end of the alley. All I had to do was get to the opening, get to the street. He wouldn't attack me out in the open, would he?

But was there even anyone on the street to stop him?

"Get your spoiled little ass back here!"

When I was less than fifteen feet from the mouth of the alley, Flint grabbed my hair and yanked. He pulled me back, tugging me away from the alley opening. Freedom was at that opening, *hope* was at that opening, but I was pulled farther and farther away from it as I struggled in his hold.

He tossed me against the brick wall of one of the buildings lining the alley, then pressed against me, forcing my legs open.

"You're kind of a dumb bitch." He chuckled, the sound like rocks scraping together. "Poking around asking criminals about your daddy. And then you come here asking all these fucking questions. Dropping names. What made you think I was gonna tell you shit?" He laughed. "Not like it matters. You'll be easy to get rid of. After some fun."

Horrific realization wracked through me as he shoved my skirt up, tearing at my leggings and ripping the fabric like tissue paper. Cold air met my skin, and the feel of his hand on my bare thigh made vomit rise in my throat. Balling my hand into a fist, I lashed out wildly, catching him across the cheekbone with a wide right hook. He grunted and stepped back, his weight heaving away from my body temporarily. But before I could try to run again, he backhanded me, knocking the sense from between my ears.

A ringing sound filled my head, and I tasted a fresh wave of blood from where I'd bitten my lip.

Struggling to stay conscious, I hit him again, but my aim was worse the second time. He barely seemed to register the glancing blow, and then one large forearm pressed against my neck, pinning me to the wall and nearly cutting off my air supply. Panic spiked in my chest, and I spit the blood drawn from my lip back at him as he tore at my panties.

"Goddammit." He grimaced, but didn't release me to wipe away the blood and spit on his cheek. Instead, he pressed into me even harder. "You think because you're daddy's little princess you can just walk around and ask whatever you want, get whatever you want, huh?" he sneered. "Well, fuck you and your daddy. You both are gonna get what's coming—"

The loud squeal of tires cut him off. An engine roared, and the sharp, bright beams of headlights fell on us like a spotlight. Then several car doors slammed. Flint and I both heard them, but I was the only one who seemed affected as I looked over, my heart leaping, hoping for a miracle.

I let out a choked breath at what I saw. Flint's forearm on my neck kept me from turning my head much at all, but from the corner of my eye, I saw three distinct figures approaching, backlit by the headlights behind them.

Bishop, Kace, and Misael.

Tears stung my eyes at the sight of them. I had no idea how they'd found us here—part of me couldn't even believe they were real—but every fiber of my being cried out with relief as they approached.

"What. The. Fuck?"

Bish's voice was tight with fury, and the three of them reached us in several long strides. He and Misael grunted as they hauled Flint off me. To my surprise, the older man didn't fight, but he did look smug.

"It's not polite, ruining another man's fun, boys." He looked between the three of them, gaze settling on Kace. "C'mon. You can't tell me you blame me."

I was still pressed against the wall, leaning against it for support as my knees wobbled beneath me, and I followed Flint's gaze.

Kace looked almost unrecognizable. Pure, unadulterated fury contorted his features, nothing like the way he'd looked when he'd fought Caleb in the hall at Slateview that day.

That had been totally controlled, strategic violence, but this was the complete opposite.

"Shut the fuck up, Flint." His voice was rough. "You better shut the fuck up."

He raised his hand, and for the first time, I saw what he held in a tight grip.

A gun.

It looked big and heavy, and the smooth metal was so dark that it was almost impossible to make out any of its details in the dim light.

Breathing heavily, Kace aimed the gun at the man who stood a few feet away from me, facing off with the Lost Boys.

"Oh. Big boy, are we now?" Flint laughed, a raspy chuckle that made my blood run cold. "Come on, kid. Put it away and leave. You're not gonna do shit to me if you know what's good for you. Nathaniel needs me a lot more than he needs you. You know she's not worth it."

All three of the guys stiffened at the mention of Nathaniel's name, and Kace licked his lips, shaking his head as if simply denying it could make it untrue.

But it *was* true. I could see it in their faces.

Nathaniel Ward didn't give a shit about me. He probably didn't even care all that much about the Lost Boys. But Flint was high enough up in the organization that he probably *did* matter.

Which meant the three boys who'd come to rescue me had their hands tied.

If they did anything to Flint, Nathaniel would probably kill them for it.

Flint's posture relaxed even more as he gave them all time to process that fact. There was something sly and predatory in his eyes as he shifted his attention back to me, taking in the sight of me with my skirt pushed up, leggings torn, and shirt askew. I shrank back from his gaze as my heart seemed to stop beating entirely.

He still planned to kill me. He still planned to use me.

Oh God. Would he make them watch?

"Besides..." He tilted his head to one side, taking a single step toward me. "Considering how much you little assholes have slacked off on work because you've been runnin' around with her, I think I deserve a sample of the goods. She's hot as fuck, I'll give you that, but she can't be that goddamn amazing in the sack. I'll just take a few turns with her, and then—"

He never finished that sentence.

A sudden *pop* sounded, so loud and sharp it seemed to fill the entire space of the alley.

Flint's whole body shifted backward from the impact of the bullet, and then he was falling, his form going completely limp as it dropped to the dirty pavement like a bag of rocks.

The headlights from Bish's car still streamed down the alley, and they made Flint's skin look washed-out and pale as his dark eyes stared up at the night sky above, unseeing.

Dead.

"I told you to shut the fuck up, you son of a bitch," Kace rasped. "She's ours."

To Be Continued…

The story will continue in Wild Girl, the second book in the Slateview High series.

Made in the USA
Middletown, DE
30 July 2021